DRESSING FOR SUCCESS

by
P. J. Wright

pjwrght@aol.com

Ὑπό Τῷ
Ἡλιῷ

HYPO TO HELIO BOOKS

Houston

Paperback ISBN: 978-1-938293-18-4
Ebook ISBN: 978-1-938293-19-1

Front-cover render art by: P. J. Wright

Front-cover cardboard-box font is CCToBeContinued, licensed from Comic Book Fonts/Active Images.

Contact the author at: pjwrght AT aol DOT com

BISAC Subject Headings:
Fic016000—Fiction > Humorous
Fic027010—Fiction > Romance > Erotica
Fic027130—Fiction > Romance > Science Fiction
Fic028000—Fiction > Science Fiction > General
Fic029000—Fiction > Short Stories (single author)

HYPO TO HELIO BOOKS, 2427 Clearbrook Dr., Missouri City, TX, 77489-6061

PART 1
Girl, Monday Through Friday

Chapter 1-1
The New Girl

In a Los Angeles apartment

"You're *insane!*" I yelled.

Josh was calm. "Look, it's a workable plan. You need a job. The firm needs a new employee with your qualifications. I'm telling you, it's meant to happen!"

"My qualifications? You claim this is not a crazy plan because of *my qualifications?*"

Josh said, "You're a graphic artist. You've got the talent. You've got the training—"

"And I've got the *wrong sex!*"

Josh settled back in the couch and grinned. "Bro, I think I can solve *that* little complication, no problem!"

****

My name is Peter James Wright, "PJ" to everyone who knows me. All my life, I've wanted to be an artist. Two years ago I graduated with honors from Julliard, with a Master's in Fine Arts.

At the time I had congratulated myself on my pragmatism, in that had I concentrated on the so-called "commercial arts." Graphic presentation, layout and design, that sort of thing. I knew it was a hungry world out there for artists, and I figured that I'd be smart and use my art to pay the bills.

Two years later, I was still looking for my first steady job. Pragmatism notwithstanding, I'd still badly underestimated how hungry it was, outside the ivy tower.

Josh Arjer, the fellow with the ominous-sounding plan, is my half-brother by my late mother's remarriage. Back in those days, he had a steady gig: He worked for an ad agency, Whitman and North.

He was in Sales, and it was a job that he'd been born to do. If I'm the "artsy" one, Josh is the "hustler." He can sell deep freezers to Eskimos, and make them wonder how they ever got along without them. When this whole sordid tale began, he was trying to sell me on what had to have been the most hare-brained scheme he'd ever come up with.

The frightening thing was, I was so desperate for a job I was listening.

Here's the deal: Back in those days, Whitman and North was a sleepy little firm that should have had its main offices in "The Land That Time Forgot," not in chic L.A. The agency's heyday occurred sometime back in the mid-Fifties. Since then, they'd been living on a steadily declining pool of regular accounts, and wondering if color advertising was more than just a passing fad.

Then by some fluke, a major multinational corporation, The Sprague Group, decided that they needed a captive ad agency for some of their smaller corporate holdings; and the name *Whitman and North* caught somebody's eye there at The Sprague Group.

But there was a catch.

Several of Sprague's companies were heavily into government contracting. There's this federal-contracting rule that says to be eligible to bid, you have to have a certain percentage of each ethnic group—*and both sexes*—in all levels of your company. And that rule applies to all of your subcontractors too.

And that was the catch with respect to Whitman and North. As I said, they were still "lost in the Fifties." A woman in management was a radical concept to the minds that ran the firm. Now, being a small firm, the number of women required to be holding management-level jobs was equally small. In fact, to be in compliance, Whitman and North only needed one woman.

They were one woman short.

As it happens, they also needed a new lead graphic artist, especially with a major presentation looming on the near-horizon. Since Lead Graphic Artist counted as a management position, somebody managed to put two and two together and the word went forth: "Hire a female graphic artist."

Which brings us back to Josh's plan.

****

Now I held up my hand, as I shook my head. "You're gonna suggest that we get me a granny dress, some socks to stuff down my bra, do a few sessions at the beauty parlor, and pass me off as the sister that you've forgotten to mention for the last twenty-two years. That's something out of a bad TV sitcom, and I'm not having anything to do with it. Period!"

Josh just grinned a predatory grin that I'd long ago learned, he had a scam he was just dying to run on somebody. (Usually me.) "Bro, would I do something like that to you?"

(History had taught me that the answer was almost always *Yes!*)

Josh continued: "No. What we need is a way to transform you into a completely believable woman, something that isn't permanent, and something we can accomplish in the very near future."

He had me stumped. He already knew the answer; you could see it on his face. I said, "You got a magic wand?"

Still grinning, Josh walked over to his laptop that was sitting on the dining table. "Maybe I have something better:

technology!" He plugged the phone line into the computer, and logged on to the 'Net.

Josh—my brother, The Salesman. He already had me, and he knew it. He knew my "button." Imagination is a large part of artistry, and curiosity is a large part of imagination. Get me curious, and you can usually lead me around by the nose. I walked to the table and looked over his shoulder.

There was a web page coming up. At the moment, the screen consisted of a tastefully understated presentation of the name "NuGen" against a subdued green-marble background, and a placeholder for some kind of graphic—a photo or something. Before it could come up, Josh turned to face me, blocking my view of the laptop.

He said, "I would have been stuck. No good idea. Except I'd talked a few weeks ago with Morrie."

(That would be Morrie Feldstein. He was something of a maverick down at Whitman and North, because he actually tried to keep up with the march of time. He'd even taken some programming classes down at L.A. City College. As a result, he was in charge of Whitman and North's modest foray into web-page design.)

Josh continued, "Morrie was telling me about this new account he was working. Seems that there's this aerospace firm that's trying to branch out. I didn't pay too much attention after I heard what they were up to, because it sounded so far out in left field. But then this job opening came up, and I did some checking."

He glanced over his shoulder at the computer. "Take a look."

The placeholder had been filled with a photo of an attractive young woman in her twenties, attired in a little Grecian toga-like costume.

She wasn't what I'd call exactly *fashion model*, though she didn't miss the mark by much. Long, shapely legs (well displayed by her outfit); nicely slender, athletic hips and narrow waist; truly impressive (though not excessive) breasts; and a softly-rounded face smiling this flirty smile at the camera.

I admired the image for a moment, but still didn't get what it was that Josh was trying to show me. Aloud I said, "Pretty girl. So what?"

Josh folded his arms and grinned triumphantly. "It's not a girl. It's a guy!"

I took another look, just to be polite, but the truth of it was obvious, even from the most cursory inspection.

As an art student, you do *a lot* of "human form" (read: *nudes*) work. You become so intimately familiar with studying the human figure that you eventually find yourself so concentrated on trying to get the length of her arm just right, you lose track of the fact that it's the arm of an attractive female. I think it was that shopworn familiarity with the female form that was at work in the back of my mind here. My studies had conditioned me to believe that the proportions of a male form are readily distinguishable from that of a female form. And here, with regard to this young woman, the proportions—leg to hip, waist to shoulder, curve of shoulder to length of arm—the conclusion was too obvious.

So I said impatiently, "Oh, come on! Okay, maybe 'she' is one of those guys that can do some makeup tricks for the face, and that's a *really* retouched photo for the body. Again: So what?"

Josh tapped the mouse, and the screen changed to a "before and after" shot.

I looked again. "Oh, bullshit!"

I was willing to admit that the male and female faces were somewhat similar. Again, it was a question of proportions. In this case, the proportion of forehead to jaw to chin were identical, though the male's face was a bit more angular. Probably a family relation. But the male was male, while the female was definitely female.

And they *weren't* the same person!

Were they?

As I say, I have the imagination of an artist. Using a little of that imagination, and after a little more study, I had to admit that there was something about the eyes—

They were the same shade of hazel, with a dark ring around the outside. But it was more than that: Behind their eyes, their souls looked the same.

Josh chuckled. He had my attention, and that was usually all he needed to reel me in. "I swear to God, Bro. I've done some checking. NuGen Transgender Appliances is a bona fide subsidiary of NuGen Stratosphere Plastics, an up-and-comer in the aerospace industry. They have kind of a 'hush-hush, black-sheep relation,' granted. Still 'in the closet,' you might say. But definitely for real."

It wasn't possible. The rational part of my brain kept reminding me of this indisputable fact. And yet—

We spent the next half-hour checking out NuGen's web site. The gist of it was, they used a new Space Age polymer—something called "memory plastic"—to create a full-body suit that would turn your hairy Uncle Jake into your sexy Aunt Jolene, with nobody the wiser.

The site had lots of photos and lots of facts, some of them patently unbelievable. (I mean, in the back of my mind, I knew none of this could really be real. Right?)

For example, on one page they were raving about attention to detail. They actually claimed, "Employing proprietary design features achieved through consultation with noted experts, it is now possible, using the new I-2000S series, for the wearer to simulate normal female sexual intercourse."

On the other hand—and I remember wondering if this wasn't just more "cleverness" on their part, pointing out things their product couldn't do, so as to thereby make the things it could do more plausible—the site also had a long list of disclaimers.

They didn't sell to anyone under eighteen, for example. Furthermore, if you were 6′8″ and weighed 380 pounds, NuGen would be happy to sell you a suit, but you had to understand that first, they charged extra for all the materials; and second, what you'd get for the increased price was a 6′8″, 380-pound facsimile of a woman.

In other words, while the memory plastic could make some changes—changes they were eager to show off—this was what Josh had billed it as: technology with some real-world limitations. Not magic.

It was all a crock. Rationality and a very natural cynicism said it just had to be.

But Josh was sold. He wouldn't listen to my protests. Soon we were looking at an interactive catalogue that you could use to place an order for your custom-fitted suit. When I got a look at the price list, I just about swallowed my teeth! The base model had a sticker price of well over six thousand dollars.

Josh and I went back to calling each other names for a while.

Have I mentioned that, given time, Josh can always sell me? He was convinced, and to be fair, NuGen's presentation was earnest and—even though it was a scam—seamlessly presented. It had more than enough "proof" offered to make it plausible.

Including a before-and-after "girls/boys on the catwalk" video! I've worked with enough image-editing software to know just what is required to do a convincing job of faking a video, and if this was faked, it would have done an entire Hollywood special-effects department proud. That's not to say that I wasn't suspicious that it wasn't all somehow faked.

It's just that, taken as a whole, all the evidence was making it more and more difficult to mount a successful defense to Josh's continual pressure.

And so, in the end, just before 6 p.m. Wednesday night, we got out the tape measure, and took a whole bunch of measurements of me. We then dickered over the specs of our new "girl."

We wound up with athletic, twentyish, C-cup (Josh had been holding out for D-cup), and over-the-shoulder length blonde hair. (I've got this thing for blondes.)

We used Josh's AMEX Gold to place our order, specifying two-day air delivery.

****

I thought a lot about what we were considering, all the following day (Thursday). I was developing mixed emotions. On the one hand, I was still convinced that this was all an elaborate scam. The pictures had been faked, or heavily retouched. Or just real women to begin with.

That line of thinking was pleasing. I'd finally have something to hold over Josh's head: the "Great Scammer" himself scammed!

They couldn't really do that—make a man look so flawlessly, believably like a woman—with just a few pounds of plastic, no matter how high-tech the material.

Could they?

What if they could?

Was I ready to hold up my end of the deal?

What was involved in holding it up? What would I be required to do? Would I be able to do it?

That really gave me pause. After all, I was a normal heterosexual male. Furthermore, while it's not like I was a complete stranger to women, I had to honestly admit to myself that I didn't have extensive, comprehensive knowledge of the fair sex.

More importantly, what knowledge I did have, was all based on the perspective of a male. Always "on the outside looking in."

I had no experience, or really any concept, of what it might take to be "on the inside looking out." I didn't know how to be a woman. I'd never even considered the prospect. I didn't know how she thought. I didn't know how she reacted to the million-and-one things that a person reacted to every day.

However, even with my limited knowledge, I was fairly certain that there was more to being a woman—a hell of a lot more!—than tits and ass, and not having to shave your face each morning.

By mid-morning Friday, I was getting a case of butterflies, watching out the window for the parcel service to show up.

But they hadn't shown by 5 p.m., when Josh got home from work.

At first he tried to put a good face on things. He called a toll-free number we had for NuGen, but all we got was a recorded message stating that business hours were from 8 a.m. to 5 p.m. CST. We called the parcel service. A professionally polite (but also clearly uninterested) woman tried to track down our package for us, but the computer was fouled up and she couldn't give us any useful information. She suggested we call back Monday.

I think Josh was beginning to suspect that he'd been "had," but he certainly wasn't going to give me the satisfaction of admitting it. In the end, I headed upstairs, and left him to rattle around looking for something to vent his growing frustration and embarrassment on.

I'm really a nice guy—I teased Josh only twice that night.

****

Josh had left for a Saturday at work—Whitman and North was feeling the pressure of preparing for the Sprague Group presentation—and I was watching an old war movie on "Nostalgia Cinema," when the doorbell rang.

I'd put the thought of the suit out of my mind. The chime jarred me back to all my previous anxieties.

Sure enough, it was the parcel service. A perky little brunette in the service's uniform apologized for the mix-up. Apparently one of their jets had engine trouble yesterday, and had to divert. The parcel was tied up all last night while they got a spare plane out and transferred the cargo. She hoped I understood; "Sign here, please."

The box was about two feet, by one foot, by six inches—and completely unremarkable.

I set it on the dining table, and used my car key to open the tape. Sitting on top of the contents was a folio-sized "Manual for Use," with the familiar green-marble background. I pulled it out and underneath was what had to be "The Suit."

I think I was actually relieved when I saw it. Looking at The Suit, you could tell that it had indeed been a scam all along. It was just a thin parcel of flesh-colored plastic with some fuzzy blonde fur at one end, all sealed in a clear plastic wrapper. I smiled, vindicated, as I picked it up and turned it over in my hands. There were lots of folds but no discernible features. And it was painfully obvious that, if that fuzz was "over-the-shoulder length blonde hair," then somebody didn't know where shoulders were. The "hair" couldn't be more than an inch long.

I was going to toss the thing back in the box, and go back to the movie, when I saw a little slip of pink paper that had been under the suit. In bold black letters, it commanded, "READ ME FIRST."

I picked it up and read it.

"Don't be discouraged by your first impressions of the I-2000S! We at NuGen assure you that if you follow the enclosed instructions, this quality product will meet or exceed all your expectations. NuGen Transgender Appliances, Inc."

Thinking that somebody somewhere must be laughing at the thought, *The damn fool might fall for that and actually read the manual,* I set the note down, and then stood there in indecision.

Indecision that lasted for all of one minute.

Have I mentioned that curiosity is one of my greatest weaknesses?

Let those NuGen con-artists laugh.

After reading the first few pages of the manual, I gathered that the whole thing depended on two factors: moisture and heat.

According to the manual, the bulk of the suit was composed of a polymer "skin" that perfectly mimicked human flesh's color, texture, and elasticity. Though it was only a few mils thick ("equivalent to tissue paper"), it was supposed to be very durable.

It also was supposed to have very little impact on tactile sensation. As the manual explained, human skin—the outer skin, that is—is actually insensitive. It's just dead tissue. Our sense of touch is based in the inner, living layer of flesh. As a result, because of the thinness and close adherence of the suit's "skin," there would be only the slightest reduction in the wearer's sense of touch. In essence, the suit would just slightly thicken that already insensitive outer layer.

(At the time, and perhaps given the context of the moment, I remembered back to one of my few experiences with a condom. That had been only a few mils thick too. But as I recalled the experience now, I wouldn't have called it "only the slightest reduction" in sensitivity! Once again, I was wondering about "cleverness" on NuGen's part.)

In any event, the manual insisted that there wouldn't be much-reduced feeling except in those areas where the suit "added tissue."

This adding of tissue was accomplished by placing numerous pads of various sizes and shapes throughout the suit. These pads were used to add "contour and feature" ("tits and ass") to the finished form. Like the skin, the pads were made out of some pretty advanced material. At a temperature exceeding 108 degrees, the pads absorbed moisture. Between 82 and 108 degrees, the pads retained moisture. Below 82 degrees, they released moisture. When saturated, the manual claimed that the pads were able to convincingly portray either fatty or muscle tissue, depending on their placement and construction.

But the real secret of the suit was something called *memory plastic*. Apparently memory plastic was a fairly new development, arising out of research into materials for use in outer-space construction. Simply stated, memory plastic could be "trained" to assume a specific shape. Bend it into any other shape, apply a specific stimulus, and it returned to its "learned" shape. Apply a different stimulus, and it "relaxed."

Woven throughout the suit were thousands of "memory threads." Supposedly they had been taught how to take my measurements; and by contracting, mold them into a "nominal female physique." The stimulus required was moist heat.

A very specific temperature too. Like the pads, the threads reacted differently to different temperatures. At 110-plus degrees, the threads relaxed into what the manual referred to as their "deployment" state. Drop the temperature to a range of 90 to 104 degrees (body temperature, more or less), and the threads contracted into their learned shape. Drop the temperature below 90 degrees, and they went into what the manual called their "dormant" (or relaxed) state. I was informed that the thing in the box was the suit in its dormant state.

The manual said that the first thing I needed to do to use the suit, was to fill the bathtub with water that was heated to between 110 to 120 degrees ("approaching the hottest of baths"), and just drop the suit in.

I shook my head, and smiled at the concept. "Dehydrated woman—just add hot water."

****

Taking the suit and the instruction manual, and leaving everything else in the box, I went upstairs and started the tub filling.

Now, at this point you have to understand that it was still only my curiosity that was driving my actions. I didn't for one minute believe that any of the claims in the manual were true. I was still positive it was all a scam. Even so, I had to try it out. You know, prove the lie so I could justify the last laugh.

When the tub was about one-quarter full, I suddenly realized that I had no idea of how to take the temperature of the water. *Approaching the hottest of baths* was rather vague. Considering the cost of the suit (and my intention to preserve it as much as possible, for when Josh returned it and demanded a refund), I didn't want to run the risk of damaging it with water of the wrong temperature.

Sitting on the edge of the tub, I wracked my brain for a solution. The thermometer in the medicine cabinet went up to only 103 degrees. I didn't have an outdoor thermometer, and I doubted it would go high enough anyway.

How to measure the temperature of the bath water?

Then I remembered we had a meat thermometer in one of the drawers, down in the kitchen. Josh and I had used it (or perhaps I should say, *misused* it) last Thanksgiving to incinerate a turkey. Leaving the water running, I ran downstairs and rummaged through the drawers till I found it. Taking it back upstairs, I was pleased to see that the tub was now half full. Shutting off the taps, I stuck the thermometer in the water. The needle quickly rose to 117 degrees, then stopped. I congratulated myself on my good guess at the faucet settings.

Picking up the suit, I worried at the plastic sealing for a moment, then finally tore off a corner with my teeth. The rest of the wrapper came off easily, and I was left holding a ridiculous-looking, papery-feeling cutout of a feminine-ish form, all topped by a bristly thatch of blond fuzz.

I stood looking at The Suit for a moment, feeling like six kinds of fool for proceeding with this farce, or for even entertaining the thought that this suit could possibly make good on any of its claims. But the money was spent, and I felt that I had to follow the charade through to the end. Besides, I didn't have anything better to do.

I gently set the suit into the hot water.

It promptly sank.

I glared at it for a moment, and then went back downstairs to get a beer. As I trudged back up the stairs carrying a nice, cold bottle of Coors Lite, I remembered that the manual said that the suit needed to soak for no less than ten minutes.

Passing the bathroom without a glance, I went into my bedroom.

I pulled off my tee shirt and jeans, then my socks. *What the hell? Why not?* I started to pull off my briefs, but then stopped. I don't know exactly why. Perhaps I'd just reached my level of discomfort, and the thought of checking on that ridiculous suit in the nude was more than I could take.

Still carrying my beer, and clad only in my undershorts, I padded back to the bathroom and glanced into the tub.

I damn near dropped my beer in surprise.

A nude woman, her head crowned by a full golden mane, floated partially submerged in my bathtub.

I stood there slack-jawed, staring. When the initial surprise—I defy you not to be at least a little surprised, the next time you walk into your bathroom and there's a naked woman in your bathtub!—had worn off, and I was capable of closer inspection, I could see that she wasn't a real woman.

In fact, she wouldn't even make a particularly good mannequin. To some extent, I was reminded of one of those inflatable love dolls—the really expensive ones. Individually, her features were nicely drawn with an aristocratically high forehead, thin, arched eyebrows, a cute little button nose, and full, sensuous lips.

But the individual parts far exceeded the whole. The face was expressionless in the most artless way. The hair was nice though, I give NuGen that. Somehow that short burr of fuzz had expanded into what would indeed be the advertised over-the-shoulder length. At the moment, it fanned out from the suit's head, gently swaying to the motion of the water.

Josh had paid six thousand dollars for a nice wig.

Continuing my inspection downward from the head, my attention was next drawn to "her" breasts. While I saw some real promise in those delightful, pink-tipped islands rising above the submerged torso, they seemed improbably high on the chest. Perhaps for that reason, they also seemed to be out of proportion to the rest of the body.

There were other problems as well. Running down from the base of the throat, there was a large, obvious slit. Clearly, this was how one put the suit on. Following the slit to its conclusion, my eyes came to rest on a small ruff of golden fur crowning the suit's groin.

That's a nice touch, I thought. *Matching the pubic hair to the golden tresses on the suit's head. At least the poor fool who's wearing the suit won't have to pretend to be a natural blonde.*

Remembering the claim of "simulated sexual intercourse," I cautiously reached into the water (which was *hot!*) and tentatively traced the exterior of the fake vagina with the tip of my finger. I felt embarrassed, and responded with a nonchalant mumble of "Nice detail."

Realizing how absurd the embarrassment was (and perhaps to prove to myself that I wasn't embarrassed—oh no, not at all), I abandoned my tentative approach and gently (I still didn't want to damage anything) spread the lips apart. Sticking my finger deep within this artificial female's make-believe womanhood, I was rewarded with an admittedly arousing touch of silky soft "flesh."

I pulled my finger out and then stood there for a moment, chewing on my lower lip.

Oddly, it was my curiosity as to how that particular feature worked—how the depth of a real vagina could be simulated, if the suit were on a male form—that decided me to try the suit on.

Pulling the (*hot!*—damn it—*hot!!*) suit out of the water, I flipped down the lid of the toilet seat, slid off my briefs, sat down, and began to wriggle my left foot down the leg of the suit and into its foot.

The material of the suit was fairly elastic, more so than the latex glove I remembered from dissecting frogs in Biology 101. The sensation of having the plastic of the suit against my skin was similar to wearing those gloves as well.

Similar, but also different. I thought about it for a moment, and then realized that for some reason the suit didn't feel as tight as the latex glove had—which I thought was rather odd, when I coupled that looseness with the assertion that close adherence to the wearer's skin was one of the things that made it all work.

In any event, though it was a bit loose, the material of the suit seemed to be a good fit for my leg. It was no great chore to slide the artificial skin all the way up to the top of my thigh. The same was true of the right leg. The only real challenge was to fit each of my own toes into the (very detailed, down to the nails) toes of the suit.

After just a few moments I was sitting on the toilet, up to my thighs in "woman."

As I was smiling at the image this conjured, my fingers encountered a—call it a "pocket"—on the inside of the suit, just behind that intriguing fake vagina.

Puzzling what it could be for (but having a strong suspicion), I picked up the manual that I'd left sitting on the counter, and turned to "Appendix B: Illustrations for Use." Figure Three made it very clear, via a painfully specific line drawing, what was expected of the wearer at this point. Well, at least now I knew how NuGen would make my "masculinity" disappear!

There was a helpful little footnote, suggesting that "The judicious application of petroleum jelly or similar is recommended, to ease any possible discomfort caused by chafing." I ignored the advice, and spent an uncomfortable moment tucking my—self—into the pocket.

That detail accounted for, I then slipped the buttocks up over my own, and spent several minutes wrestling with getting each arm into the arms of the suit. The experience was not unlike donning a somewhat tight pair of coveralls. I puzzled for a moment on how to proceed with the head, but could think of nothing else than to pull it over my own head, like a hood. I was a little worried that the material of the suit, as stretch-y as it was, wasn't elastic enough to do this and it would tear, but this didn't prove to be the case.

It was here that I realized the suit's eyes were closed.

I stood for a long moment, trying to figure out what to do, now that I was effectively blind. I started to reach for the manual, realized that I couldn't see to find it—and realized further that even if I did find it by touch, it would hardly do me any good in my present predicament. (Hard to read with your eyes closed.)

The absurdity of my situation finally hit home, and I began to laugh.

It was a muffled laugh. The suit's mouth was closed too.

Fortunately, I could still breathe through my nose.

All through the donning process, the suit had been gradually cooling. What at first had been uncomfortably hot passed through pleasantly warm to no perceived temperature. In other words, body temperature.

Or, to put it another way, *the activation temperature.*

Suddenly I was being squeezed from all sides. The pressure was incredible. It was not painful—at least not noticeably, say rather, it was *uncomfortable*—but the pressure was frightening, nonetheless.

For a moment, I panicked, unsure as to just what was going on. Then I remembered the manual's description of the operation of memory plastic. Clearly the pressure I was feeling was the memory threads contracting into their learned shape.

Knowing what was happening eased my initial fear, but it was still a decidedly unpleasant experience. I had an odd memory of a toy called a "shrinky-dink" that I'd had as a child. It was a sheet of plastic, with the outlines of cartoon characters that you could color and cut out. Pop the cutouts in an oven, and they shrank to one-eighth their original size, becoming dense figurines you could play with. I suspected I now knew how they felt about the process.

It was at this point that my patience finally wore out. It had been amusing for a while, and I'd finally satisfied my curiosity, but now things had gone too far. I'd played along. I'd embarrassed myself, and I was just being made more and more the fool.

I was reaching for the donning-slit—which, of course, I now couldn't find!—to begin removing the stupid suit, when two things happened at once. There was a distinct, and again not entirely pleasant, pulling sensation at my crotch; and the eyelids and mouth of the suit seemed to adhere to my own (by some mechanism that I haven't figured out to this day).

With a tearing sensation, both the eyes and the mouth popped open. I happened to be facing the mirror when they did.

If I'd been holding the beer at that moment, I would have dropped it again!

Staring back at me from the mirror was—

A woman.

A beautiful, blond, naked woman with her jaw hanging open in slack-jawed amazement, as she stared at the vision staring back at her from the mirror.

A vision with wistfully attractive features and just the cutest little button nose.

A vision with slender, rounded shoulders that led naturally, gracefully, to the gentle rise of a pair of perfectly proportioned breasts. (Not too high on her chest or "artificial looking" in any way!) Breasts crowned with a pair of impertinent, "perky" nipples that teased my male libido with their demand for attention and admiration.

A vision with a narrow, hourglass waist that led again, naturally, gracefully, to the swell of feminine hips, thighs, and a pair of flawlessly gorgeous legs.

And crowning it all—irresistible—alluring—

That "fake" vagina that now didn't look fake at all. In fact, that vagina now looked, like everything else, so undeniably real and natural that once again I felt a distinct twinge of embarrassment for—

—for—

Me!

I knew, in a detached, objective corner of my mind, that it was *me* staring back from the mirror. But the illusion was so perfect, the woman in the mirror was so *real!* I distinctly felt—*disconnected* is the only word.

Looking at this reflected vision, my subjective knowledge that it was all just illusion, that it was really only me in the mirror, simply couldn't overcome the objective "reality" of what I saw. This woman wasn't me; I wasn't anywhere in sight; there was only this beautiful stranger.

So I played with the woman-reflection.

I raised my right arm—she raised hers. I dropped my arm—she dropped hers, and those gorgeous breasts jiggled in the most erotic fashion. I could feel their weight move against my chest.

A sly little smile curled her luscious lips. With a toss of her head, she flipped the long, wet hair off her shoulder. Then, making a pouting little moue with her mouth, she reached up and cradled her left breast in her left hand, the nipple peeking out between her middle fingers, her right hand twined in the hair over her right ear.

(More disconnection. In the mirror, it was that beautiful wanton caressing soft flesh—but I could feel the weight of it cupped in my hand.)

Still fondling that exquisite breast with her left hand, she stretched out her right hand. Seeking my touch. Her expression changing from that pouting little moue to an almost desperate "Take me *now!*" plea.

And it was me doing it!

And that was the greatest disconnection of all!

I didn't know how to mold my features into a feminine "Take me now" expression. Or at least up until now, I would have thought I didn't.

I leaned forward toward the mirror, to examine the expression more closely and objectively; and of course immediately traded "sultry sexuality" for "studious inquiry." With a mental *Tsk!* I again tried to mold my—or rather, "her"—features into that "Take me now!" plea. (Making a mental bet with myself that the first success had just been a fluke, a one-time example of beginner's luck.)

I was both pleased (and a little surprised) to see that my doubts were unfounded, and I apparently had the knack after all. Now the hand that had been fondling the breast was wrapped across her chest beneath both breasts, lifting them into greater prominence; and the hand that had been reaching out was now pressed against the base of her throat. (I was copying a pose, though I couldn't immediately place where I'd originally seen it.) Her head tilted back, her lips parted, and her eyes closed. (But not all the way. Only far enough to still allow a sly little peek through the lashes. The little slut was toying with me, and she wanted to be able to continue to gauge my reaction to her performance.)

Again, it was more than a little disconcerting when I gauged my reaction for myself.

On a man, the pose and the expression would probably have been ludicrous. But on the beautiful temptress in the mirror, that expression of equal parts plea and command just about stopped my heart!

In some little still-rational corner of my mind, I realized with a shock that—

This was fun!

****

Minutes later, I'd realized that I had my own personal live sex show! Anything I wanted, this sizzling siren would do. No embarrassment. No questions asked.

The little temptress in the mirror pressed the arm supporting her bosom tighter against her chest, lifting those breasts into even greater prominence. Then, again closing her eyes in anticipation (well, again slitting them so I could still enjoy the show), she reached down with her right hand—the hand that she had been pressing against the base of her neck—and began teasing herself, circling the mound of her sex with long, shapely fingers.

Slowly—slowly—those fingers insinuated themselves into her.

(That still-rational corner of my mind was curious how the illusion of depth could be created. Apparently, the "pocket" was doing whatever it was supposed to do. I could feel a slight pressure against my groin as her fingers probed deeper and deeper, but from my/her fingers' point of view, everything was just as it should be.)

The brazen little slut! She was rapidly teasing herself into climax. I could feel a tightness in my chest as she moaned deep in her throat, opened her eyes, and again stretched out her hand to me.

"God, Peter, I *need* you so bad!"

BAM! That took care of the illusion.

****

I'd tried for a breathy falsetto. I wound up sounding more like Marilyn Manson than Marilyn Monroe.

The sense of disconnection collapsed. It *was* only me, after all. Hearing my own voice had proved it, beyond any hope of recovery.

I strode over to the counter and grabbed the manual, then I thumbed through it for a moment, pausing once to flick "my" rapidly drying hair out of my eyes.

Sure enough, here it was: "Voice", Section 8, page 19. Sitting back down on the toilet, I began reading the indicated page—

"One of the most difficult facets of convincingly impersonating a female is the voice."

What an understatement that was!

"It is interesting to note that physiologically, male and female vocal apparatus are almost identical."

Not in the mood for a physiology lesson, I skipped ahead.

"NuGen has therefore perfected a harmless, temporary method of achieving the necessary tightening of the male vocal cords to produce a completely believable feminine voice. The enclosed sample of 'Formula A18, Vocal Aid, Contralto' in its convenient spray bottle, contains sufficient formula for at least twenty applications. Refills are easily obtained by contacting our Service Department at Area Code—"

"Convenient spray bottle"? It must still be in the box.

I set the manual aside, and quickly padded back downstairs. Now, you have to understand: At that moment, I wasn't thinking about my appearance. I was anxious to see if I could complete the illusion that I'd made such an unbelievable start on. That's what I was concentrating on. If

I'd thought about it at all, I certainly wouldn't have felt nude at that moment. It's not that I necessarily felt dressed—the suit didn't feel like clothes.

In fact, if I'd taken the time then, as I have since, to explore just what wearing the suit felt like, I'd have realized that it didn't really feel like much at all. In some respects, the manual had been correct that the suit did little to diminish a person's sense of touch. On my hands and feet, my shoulders, my legs, areas where there was just a very thin layer of plastic—plastic that, with the activation of the memory threads, now adhered *very* closely to my skin—the loss of sensation was actually less than from those latex exam gloves.

True, there was a feeling of pressure over my body. Of constriction. But like wearing a really tight pair of pants, after a while, and even though the pants were still tight, the tightness wasn't at the forefront of your awareness. Especially when you were focused on something else.

Like finding a spray bottle, for example.

The box was sitting on the dining table where I'd left it. I began to paw through the contents (again flicking hair out of my eyes), looking for the voice-spray. I soon found it, snug in its own Styrofoam packing.

I pulled it out and began reading the label. The directions were pretty straightforward: "Depress applicator ONCE while aiming at the rear of the mouth. Inhale deeply as formula is introduced. Allow five minutes for operation of active ingredients. NOTE: A slight, transitory discomfort is not unusual. DO NOT EXCEED RECOMMENDED DOSAGE. Results should continue for not less than eight hours with decreasing effectiveness thereafter. Effects disappear in no more than ten hours from application. For a list of possible adverse reactions, refer to—"

I couldn't read further. Suddenly I had the feeling that someone was watching me.

****

I looked up and realized: I was standing in full view of the kitchen window that overlooks our building's parking lot. More to the point, I was standing in full view of Kyle Tyler, the fourteen-year-old boy from three doors down, who was just then walking past my window after returning from some errand.

He and I stared at each other for a second. I felt puzzled as to why he was just standing there, his arms hanging limp at his sides, gaping at me with such huge, round eyes. Then I realized:

Kyle wasn't staring at me, he was staring a *nude woman* staring back at him from the window of PJ and Josh's apartment!

I had two choices. First: I could give Kyle a cheap thrill. A little something for his fantasies, besides what he found in the *Playboy* he smuggled home every month. Or second, I could teach him he really shouldn't be staring in other people's windows.

I chose Option Two.

The blonde of Kyle's dreams suddenly shrieked (in a jarringly discordant male voice, but being on the other side of the window, Kyle wouldn't know that), grabbed a wholly inadequate dishtowel off the rack, and tried desperately to use it to simultaneously conceal both her naked breasts and equally naked pussy. (I made sure she failed at both endeavors. Hey, I'm not so cruel as to deny Kyle all pleasure at this encounter!) Waving her hand furiously (which set those beautiful breasts jiggling), she shooed Kyle away. To his credit (he's a good boy), he turned crimson and fled to the safety of his own apartment.

****

Seconds later, *after* I closed the blinds, I picked up the "convenient spray bottle" and resumed the business of girlifying my voice.

Taking careful aim, I gave myself a healthy spritz while taking a deep breath. I gagged as the spray seemed to go down the wrong pipe. I wheezed for a few seconds, but finally caught my breath. The stuff tasted awful! It had a pungent chemical taste that somebody had tried to mask with a sickeningly-sweet, clearly-artificial cherry flavor.

I waited for what seemed like five minutes, but nothing happened as far as I could tell.

"Testing, one two—" (Hey, it was all I could think of.)

No change from my normal baritone.

I said, "Fuck! And everything else was working so—"

I had intended to say *working so well*, but I never finished the sentence. At the word *everything*, my voice started to crack and fade. By *so*, it was gone completely.

I raised one delicately feminine hand to my slender throat, and winced at the "slight discomfort" I was suddenly experiencing. It felt like some lunatic was gleefully scrubbing the inside of my larynx with broken glass that was embedded in steel wool. I swallowed several times, trying to ease the suffering, and it finally subsided.

I took a deep breath and tried again. *This crap had better work* was what I'd intended to say. Again, I never finished the sentence.

The voice coming out of my throat—the voice speaking in a throaty, seductively feminine contralto—

I could feel that sly little smirk again curling those full, sensual lips. I was there; I'd done it; there was no doubt remaining. With the final element of an undeniably feminine voice, to match the undeniably feminine body, everything was perfect.

If anybody could spot me through this disguise, I'd eat my bra!

I remember this got me thinking that—flawless as the disguise might be—I couldn't accomplish much with it while I was in the nude. I wondered if the folks at NuGen—having done so well with all the rest—thought to provide for this final detail.

And of course they had.

Nestled in the very bottom of the larger box was a smaller, boutique-style box. Pulling it out, I carried it over to the couch and, making sure I wasn't in the line of any other windows, opened it and examined the contents.

Panties, a bra, a flowery blue dress, stockings, high-heel shoes—women's clothing that was ordinary in every way.

Except that now this women's clothing belonged to me, and now I was about to put it all on.

****

To this day, I still have vivid memories of my first experience donning woman's clothing.

Why is that, do you suppose? Why should something as simple as fabric and buttons and zippers imprint so heavily on a person's memory? I don't have any lasting memories of putting on a pair of men's jeans or a pullover shirt.

Was it a function of the—What's the word I'm searching for? The *newness*? The *exploration*? Surely it's not all that surprising that doing something rather extraordinary for the very first time sticks in your memory.

And being the innocent about such matters that I have already freely confessed that I am, this was the first time I'd ever held a bra, or panties, or a pair of women's stockings in my hands, much less gone about putting them on.

Of course another, alternative explanation exists. Was it in fact memorable because the clothing was "feminine" and I'm "masculine"?

That's an odd notion: that clothing can have gender. Well, of course it does—in a way. I mean, it's women's clothing, so I guess you could say it has "gender relevance." But it's not like the panties I found in that box were "girl panties"—that is, panties with a feminine gender. They were a genderless inanimate object that was intended for use by girls.

In the end, perhaps it was all just the combination of factors and circumstance.

The memories might not have been so vivid if I—that is, me, Peter, the masculine me—had been handling that pair of panties. However, as mentioned, it wasn't "Peter" handling those panties, it was me gazing down over a pair of perky, rose-tipped breasts at a slender pair of feminine hands that were fondling those silky little panties. It was watching those panties slide up a pair of sleek legs and snuggle against that perfect little pussy.

It was having to continually brush back the fall of blond hair as I tried first to get that lacy bra properly aligned on my shoulders, and then wrestle with getting the three hooks fastened in the three eyes by touch alone. And then, once it was on and more-or-less properly aligned, it was me watching those same slender feminine hands insinuating themselves into the cups to rearrange those perky breasts more "comfortably."

It was the realization that I could manipulate the operation of those breasts and that bra. That is, with some "rearrangement," I could produce either a little less or a little more cleavage. I had feminine "options." Set things up one way, and I was prim and modest. Set them up another, and there was just a hint of wanton and sexual.

And speaking of alluring and sexual, and the gender of clothing: There was just no other way to think about it when I rolled up a stocking, slipped those (disconcertingly realistic!) toes in, and then gently coaxed that shiny fabric higher and higher up those curvaceous, female legs.

Mrs. Robinson. *The Graduate.* Seduction. Feminine wiles.

It was raising my arms and feeling the lightweight, floral-print dress slide down over my head. Bunching for a moment atop the thrust of my bosom, before cascading down to caress the curve of my hips. Gliding with an almost *liquid* touch over the fabric of those nylons to finally swirl around my knees.

And it was the memory of finally gazing in the full-length mirror, on the inside of my closet door, at the young woman gazing back. It was watching her fluff out that long blond hair in a completely casual, completely feminine gesture, and then stand there with her hands casually folded behind her back, appraising me as I appraised her.

It was the again oh-so-*disconnecting* realization that, though I might fantasize about it (and given what I was looking at, how could I not), I—the male PJ me—would never actually know what lacy little treasures she might be concealing beneath that print dress. Or what treasures within treasures lay concealed beneath that lace.

Because she was a stranger.

I didn't know her. She didn't know me. As a result, modesty on her part, and propriety on mine, dictated that even a long, lingering glance was taboo, much less any expectation on my part that she'd freely display what propriety demanded that she conceal.

She did allow me to watch, however, as she tried out various poses. Hands on hips. Hands folded behind her back. Arms crossed—beneath breasts, after a momentary fluster when she discovered the need for a woman to consider the difference in anatomy between herself and a male. "Flirting" with that skirt: pulling the fabric out, away from her leg on the right, thus drawing it tight against the left. Casually swinging the hem back and forth while rocking her shoulders from side to side, the little finger of her free hand tugging at the corner of her lower lip. Then gathering the skirt against the back of her thighs and leaning over, slightly, from the waist, her shoulders rocked forward, her neck arched backward, giggling softly at her "innocent shamelessness."

Her flirting.

I finally glanced at the clock. It was almost 2 p.m. Where had the afternoon gone? (Where, indeed!)

Josh would be getting home in just over three hours. I just couldn't wait for him to see what his money had purchased. I couldn't wait for him to share in the wonder of the stranger that I had become.

This plan was going to work! I could fool anybody! *Anybody!*

Then a devious little thought entered my mind, and my grin must have doubled in size.

Rushing downstairs (struggling not to be distracted by bounce, jiggle, and skirt swirling around nylons), I ransacked the drawers for a paper grocery bag. Finding one, I then began looking for the scissors. I had some delicate work to perform, and some practicing before the mirror to do, if I was going to pull off what I intended.

Chapter 1-2
Women Are From Venus

Josh wheeled his Taurus into the parking lot of the apartment, pulled into his space, and shut off the engine. It had been a long day in a long week, and he was worn out. The pressure of landing the Sprague Contract was starting to build. He massaged his tired eyes and opened the door.

As he was climbing out of the car, he caught sight of a gorgeous twenty-something blonde coming toward him down the sidewalk between the apartment blocks, struggling with a heavy looking grocery bag.

She was wearing a print dress that Josh could see was fairly low cut, but because of the way she held the bag against her chest, he couldn't get more than an occasional glimpse of what had to be a truly spectacular pair of tits. Tits that he imagined bouncing in counterpoint to the long, honey-blonde hair that swung and bobbed with each of her determined steps.

What a babe! was Josh's thought as she turned the corner and strutted past, apparently oblivious to the rapt attention she was generating.

The rear view was just as pleasing as the front. A heart-shaped ass wiggled beneath the filmy fabric of the dress, as the skirt swirled around a flawless pair of legs.

"Baby, where have you been all my life?" he muttered, enjoying the show.

She had just reached the path to his apartment block when it happened. The bag split wide open, spilling groceries all over the lawn, sidewalk, and parking lot.

She wailed a delightfully helpless "Oh, oh, *shoot!*" and stamped her foot just like a petulant little girl. Then, gathering her skirt primly against her thighs, she squatted on her heels and began retrieving the spilled items.

Josh whispered, "Thank you, God!" and then rushed to the aid of this damsel in distress.

"Hi. Need some help?" Josh asked.

She glanced up, startled, her cornflower-blue eyes flying wide. "*What?* Oh, uh, would you?"

Her startled expression changed to an alluring, demure little smile, as she flicked an errant wisp of honey-colored hair behind her left ear. Her voice was a smoky, breathy contralto.

Josh expected he'd be hearing that voice whispering "Fuck me, *now!*" in his dreams for a long time.

He bent down and began helping pick things up. "No problem! Happy to help out a neighbor. You *are* a neighbor, right?"

She nodded, her smile becoming even more open and friendly with the implication that this stranger might be a neighbor, and therefore at least potentially "okay."

That sexy contralto voice replied, "Yes. I'm brand-new here. Thank you so much for helping. It's been such a weird day, and now this!"

Josh chuckled, turning up the masculine charm. (*Hot Damn! New meat in town, and I might just be getting first crack at it!*) "Well, welcome to the neighborhood!"

He stood. "I'm Josh, by the way. I live right over there in 27F."

As she straightened back up, she had to lean forward for just a moment to maintain her balance, and Josh managed to steal a fleeting glimpse down the bosom of her dress.

God, those tits! They're spectacular! A deep cleft of cleavage, and full, soft curves, pressed against a teasing glimpse of white lace. Josh felt a stirring at his crotch.

She reached out for the bag of groceries in Josh's arms and started to reply to his introduction, but then something distracted her. With her arms still outstretched, she glanced down at something that was apparently on the ground at her feet. Josh followed her gaze but didn't immediately notice anything.

She lowered her arms, placed her hands on her hips, and glared down at the "something" that Josh still didn't see. In a return to that pouting, frustrated tone, she grumbled, "Oh, for goodness sake! If it's not one thing, it's another. Look at that!"

"I'm sorry. I don't see—"

"Would you mind holding that bag just a moment longer?"

"Not at all. What—?"

But instead of replying, she was suddenly bending forward from the hip, and reaching down toward her left foot. This time the glimpse of cleavage and curves and lace wasn't fleeting.

She muttered, "Silly things! It must have happened when I was picking up the groceries."

The still unanswered question froze on Josh's lips as the blonde beauty ran her hands up her leg, starting at her ankle and ending at her upper thigh, her skirt rucking up in the process to the point that Josh caught a glimpse of more silk and more lace. She smoothed the stocking on her left leg, and then fussed for a moment, rearranging the tension on the garter tabs supporting it.

Josh could only stand there, gaping in astonishment.

Her stockings apparently adjusted to her satisfaction, and as casually as if nothing at all had just happened, the blonde then smoothed out her again modestly arranged skirt, again tucked that flyaway strand of hair behind her ear, and smiled a polite and completely innocent little smile at Josh as she once again reached out for the bag of groceries.

"I'm sorry. You were saying?" she said.

"I—um—Josh. Apartment. Twenty-Seven. F."

Still smiling that friendly smile, she batted her long lashes and purred, "Oh, yes. That's right. And isn't that the most *amazing* coincidence? You see, I'm PJ. I live in 27F too!"

For a second the words didn't register. It wasn't until her demure smile melted into a wicked grin that Josh's jaw dropped open, and he actually staggered back a step.

She folded her hands behind her back and gave her shoulders a playful shake. It would all have been very "little-girl-fetching," but for the evil glint in her eyes and the vicious smile on her lips. Not to mention, she wasn't shaped like a little girl.

Josh's brother the temptress said, "That's right, you horny bastard. It's *me!* What do you think of the new suit? Wanna go inside and fuck?"

****

Several minutes later, I was sprawled out in my favorite spot on the couch. With the need to pretend modesty gone, I ignored the fact that the hem of my skirt currently rested a daring three-quarters of the way up my thighs, the material sagging between my legs. Glancing down over those amazing counterfeit breasts, I could just glimpse the lower hem of the stockings once again peeking out.

Still giggling (you couldn't call that girlish sound a chuckle!) over Josh's discomfort, I took another sip of my beer. "Admit it, man, you didn't have a clue! By the time I had my skirt up to my hip, you were staring so hard at my panties that your eyes were about to pop out of your head!"

Josh finished putting away the last of the groceries (for the second time since we'd bought them), and popped open a beer of his own. "Okay, okay—I admit it. But I had good reason! Have you seen yourself in a mirror?"

It was probably a good thing at that moment that all Josh could see were the suit's smooth, downy cheeks. My own stubble-covered cheeks were probably flame red with the guilty memory of blond, girlified me "performing" before the mirror.

Aloud I replied, "Yeah. I've—uh—yeah. I checked it out after I first put it on."

Josh apparently caught the note of guilt in my tone, and deduced (correctly) just what I might have been doing with that mirror. A smug little smile quirked the corners of *his* lips.

I quickly moved to recapture the initiative, before it strayed too far out of my favor. I again hiked up my skirt, shifted my hips, and used my counterfeit voice to pout, "Well, what do you expect? I like a free peek at a girl's panties as much as the next guy!"

Josh flopped down in a chair across from me, looked me up and down, and took a healthy pull on his beer. "All right. All right. Could you please not—? I mean, this is more than weird enough already without you—"

Obliging, I stood, repeated the carefully rehearsed smoothing gesture that had been part of the bait for my practical joke out on the sidewalk, and sat back down, thighs primly pressed together. I even tugged on the hem till it fell over my knees. Then I smiled as innocently as I could.

I batted my eyelashes and asked, "Better?"

Josh just frowned. "I still can't believe it's you. I keep expecting PJ to come down the stairs, laughing at the joke."

I nodded. "I know. But it's me, all right. If I could take this thing off easily, I'd show you." Glancing at the clock over the TV, I realized I'd been *en femme* for over six hours. It probably was time to shed the suit, so Josh and I could seriously consider our next moves, and I said as much.

Josh considered that for a moment, took another swig of his beer, and cleared his throat. "Um, before you take it off, I was wondering—I mean, nice face, nice hair, nice— uhh—" He gestured vaguely with the can. "But, uh, what about—? I mean, underneath the clothes. Is it, um—?"

That was just too good an opportunity to pass up. Without saying a word, I stood, flipped my hair over my shoulder, reached around behind, and unzipped my dress. Teasing off first one shoulder then the other, I held the material against my breasts for a moment, then let it fall in a heap around my ankles.

Needless to say, I suddenly had Josh's full attention.

Again reaching behind myself, I breathed a silent prayer to the gods of lingerie, and flicked the catch of the bra. To my surprise, it immediately came undone, and released those two remarkable fake boobs, which promptly bobbed and swayed in newfound freedom.

Josh's eyes were getting wider by the moment.

Letting the straps of my now-unfastened bra slide down my arms, I allowed it to fall to the floor. Next I slid my hands down my sides, slipping my fingers into the sides of my panties. I looked right into Josh's eyes, gave him a breathy sigh of make-believe passion, and bent over from the waist, sliding the panties down around my knees as I went. Straightening, I ran my fingers through the hair at my temples, and struck what I hoped was a dramatic pose.

Considering Josh's reaction—the sudden and quite noticeable bulge in his pants to go along with his bulging eyes—I evidently succeeded.

He whispered an amazed, "Holy smoke!" and stared open-mouthed at a point just below my navel.

I gave him my best sexy purr. "Like what you see, big boy?"

He looked up and pointed at my crotch. "Does it—I mean, can you—?"

I shrugged. "How would I know? I haven't had much of a chance to try it out. The manual says it should work like a charm, and the manual hasn't been wrong yet."

I switched back to that sultry purr. "You wanna find out, you big, hot stud?"

His look of embarrassed, indignant anger set me laughing again.

I relented, slid the panties back into place so I could walk, collected the dropped items, and headed for the stairs. "Put on a couple of burgers and I'll see if I can get out of this thing. Then we'll figure out the next step."

****

Passing my bedroom door, I tossed the female clothing onto the bed. Remembering I was still partially dressed, I also slid out of the panties and hose and tossed them in as well.

Whistling a little tune (and noticing that a woman whistling sounds pretty much like a man whistling—funny, I'd never noticed that before), I strode into the bathroom. In all the excitement, I'd forgotten to drain the tub and it was still half-full of now-cold water. Opening the drain, I picked up the manual, and began looking for the instructions on removing the suit. I easily found the relevant section.

"Removing your I-2000S is, in many ways, simply the reverse of donning it. CAUTION: to safely remove the suit without damaging the memory threads, it is *imperative* that the suit be heated in water of between 110 to 120 degrees temperature for not less than ten minutes prior to removal. *Failure to follow this instruction will result in damage to the I-2000S and will void the manufacturer's warranty!"*

I remembered how hot the water seemed earlier. This time, I got to be inside the suit when it went into the cauldron. The tub had finished draining. Closing the drain, I started the taps running.

The manual continued: "It should be borne in mind: The head of the I-2000S also contains a significant number of memory threads. Therefore, the head must also be immersed in heated water prior to removal. DANGER! It is *not* necessary for the head to remain submerged for a continuous ten-minute period. It is sufficient to submerge the head for several consecutive brief periods, provided that ultimately the head is thoroughly saturated and attains a temperature in excess of 110 degrees. (NOTE: some users of the I-2000 series have reported excellent results employing an easily obtained diving snorkel.)"

A snorkel? I set the manual aside with a chuckle. (Well, actually a giggle.) I could just picture myself, wearing the suit, submerged in the tub, a snorkel jammed in my pretty little mouth. The things a person would do to land a job!

****

All this time, the hot water had been splashing into the tub. Listening to the gurgling, bubbling fluid, I suddenly became acutely aware of the several beers I'd consumed throughout the day.

I stood up, and by reflex lifted the toilet seat. I reached down for my—

And realized that I was in trouble!

I had to go. *Now!* But my "drain" was deeply ensconced within the confines of the suit. To get at my tool, I had to get out of the suit. But to get out of the suit, I had to soak it in hot water for at least ten minutes! I grabbed the manual and began looking for a solution—a *quick* one!

I found the "U" section and almost immediately spotted "Urination—see 'Elimination' " More frantically-turned pages. C . . . D—Ah! E—"Elimination, Section 29, pg. 36."

By the time I found the right page, I was doing a panicky little dance. It's funny how the realization that you need to go starts building that need in a rapid, geometric progress. Need fuels anxiety, which fuels greater need—and so on.

"The designers of the I-2000S have taken great lengths to ensure that the illusion of femininity is perfect in every respect. Realizing that during prolonged periods of use, it may become necessary for the wearer to attend to normal bodily functions, the designers have provided a uniquely advanced—"

A little voice in my mind was whimpering, *God! Spare me the sales pitch! I've already bought the damn thing!* I scanned further down the page till my eyes lit on a sentence halfway down.

"Wearers may therefore use female accommodations secure in the knowledge that, even here, the appearance of normal female anatomy will be preserved."

To hell with this! I was at the point where I could only hope that the manual was saying what I hoped it was saying. Dropping the seat, I sat back down and—

The sensation was rather odd. It didn't particularly feel any different. I could hear the urine striking the water. But I couldn't tell how it was getting from point "A" to point "B". I sneaked a quick peek between my legs.

So—that's what it looked like when a woman took a leak. Interesting. I could see that this suit was going to be a real educational experience, in ways I hadn't even considered.

****

Sitting at the dinner table, I finished off the last of my burger while still toweling my hair.

The suit had come off with surprising ease, if you discounted the difficulty I'd had holding my breath while soaking my head. Suddenly, that snorkel idea didn't sound so ridiculous after all.

The suit was now hanging from the shower rod, peacefully dripping into the empty tub. All in all, not a bad afternoon's work. I was looking forward to my next "foray into femininity."

Josh was idly tapping his fork against his plate, thinking. I washed down the last bite of burger with the last beer from the fridge.

I asked, in that (now more than a little distracting) contralto voice, "So, what's the plan?"

I glanced over at the clock on the stove. Another two hours till my voice returned to normal.

Josh glanced up and frowned. "You have no idea how weird it is, sitting here listening to that sexy voice come out of your head!"

I nodded. "Think how it feels for me. From now on, I'm gonna make it a point to leave the suit on till my voice starts to change back. Don't want to freak out the mailman if I have to talk to him to accept a package or something."

Josh nodded. "That's a good idea. We've both got to start thinking that way. If we're not careful, and somebody figures out what's going on, we're both gonna be down at the unemployment office!"

We sat quietly for a moment.

I said, "Josh?"

"Yeah?"

"Uh, I want to thank you for putting up the money for this, and for the idea. You know, for everything."

He seemed lost in thought. "Don't worry, Bro. I trust you. You'll pay me back. Besides, you'll be doing all of the work."

"Just the same—thanks, man. So, what's next?"

Josh looked up and smiled. "Tomorrow's Sunday. Since I don't have to go in to work, I thought we'd blow more of my money and get you some working clothes."

I just grinned.

****

By the second day, I was beginning to discover some interesting changes in my behavior when I wore the suit.

Now, I don't mean any kind of Jekyll/Hyde transformation, or anything like that. It was still me in there. I was still conscious of my actions and I was in control of them.

The changes were more subtle. Wearing the suit brought out a—I guess the word would be *playful* or teasing aspect of my character that I'd never seen before. Again, the suit didn't create this aspect; I suppose it was always there. The suit just let it "come out and play," so to speak.

The trip to the Mall turned out to be "playtime" in a big way.

All during the twenty-minute drive, I was trying to pull the same prank I'd pulled on Josh yesterday. I gave a languorous stretch, arching my back and really sticking those boobs out. Then I quickly glanced sideways to see if Josh was obediently staring at them.

He wasn't. He was concentrating on making a left turn from one street to another.

Realizing that trying to make more out of my already exaggerated pose would only make the game obvious, I relaxed to a natural sitting posture with my hands folded in my lap. The weight of my hands caused the material of the skirt to climb a fraction of an inch higher up my thighs. I primly slid the hem back down.

No reaction from Josh. He continued to pay all of his attention to his driving and none to me.

I wriggled in my seat, freeing up more loose skirt to tug all the way down over my knees.

Nothing from Josh.

I glanced down to see if, perhaps, all the activity had caused a wrinkle in my stockings and I could do the "girl straightening her nylons" routine again.

(Though in the back of my mind, a little voice was warning me that was probably a trick I could only expect to get away with once. At which point a second little voice smirked, *Wanna bet? I bet that works as many times as you want to try it.*)

It was as I was arguing back and forth with myself that I realized that at some point during all the hem-tugging and butt-wiggling, the left strap of my bra had somehow slid down off my shoulder. Without even thinking about it, I casually reached inside that flirty little dress and tugged the strap back up where it belonged.

My reward was a growl from Josh. "You can keep playing those tricks if you want, but you need to realize that your reward will probably be a broken neck in the car crash when I finally get distracted to the point that I can't pay any attention to my driving at all."

I meekly folded my hands in my lap and behaved.

At least for the rest of the trip.

But when we pulled up in front of one of the Mall's department stores, and Josh no longer had to concentrate on his driving, the teasing resumed.

He got out, but I just sat in the car.

Josh had gone about a dozen steps when he realized I wasn't following. Leaning in the driver's window, he asked, "What's wrong?"

I gave him that sexy pout I'd perfected in the mirror, and in my best little-girl voice I whimpered, "A gentleman always opens a door for a lady."

Josh glanced to Heaven for strength, stomped around to my side, and flung my door open.

I giggled, gave my shoulders a shake setting those boobs jiggling, swung my legs out the door (just like that hosiery ad on TV), stood, and pranced off toward the entrance, swinging my hips in victory.

I made damn sure I beat Josh to the Mall door, then just stood there, hands clasped behind my firm little butt, smiling innocently. Give Josh credit, he knew when to admit defeat. Without comment, he opened that door for me too.

****

We walked through the women's-wear section of the department store, but Josh quickly pronounced all those items too low-budget. I thought some of the suits and dresses were quite nice, and said so, but Josh insisted that we go first-class if we did this. He wanted the woman who appeared for the interview to be a "Class Broad" (his words), and felt that she should dress accordingly.

Who was I to argue? We finally wound up in an upscale woman's clothing store.

I've never been what you'd call a clotheshorse. I like my tee shirts and jeans. Occasionally you can force me into a suit and tie, but it takes a lot of effort.

But now things had changed. I was seeing the world from a whole new perspective. I was wearing a gorgeous, sexy body, and I wanted clothes that would show it off.

Josh and I spent almost three hours conducting a mini-fashion show, with me as the star model. The saleslady, a professional looking woman in her fifties, was very helpful. Josh explained that his "little sister" had just landed a job with a prestigious firm and needed a starter wardrobe, and off we went.

I was having a blast. It can be fun to have people staring at you, admiring how you look. I can see why women like to be fashion models.

Jennifer (the saleslady) would inspect each outfit, while Josh watched over her shoulder. They'd quietly confer as I strutted my stuff around the aisles. In the end, we picked out four complete suits, three dresses, and several blouse/skirt/slacks combinations that Jennifer assured me I could mix and match with the rest to create an adequate wardrobe. She carefully measured my feet and picked out four pairs of shoes, mostly conservative, low-heeled pumps in goes-with-anything colors. Finally, she selected a nice, leather, shoulder-bag type purse.

I just about choked when she tallied it up and presented Josh with a bill for just over *two thousand dollars*! Josh, bless him, didn't even bat an eyelash. He just plopped down his Gold AMEX.

I was so chastened by the amount that I quickly picked up the lion's share of the boxes and began toting them out to the car. I suddenly didn't feel like playing mind games and insisting that Josh be a gentleman and carry everything for his "delicate little sister."

We were just about out the door when Jennifer called out, "Why not stop off at Victoria's on the way out? Nothing like a little sexy underwear to give spark to a power suit!"

Now it was Josh who was grinning.

****

If "clothes make the man," then sexy, slinky, silky underwear makes the woman.

In some ways, I was the "kid in the candy store." Be honest, what normal male can walk by the window to Victoria's Secret and not steal a sly, sidelong glance?

But now, and unlike poor Josh, I didn't have to be sneaky. I could stare. I could walk right up and touch the items. Hell, I could lift them off the rack and actually hold in my hands the intimate little bits of silk and lace that men weren't supposed to know existed. After a moment, I realized I could even hold them against myself and imagine what they would look like on the female form beneath the dress.

And then I realized I didn't have to imagine. There were several changing rooms in the back.

Bras of every description: lightly padded, push-up, "miracle," demi, and strapless. Panties in every color of the rainbow: lacy, frilly, satiny, virginal, daring, and sleazy. Thongs, hip-huggers, g-strings, half-slips, full slips, camisoles, corsets (ouch!), body-hugging teddies, garter belts, stockings—

I tried them all.

And as I say, poor old Josh didn't get to play this time. The all-woman sales staff made it clear that while he could pay the freight, the changing rooms were off-limits. Strictly "woman's country." Perhaps that added a little extra thrill for me.

That is to say, a little extra thrill on top of the wonderful turn-on of having a live-action Victoria's Secret catalog to play with. Standing there at the mirror, looking at that amazing body as it displayed all those forbidden views of woman's under-dress, I felt like a spy in enemy territory. Undiscovered, and getting away with something.

At this point, I should probably say that I'm about as sexually straight as a guy gets. A real "plain vanilla," "XY-chromosome," "bowling with the guys" type. I'm not a cross-dresser, or transvestite, or whatever the currently politically correct phrase is. At least, I truly don't think I am.

It's not that I have any problem with cross-dressing, mind you. The folks who are into it have never done anything to hurt me; and despite the ranting and raving of the conservative right, I sincerely doubt they're contributing significantly to the decay of Western Civilization. So I don't find it particularly hard to take a "live and let live" attitude. I just honestly think that while I don't object to their choice of lifestyle, it's not one that I'd have ever been attracted to, in the normal order of things. I'm not one of them.

I suppose that doesn't seem too believable when I recount my breathless fascination as I stood there before the mirror, feeling all "hot and bothered" over the basque, g-string, and white stockings adorning my body.

Perhaps that's the answer. "Body." What normal male wouldn't be "hot and bothered" by the images I was seeing? After all, it wasn't Peter James Wright preening and posing in the mirror.

But it was even more than that, than the surface appearance. It didn't feel like I was the one standing there in all that lace and satin. That is, it didn't feel like "me." And by *feel*, I mean—well, I'm not quite sure what I mean. That mental detachment again. If it had been me, "in my own skin" as it were, I wouldn't—*I couldn't*—have been doing that. Peter in those frilly little undies? No. I'd dry up and blow away from embarrassment. But put me in the suit, *give me some mental distance,* make it not "me," but rather the sexy little vixen who was most definitely not me—just look in the mirror if you have any doubts!—and look out, boys!

****

Four hours from the time we started, we were back in the car heading home, several dozen boxes heavier, and Josh, two-thousand-dollars-plus lighter.

We made one last stop at one of those chain drug stores. I browsed the makeup aisle for a bit, then selected a complete cosmetics selection from—well, one of the major designers. I also picked out several fairly neutral shades of lipstick. Finally I scanned the periodical section and grabbed two woman's magazines. One promised "complete makeup tips for work or play," and the other advertised a "beginner's guide to fabulous makeup."

****

And so, finally, we came down to it. The big interview was scheduled for 11 a.m. Tuesday morning.

Chapter 1-3
Playing "The Game"...

I spent all morning Monday *en femme*, trying on my various outfits and practicing my makeup. Makeup's not as easy as you might think. I've got a natural artist's eye and touch. Still, the first few attempts were—

Well, *striking* might be a polite term. By the third try, I was up to *cheap streetwalker*. However, by mid-afternoon, I'd finally arrived at something that I felt closely approximated the pictures in my magazines. I'd also made a pretty good dent in my supply of cosmetics, and used up a whole jar of cold cream.

Tired and somewhat on edge, I went through the ritual of removing the suit, and carefully hung it up to dry. I then went for a long walk. Usually that cleared my head, but not today. I was just as edgy when I got back home and saw that Josh had come home early.

I found him stalking around the kitchen.

"Where the hell have you been?" he demanded. "I came home early just to prep you for tomorrow."

I collapsed on the sofa. "Back off, Josh. Since when do I have to tell you when I'm coming or going?" Almost immediately I regretted my words. "I'm sorry, man, I'm just nervous, is all."

He walked around to his chair and sat down, his "businessman mode" clearly evident. He even had his briefcase with him.

He said, "You should be nervous. This is a big interview you're going to, and it's already cost me a fortune to set it up." Seeing me tense up to strike back, he quickly continued. "But, nervous is good. It'll give you quick reflexes tomorrow. Besides, I know Old Man North, inside and out. I can get you past him, no problem."

I felt my heart pressing against the walls of my throat. "You mean the *owner of the firm* is gonna be conducting my interview?"

Josh grinned. "Don't sweat it. That's actually a point in our favor. Old Man North has been around two years longer than dirt. He's one of the last surviving relics of the Old School. That's one of the reasons we're in the mess we're in, down there. That's why we don't have female executives. North still clings to the notion that women are inherently evil creatures, put on this Earth solely for the purpose of tempting men into sin."

I scratched my head. "And this *helps?*"

Josh nodded. "I've been checking into the other two candidates for the job. We've lucked out. They're both 'new corporate women.' Real hard-chargers, out to climb the business ladder. North gets one good look at them, and he'll probably have a coronary on the spot!"

"While I, on the other hand—?"

"All you got to do is wear that conservative gray number, keep your hands folded in your lap, bat those big baby-blues, and play the naïve little virgin. Like I say, after seeing the other two, North will hire you on the spot, guaranteed!"

I went to bed early that night, and tossed and turned for hours. Somewhere around 2 a.m., I finally drifted off to sleep. A terrible nightmare woke me just as the alarm went off at 7. I can't remember exactly what the dream was about, except that it had something to do with being sacrificed to a volcano.

****

Josh had left for work early, and I pretty much had the place to myself as I went about my conversion into female mode. I took extra time with everything, carefully measuring the water temperature, being unusually careful about slipping into the suit, and drying myself off completely. I even brushed out my long, golden hair—three hundred strokes—till it was a glossy, shimmering cascade flowing over my shoulders.

It took three times for me to get my makeup right. I wanted to accentuate my beauty, without looking like I'd done anything, just like the magazines said. I finally got the look I was trying for: *farmer's daughter waiting for her very first kiss.*

I had laid out my clothes on my bed before I started with the suit. But now, at the moment of decision, I folded my arms under my ersatz bosom and tapped my foot, thinking.

The outfit was a conservatively cut charcoal-gray blazer with matching skirt, the hem falling just below my knees. I had a bone-colored silk blouse to go with it, which I intended to wear buttoned to the throat. I'd selected a simple white bra, one that didn't emphasize my breasts and that held them firmly in place. (Somehow, based on Josh's briefing, I didn't think my "bouncing boob" routine would win me any points today.) A full-cut panty brief, plain except for a delicate lace panel on the front, and a full slip with elegant lace detail at the hem and breasts, completed my underdress.

Except, that is, for my stockings.

Originally, I'd intended to go with a pair of sheer black pantyhose. I thought about it for a while, and even went so far as to put on the panties, then the hose, then slip into the skirt. Checking out the effect in the mirror, I decided that it would be too provocative for Old Man North. (After a moment, I also realized that here I was, staring at a half-nude woman wearing silky black stockings, a gray skirt, and a stern little frown of concentration, her golden hair flowing down over her shoulders, and around two lovely little nipples bobbing about atop two exquisite breasts—and I wasn't even noticing the breasts!)

I unzipped the skirt, stepped out of it, and slid the pantyhose off. Rummaging in my new "unmentionables" drawer, I found a pair of nude-to-the-waist, "silk mist" pantyhose, and started to slip into them.

Without really knowing why, I stopped, pulled them back off, removed my panties, put the hose back on, then pulled the panties up till they completely concealed the dark waistband of the hose. It was disconcerting to realize that I found wearing the hose and panties this way was reassuring. *If I screw up somewhere along the line, at least they won't see the pantyhose. Only the panties.*

Once consciously recognized, that thought was so bizarre that I had to stop for a moment and try to determine the underlying rationale. For the first time, a new little voice in my head chided me with what was an apparently obvious truth. *It's modesty, stupid. Can't you see? If it goes really, badly wrong. If I screw up so badly that they can see all the way up my skirt, at least I've still got one secret left. I won't have given the whole show away.*

Strangest of all (in retrospect), what I would have called "woman's logic" on any other occasion, actually made sense to me here.

The bra came next. I still fumbled with it for a moment, but I was already becoming much more adept at this particular facet of the dark art of donning female attire.

I pulled the slip over my head, then put on the blouse. I slid the skirt over my head, so as not to ruck up my slip, and zipped it up. Finally, I stepped into the conservative black pumps that I'd chosen, then shrugged into the blazer.

I very carefully checked out the result in the mirror, turning this way and that, making sure that my stockings weren't baggy and that my slip wasn't showing. I primped my hair a bit, checked my makeup one last time, and decided I was as ready as I was ever going to be. Slinging my purse over my shoulder I strode (confidently, I hoped!) out the door.

I was halfway down the sidewalk when I realized that I hadn't done anything about my voice!

Practically running back inside, I grabbed my "convenient spray bottle" then spent an anxious several minutes waiting for the "slight discomfort" to announce that I was indeed ready to face the world on feminine terms.

I was still trying to swallow the pain away several minutes later, waiting for the bus to arrive.

****

The advertising agency of Whitman and North occupied a large suite on the fourth floor of an old gray stone office building downtown.

In its heyday, this building had been a prestigious location, and the size of Whitman and North's suite was a cachet of its success.

But nowadays all the fashionable firms were long gone, in favor of the new glass and steel towers several blocks over. The old gray stone was left with a few travel agencies on the ground floor, some small-time insurance brokerages, dentists with waiting-room furniture from the Sixties, and tenants that leased space by the month. That isn't to say that the building was seedy. It wasn't. It was just sleepy—out of the mainstream.

A good analogy for Whitman and North.

All that would change if they managed to land the Sprague contract.

I checked the directory in the lobby, then boarded the elevator. When the doors opened on the fourth floor, a kindly looking older gentleman actually stepped out and held the doors for me. I gave him a genuine smile and nod of thanks. Not so much for holding the doors, but for reminding me that, to the rest of the world, I appeared to be an attractive young woman. He wouldn't know that was the reason for the thanks, but he deserved them anyway.

I paused outside the door labeled "Whitman and North Agency," smoothed my skirt, took a deep breath, and—while silently repeating, "Naïve virgin, naïve virgin"—I stepped inside.

I was in a large reception area with several couches against the walls. Low coffee tables offered magazines for guests' perusal. A middle-aged woman seated behind a receptionist's desk glanced up at my entrance, and smiled. "May I help you?"

"Yes, please. I'm—Pamela Wright. I have an appointment with Mr. North."

I'd almost said *Peter Wright*. Josh and I had discussed names the night before last while preparing my résumé. I'd started suggesting some completely fictional name, something like *Cathy White*, or *Jeanette Peterson*. Josh had overruled that idea. "Remember, this may be 'your' name for a long time. And more than that, we need to keep the possibilities for mistakes as low as possible. One slip—if you forget and automatically sign 'PJ Wright' instead of whatever you make up—the game's over. You should probably pick something that we can abbreviate to 'PJ'—you're used to responding to that. It's a nice unisex name that you can now use to advantage."

And that's how "Pamela Jane Wright" was born.

Apparently the receptionist didn't notice my hesitation, because she casually reached over, picked up the phone, and pressed a button. "Mrs. Huddleston? The young lady is here for the eleven o'clock. . . . All right."

She hung up, gave me another smile, and indicated the passage to my right. "Down that way, last door at the end of the hall." Then she winked and whispered, "Good luck!"

I thanked her and—still silently repeating, "Naïve virgin"—I headed off down the hall.

The door read "Wilson North," nothing else. I opened it and peered inside.

It was another reception area, smaller this time, with a matronly looking black woman behind the receptionist's desk.

She glanced up and gave me the oddest, most piercing stare I've ever received from a stranger. "Miss Wright?"

I nodded and stepped in. "Yes, ma'am. I have an appointment with Mr. North."

She nodded, and indicated a sofa against one wall. "He'll be with you in just a moment."

Then she went back to her paperwork, and pointedly ignored me. I sat down, placed my purse in my lap, and concentrated on keeping my knees together.

The black woman, whose nameplate suggested that she was indeed Mrs. Huddleston, finally glanced up at the clock on the wall, then picked up her phone and punched a button. "Mr. North, your eleven o'clock interview is here . . . yes, sir."

She indicated the door behind her with the end of a pencil. "He'll see you now."

****

Old Man North was a patrician-looking gentleman of indeterminate old age. Clearly over fifty, *probably* under a hundred. He rose from his chair when I opened the door (Old School manners: A gentleman always rises when a lady enters the room), and walked around his desk to greet me. "Miss Wright? Welcome."

He offered his hand, and I again used that "fingertips in the palm" technique.

He seemed to like that, because he didn't try to shake my hand, he just held it for a moment. (I had the strangest image of him actually kissing my hand. He was such a courtly old gentleman, it would have seemed perfectly normal if he had.)

He smiled and said, "Sit down, won't you?" He indicated a chair opposite his own massive throne.

I remembered to press my skirt against my thighs as I sat down, then resisted the urge to cross my legs. (Not ladylike!) Instead, I tried to copy a posture I'd seen elegant women adopt sometimes. Sliding my little butt to the left, I pointed my knees to the right then angled my legs back to the left, crossing my ankles. For good measure, I further protected my modesty by placing my purse squarely in my lap.

North indicated my portfolio on the credenza behind him. "I've examined your work. Very impressive!"

I lowered my gaze, and tried to look pleased beyond measure. I wish the folks at NuGen had figured out a way to incorporate a blush-response into the suit. A maidenly tinge to highlight my delicate cheeks would have gone perfectly right then.

I murmured a shy little "Oh, thank you *very* much, sir!"

For the next half-hour or so, North and I chatted about my background, my education, my likes and dislikes. Surprisingly, I found I could answer most of the questions honestly, particularly the questions relating to my art and education.

The old man finally paused, steepled his fingers beneath his chin, and asked "The Question":

"Tell me, my dear, what do you feel you can bring to our firm if we choose to hire you?"

Peter James Wright would have been out of the gate like a shot, off and running. False modesty aside, I'm a damn good graphic artist. And that's not just me talking. Noted critics and teachers, people whose opinions really matter in the industry, have praised my work. I've been told that I have a natural artist's command of line and color, and the imagination to make them work for me. I'd have shown the old man the depth of my talent by drawing his attention to the pieces in my portfolio. I'd have raved about past reviews I've received. In short, I'd have been sitting there singing my own praises long after the old geezer had crumbled into dust.

But Pamela Jane Wright? The shy young woman who was struggling to maintain her modesty, meekly reminded Mr. North of her portfolio, mentioned (in as few words as possible) her impressive academic credentials, and then quickly wound up by almost whispering, "And I hope I'd be a valuable addition to any creative team that your firm would wish to form. I promise I'd try very hard." Then she dropped her gaze back down to her lap, and prayed that Josh had read the old man correctly.

North placed his hands on the desk, palms down. he reminded me of an Old Testament judge preparing to pass sentence. He declared, "At this point, I see no need to continue this interview."

My heart thudded down to the pit of my stomach. I knew I'd blown it. All that money and effort wasted. Josh was going to pitch a fit, and he'd be well within his rights.

I was so sure I'd lost that I just about slid out of my chair when North stood, again offered his hand, and said—

"Miss Wright, welcome to the firm!"

****

I can't remember much of the rest of the day.

Old Man North escorted me to the other end of the floor, and showed me my new studio. (*My* studio!) He nattered on for a while about the proud heritage and past success of the firm. He gave me a lengthy pep talk about the ongoing Sprague Contract negotiations, and then he left me with a paternal little pat on my shoulder. To this day, I can't remember a word he said.

I was in a happy little fog.

I'd landed my first real job as an *artist*, something I'd worked for all my life. The fact that I was standing there, encased head to toe in space-age plastic like some kind of freeze-dried entrée, balancing on my high heels as my bra straps dug into my shoulders—it all seemed such a small price to pay.

To feel the pride and accomplishment I felt at that moment, I would have happily dressed as a Shetland pony!

****

There was a procession of people coming by to meet "the new girl." I missed most of their names.

I do remember Mrs. Huddleston coming by at one point with some forms for me to sign, treating me to "The Stare" the whole time. I remember wondering, *What the hell is her problem, anyway?*

Josh came by with the rest of the Sprague Team, and he and I played "strangers meeting" till the rest left—

Then he shut my door, just about whooped with joy, grabbed my hand and began pumping it in a most ungentlemanly fashion. "*God damn, bro!* You did it! You did it!"

I grinned like an idiot and shook his hand so hard my boobs just about jumped out of my bra (in a most unladylike fashion!)

We laughed and talked for a while longer, then Josh got down to business. "Okay. Take the rest of the day off. Rest up. You're really gonna hit the ground running tomorrow morning."

I smiled, too happy to care about the workload hanging over my head, collected my purse, and headed for the door.

****

On my way through the main lobby downstairs, I glanced up at a clock on the wall and realized I'd missed the next bus home. I was too happy to let that bother me, though. After all, there'd be another along in twenty minutes.

Thinking about that and about the thirty-minute ride, I figured I'd better find a restroom, rather than sit and squirm and hope to make it home in time.

Spotting one of those blue and white men/women signs over a side passage, I headed off to take care of business.

I was actually standing in front of the urinal before I realized my blunder.

Staring around in panic, I was relieved (no pun intended) to notice that, but for me, the men's room was empty. I spun on my heel and fled. My luck continued to hold. No one saw me come out the door, pause to gather my composure, then casually stroll into the ladies' room where I belonged.

Chapter 1-4
...And Paying the Price

We had ten days till the Sprague Delegation arrived for the final presentation.

The work hit me like a ton of bricks. Ten days to create all the artwork for a major presentation. I'd always wanted to be a graphic artist—and brother, that's how I spent most of my waking hours for those next ten days!

There were two bright spots to all this.

First: Word quickly spread around the office, "Don't bother the new girl, she's busy!" Except for Josh, who seemed to be coming into my office every five minutes to demand a rework on my latest piece, (my loving brother— God curse him with terminal boils!) and for Beth, our work group's secretary, I was pretty much left alone.

Beth was a real piece of work—emphasis on "piece." If I was struggling to create the impression of a naïve virgin, Beth should have been wearing a sign around her neck reading *Come and Get It!* Sometimes she was so shameless around the men that it made *me* embarrassed to be a woman! I got a pretty chilly reception from her too.

I asked Josh about her one night, before I went upstairs and tried to drown myself by soaking my head in hot water.

"Beth? Yeah, I bet you got the cold shoulder from her. There's a girl determined to screw her way to the top of the secretarial pool. I guess she's kind of stumped on how to curry favor with you."

The second bright spot was: I was so distracted with work, I wasn't constantly thinking about being Pamela. As a result, things started coming naturally, much sooner than I think they would have otherwise.

That may sound a bit odd, and I'm not sure quite how to explain it. Initially, I was constantly being reminded that even though the suit was an amazing replica of a woman, it was still me inside it. I was a guy in a very convincing drag. But as the days passed, I no longer felt that way. It's not that I actually started to believe that I was really a woman either. My mind was elsewhere, and I just didn't think about it at all.

I started to develop feminine habits, completely without design. Where Peter would absently chew on the end of a pencil while thinking, Pamela would twirl a strand of her hair around her finger, or spin the bracelet around her wrist. I started crossing my legs when I sat, completely without realizing I'd done it. In the restroom, I'd check my makeup without even thinking about it.

Speaking of the restroom, at home I took no notice of my ability to relieve myself while standing (when I'd finally managed to shed Pamela). What you'd expect, right? Yet at work, it was just as natural for me to always be sitting down when peeing. By the fifth day at work, the mistake with the lobby restroom could no longer occur. When I was Pamela, it would have seemed strange to look up and not see the tampon-vending machine.

Unconsciously, I was undergoing a change in the way I related to the world outside of work as well.

The best illustration of this is something that happened during my seventh day as Pamela. Josh sometimes took the team out to a "grab it and run" lunch. I was in the ladies' room, washing my hands, when I noticed an attractive businesswoman coming out of one of the stalls. She was turning to leave when she noticed that there was a crease in her stockings behind her knee. Stooping from the waist, she placed her hands on that ankle and repeating the action I'd once employed myself: She ran her hands up her leg, rucking up her skirt in the process, till finally she was hiking up the panty of her pantyhose. As I stood there gawking at her in the mirror, the only thought in my mind was, *Ooh, those look like nice stockings! I wonder where she got them?*

****

Slowly but surely, the presentation began to take shape. I was quite pleased with it. Everything was going well.

Then, on the day before the meeting, it all seemed to come crashing down.

****

I was going nuts, trying to finish one last illustration that I just couldn't seem to get right, when Mrs. Huddleston (she of "The Stare") came into my office.

She laid some papers right under my nose, and said, "I have some forms that require your signature, Peter, do you have a moment?"

I glanced up from my interrupted work and tried not to snap. "I'm just swamped Emma, could you set them on my desk?"

And there I was, getting "The Stare" again. If Emma Huddleston had been a man, I'd have slapped her for trying to undress me with her eyes. I was about to demand an explanation for her behavior when it hit me: *She'd called me "Peter," not "Pamela."*

And I'd responded.

I began to wrack my brain for some way out of this latest slip, and it must have shown on my face. She raised an imperious hand and silenced me. "Spare yourself the effort. I've figured it out. I was just on my way out to lunch. Join me. We have some things to discuss."

****

There was a little deli in the same block as the office, and Emma selected an intimate booth in the back. I'd been thinking that the best defense in my case might be a good offense, so before we'd even gotten settled, I demanded, "How did you know?"

She stared at me, her face quite neutral, and said, "I'm the personnel manager. I first became suspicious when your brother brought in your résumé and insisted it go on the top of the stack. I really started putting two and two together when I remembered an application submitted two years ago, by Josh's half-brother Peter James Wright."

I wanted to slap my forehead. The résumé I'd sent in right out of college. They'd round-filed it so fast, I'd forgotten I'd sent it in.

Huddleston just pinned me in The Stare. "Quite a coincidence, I thought. Josh Arjer putting in another résumé from someone with the same initials as his brother, even if that someone was supposedly a woman. I must admit that I was quite surprised when you walked in the door for the interview. I was expecting something from *La Cage Aux Folles*. Seeing you, I wondered if I might be wrong—if it might just be a coincidence after all. Then yesterday I got some paperwork from NuGen, and all the pieces fell into place."

She had me. We both knew it. I put on my best "businessman manner" (not easy when you're wearing a blue knit dress, "scanti-hose," and a damned uncomfortable bra). "All right, Huddleston, you've got me. What do you want to keep quiet?"

She looked at me for the longest time. Not The Stare. Just looking.

When she broke silence, she said, "What do you think of Beth, your work-group's secretary? Be honest, please."

The non sequitur brought me up short. I stammered something about "efficient, hard-working," something inane. I don't remember what I said exactly.

Mrs. Huddleston sighed, and spoke quietly. "An honest answer, Peter." She put just enough emphasis on *Peter* that it felt like a slap on the face.

"I think she's a little slut who's collecting sack time like bonus miles. Just waiting to trade them in for another step up in the secretarial pool. The only reason she's paying any attention to me is to see if I might be a lesbian, so she can work me too."

Emma got the saddest expression on her face, and looked away. Then she just sat there, thinking.

Finally, still gazing off into the distance, she murmured, "Did you know that Beth has a degree in Literature? That she minored in Romance Languages; and as a result, she speaks both Italian and French like a native? I was here the day she came to work. I did her interview. She was such an eager, intelligent, personable young woman. She wanted to be a writer. She was applying for the secretarial job to get her foot in the door for the first copywriter's slot to open."

Emma finally met my eyes. "But opportunities for women in business aren't that common, no matter what the papers say. The days turned into months, the months into years—and Beth's opportunity never came. She just sat in the secretarial pool. The only writing she did was correcting grammar errors in someone else's letters."

Huddleston paused, and there was something else in her eyes now. I couldn't quite read what it was. "You know how it can get, don't you, Peter? The growing desperation as it all passes you by? Beth's mind wasn't taking her where she wanted—where she *needed* to go. So she started using her body instead. Beth started playing 'The Game.' If you can't see that for the tragedy it is, then I pity you more than I pity Beth."

We sat there in silence for the longest time. Emma's words had painted a picture that I didn't like. They hit too close to home for comfort. Finally, to break the silence, I grumbled, "So you're going to blow the whistle on me because I stole one of those rare opportunities?"

"I'm not going to blow the whistle on you. It's not really my place to do so. I understand you're doing some very good work on the Sprague Proposal, and I want to see the firm land that contract as much as anyone else. You've chosen to do what you're doing. You've joined The Game, whether you realize it or not. It's your decision, and you'll have to live with it. I hope you remember that in the coming days. That's all."

She started to get up but I stopped her.

"What do you mean, 'live with it'? What are you threatening?"

"I'm not threatening anything, *Pamela*, I'm just saying: Remember, it's your choice to be here, in The Game, when it starts getting ugly."

With that, she was gone. I sat there for a long time trying to figure out what she meant.

I began finding out the very next day—the day of The Big Presentation.

****

We'd rented a private dining room at one of the swankiest hotels downtown. All the presentation materials were in place. The room was ready. The curtain went up at 6 p.m. with a formal "black-tie dinner" for the Sprague Contingent. Josh and I spent the morning making sure all the details had been attended to, then we went home around noon, to change into our best evening wear.

I spent two hours in the bathroom, struggling for a sophisticated look. I even put my hair up in a "French braid" that I'd seen described in one of my magazines. It just about wore my arms out of their sockets before I finally got it done, but I loved the elegant look it added to my open features. In the end, I have to say: I was getting good at this makeup thing.

Pamela was a very impressive sight there in the mirror. (Well, at least from the neck up. I'd taken off my business suit when I got home. I didn't want to get makeup all over my blouse. I'd just thrown an old tee shirt over my bra and panties.)

I winked at myself in the mirror. I had a very chic evening gown that I'd shopped for on a rare afternoon outing from work. It was Basic Black with just enough of a slit up the side to show off one shapely knee, and just enough décolletage to show cleavage, but not enough to be obvious about it. A string of faux pearls around my neck, some pearl studs in my (recently) pierced ears, my "silken mist" pantyhose, and three-inch black heels—and I'd wager I could stop a conversation just by strolling by.

Josh was rummaging in my "unmentionables" drawer when I walked into my bedroom. Stifling a giggle, I barked, "Hey, how many times have I told you? If you want to wear my panties, you've got to ask first!"

He glanced up, and his expression stopped me cold. "This isn't funny, and you better pay attention now. This is important." He looked back into the drawer, and finally found what he wanted. He tossed me a pair of sheer black stockings with very lacy hems, and my black lace teddy. "Put those on."

The teddy was mostly sheer black nylon with a few strategically placed lace filigrees over the nipples and the crotch. Together with the matching stockings, it was a little treat to myself. For the occasional encore of the "live sex show." I'd never intended to wear them in public.

I sputtered, "You want me to wear *that* to an important dinner?"

Josh sat on the edge of my bed and wouldn't look at me.

"Just put it on, damn it. It's time you understood something."

His sharp tone was really beginning to worry me. I pulled off the tee shirt, took off my bra and panties, and started to slip into the teddy.

Josh went on, still staring out the window: "The Sprague Bunch is being headed up by Kevin Sprague, the Chairman's eldest son and 'heir apparent.' He was down here last month, scouting us as one of the possible candidates for the contract. I got to take him out—wine and dine. As the evening wore on, it became apparent that dinner wasn't the only thing I was expected to provide."

Suddenly, I couldn't believe what Josh might be suggesting. I paused, one stocking halfway up my leg and snapped, "You can't possibly be suggesting that I—?"

Josh spun around and glared into my eyes. "This is a make-or-break deal. It's that simple. Old Man North is going to be retiring in the very near future. If he goes, and if we don't get this contract, that's going to pretty much be the end of the firm. PJ, I can't make you do this. I don't even know if anything like what we're both thinking is gonna happen. I'm just saying that it might be necessary to—be nice to Sprague. That he might expect—"

Who was this person, sitting on my bed, suggesting this? I couldn't speak. I couldn't find the words.

After a moment, Josh stood and started to walk out the door. He paused, and without turning, said, "Do it or don't. It's all up to you at this point."

Then he was gone.

I stood there, one stocking halfway up my leg, trying to make sense of what had just happened.

I couldn't. How do you make sense of something that makes no sense at all?

I pulled the stocking up the rest of the way, fastened it, repeated the process on my other leg, and finished getting dressed.

****

The dinner was a huge success.

The Sprague Contingent (several division directors, some legal types, and even a secretary) all listened politely, asked good questions at appropriate times, and generally expressed sincere interest in the presentation. At the head of the table, Old Man North nodded and smiled and played benevolent patrician.

Seated on his right was Kevin Sprague.

Kevin's age was hard to determine; I'd guess early to mid-forties. He was tall (at least six feet) and trim. He had dark wavy hair and piercing brown eyes. I suspect that if I'd been a real woman, I'd have been paying more than "professional" attention to him. As the dinner wore on, it became apparent that he was paying more than that to me.

Several times, he steered the conversation toward the graphic elements of the presentation, so that I had to take the spotlight. He always paid close attention to what I was saying, and remarked twice how impressed he with the quality of my work.

Josh's story of Kevin's previous visit had me rattled, and I tried to convince myself that I was overreacting.

Kevin's attention was certainly well within the bounds of polite society. He didn't leer at me, or make any kind of innuendo. He was always urbane, sophisticated, and personable. I began to believe that he might be just what he appeared to be: a charming man reacting normally to an attractive young woman.

I remembered my "sex shows." Pamela Wright was one hot little number. *What did I expect?* I started to relax a bit. I even glanced over at Josh once, and he gave me a reassuring smile.

****

The formal presentation ended at 9:30, and the dinner began to break up at 10. I thought I was going to get out unscathed when I saw Kevin speaking to Josh.

They exchanged some words. I saw Josh stiffen, say something to Kevin, then walk out of the room without a backward glance.

I felt something cold slither down my spine, and began collecting my things for a hasty retreat.

Suddenly, Kevin was at my shoulder.

"Pamela, I have some questions regarding your part of that marvelous presentation. Would you care to come up to my room for a few minutes and answer them for me?"

I stammered and flailed for an escape from the trap, and finally managed a lame "Oh, thank you, Mr. Sprague, but it has been such a long day, and I'm so tired—"

"Call me Kevin, please. I'm sure it won't take long. I've so wanted to meet the young lady responsible for all this wonderful art. How can I make any informed recommendation to the Board, if I don't know at least a little something about the people we're considering hiring?"

The implied threat was obvious: *Play ball or blow the deal.*

I retrieved my purse, nodded ,and tried to smile. "Well, for a few moments, certainly."

He smiled, all urbane gentleman again.

"Excellent!"

****

Kevin had a suite of rooms on the eighth floor. He escorted me up, unlocked the door, and motioned me in with a courtly little bow.

I was still trying to believe that this was all quite innocent, that he really did have some questions; or at worst just wanted a little more of my company all to himself.

He indicated a large sofa against one wall. "Please, make yourself comfortable."

I sat down and tried to keep both legs in my dress, but the damn dress kept falling away from my left leg. God! Did it look like I was flashing that calf at him intentionally?

He opened a large armoire, revealing a wet bar. "What can I offer you? Sherry? Some white wine? Something stronger?"

"Oh, no thank you. Nothing, please. I really must be going soon and—"

"Nonsense! The evening is still young." He came over carrying a glass of sherry for me, and what looked like bourbon for him. He offered me the wine, and of course I had to accept. Damned if I was going to drink any of it!

Then he sat beside me on the couch.

Not right beside me, but there were several other chairs he could have used just as easily.

Dear God.

His voice was suave: "I must say again how impressed I was—we all were—with your presentation tonight. You're a fine young talent, and I think you'll go far in this business."

I managed to contain my growing panic. "Thank you, sir. That's very kind."

He laughed. " 'Sir'? Goodness, you make me sound like your father! I'm not that overbearing, am I?"

I tried to smile, to find that teasing, playful air that had come so easily before. But it was gone.

I was scared.

Of what?

I wasn't Pamela, I was Peter. I was a man, just like Kevin. Why then did I feel so powerless, so vulnerable?

There were big stakes riding on the next few minutes, but that wasn't what was pressing against me. That wasn't what was making me want to grab my purse and start running. There was an animal threat emanating from Kevin: predator and prey. It didn't revolve around sex, it revolved around conquest and possession.

Suddenly, I couldn't take any more. I started to rise. "I'm sorry, Mr. Sprague, I've really got to be—"

He grabbed my wrist. Hard.

"Pamela. You really must learn that beautiful young women need to make time for some things if they ever expect to get anywhere in business."

I tried to free my wrist, and found that Kevin was stronger.

"Let go of me," I demanded. But the sudden tremble in my voice robbed the command of any weight.

His grip just tightened painfully. "You really must learn how the game is played."

Then he had my other wrist.

—forcing me back down onto the sofa—

—forcing my arms back over my head—back against the wall—

—forcing a kiss.

I tried to turn away.

He just continued down my throat, my chest; I could feel his tongue through the thin material of the suit.

—"So beautiful," he growled—

—releasing my right wrist, freeing his hand to insinuate itself into the slit of my skirt—

—up my thigh—my hip—

I tried to push him away. He was too strong, too heavy. I was pinned beneath him.

—his hand now pushing the material of my dress up my legs—

—my other wrist free—his other hand fondling my breast, squeezing, grasping—

—my skirt now completely up around my hips. His weight forcing my legs apart—

"Please—stop. *Please*, I can't—I'm not really—"

A snap. The fastenings on the crotch of my teddy.

—pressure against my groin—rhythmic—painful—building in intensity—

"Stop." It was a plea. "Stop." This time, a whimper.

—a final thrust—

His eyes—animal—peering into mine. "You like it, don't you?"

Can't answer—can't breathe—can't think.

"Say you like it. Say it, bitch!"

—his hand on my throat, squeezing and grasping; the pressure against my hips, my groin—

"Say you like it, you filthy little cunt!"

Anything to make it stop. "Yes—yes—" A sob—a plea—

Then he was off me. A second later, the bathroom light came on.

My right shoe had fallen off. I grabbed it and ran. He didn't follow. Why would he? He had what he wanted.

****

I put the shoe back on in the elevator. Maybe the lobby was crowded, maybe it was deserted. I didn't see, and I didn't care.

There was a taxi by the curb. I huddled in the back seat and managed to whisper my address. Once, on the way home, I saw the cabby leering at me in the mirror. What did he see? What did he think?

The snaps on my teddy were still open. I couldn't bring myself to touch—

Somehow I got home—got inside—got out of my clothes and into the bath.

The hot, hot water felt good—cleansing. I stripped off the suit—not caring if I was damaging it, hoping I was—and flung it into a corner.

Then I crawled into bed, pulled up the covers, and slept.

Chapter 1-5
Success (Quote-Unquote)

I never heard the alarm go off the next morning. The phone rang sometime later. After a while, it rang again. I ignored it and just lay there, staring at the ceiling, trying to sort out my thoughts.

The clock on my nightstand read 11:18 when I heard the door downstairs open.

Josh.

In a moment he was standing in my bedroom door.

"What the hell are you doing still in bed?"

I rolled over and tried to ignore him. He walked around and looked down at me, concern starting to appear on his face. "Hey, PJ—are you alright? What's wrong, you sick?"

I wouldn't answer or look at him.

He asked, "Did something happen last night?"

By the tone of his voice, I could tell. The business. He was more worried about the deal than about me.

I snarled up at him, "Yeah. Something happened alright! After you threw me to Sprague, he took me upstairs and—and—"

"What?"

"The son of a bitch *raped* me!"

Josh's mouth dropped open. "Dear God! You don't mean he found out you were a guy and he actually—"

"*No!*" I shouted in frustration. "Man and woman."

And Josh—my brother—visibly relaxed. "Christ! You had me scared for a second. So what's the big deal? So what if Kevin had some fun with a plastic pussy? You faked a little dirty dancing and—"

I think at that moment I truly hated Josh. More perhaps than I hated Kevin Sprague. I threw off the covers and fled to the bathroom.

I heard Josh standing for a minute outside the bathroom door. When he spoke, his tone was cold and commanding: "Now you listen to me. I'll be damned if I'm going to let you blow this *now*. It's too late for you to see the Sprague delegation off. They're already on their way to the airport. Old Man North was looking for you all morning. Everyone was. You get your act together, put on your little-girl suit, and get your ass down to the office. And I mean *right now!*"

A moment later I heard the front door slam.

I stood there, looking at Peter in the mirror, trying to read something in his eyes.

The suit lay in a heap in the corner where I'd tossed it last night. It took a second before I could bring myself to touch it, but I finally picked it up and gave it a thorough inspection. It didn't appear damaged. It was what it had always been. A ridiculous looking, papery feeling, vaguely feminine-shaped outline with a short brush of yellow fuzz on top of the head.

I carefully hung it in its accustomed place on the shower rod, and reached for my "convenient spray bottle." Somehow, the pain in my throat felt good—felt "right."

A few minutes later, I was on the phone.

"Mr. North's office, Mrs. Huddleston speaking."

"Emma, it's"—Pamela? Peter? I didn't know what to say to her—"it's me. I need to speak to Mr. North."

There was a brief pause, then her brusque tone was replaced by a gentle murmur. "One moment, child, I'll connect you."

She knew, or at least she had a good idea.

Seconds later, I heard, "Wilson North speaking."

"Mr. North—it's—Pamela. Pamela Wright. I'm sorry about not coming in this morning. I—I'm not feeling well."

"Ah! Of course, my dear, of course."

Is that answer too quick? Does he know about last night as well? Does he even care?

He continued, "Don't concern yourself. You just stay home and rest. But while I have you on the phone, I wanted to say how pleased I am with your work. You should know that the Sprague people were impressed with it—most impressed! If we should get the contract, it will be in large measure due to your contribution."

Is there a hidden meaning in that?

He said, "I just wanted to say: Thank you, my dear, thank you very much."

I said, "Thank you, sir. I—I'll be in tomorrow morning."

****

The next morning, as Pamela stepped off the elevator, you could feel the electricity in the air.

I walked through the door into the reception area and Mrs. Blane, the receptionist, greeted me with a delighted shriek. *"Pamela! We got the contract!!!"*

I tried for a bright, enthusiastic smile. I guess I either succeeded, or Mrs. Blane was so far gone in the moment that she didn't care if I stuck out my tongue and wiggled my ears.

There were little parties going on all throughout the firm. As I made my way to my office, I was bombarded from all sides by joyful excitement and congratulations.

I smiled and said, "Thank you, congratulations, isn't it wonderful?" till the words lost all meaning.

I finally made it into my office, and collapsed behind my desk. My mind was drifting when I heard a gentle tapping on the doorframe. Glancing up, I saw Beth, the secretary, standing there.

"Ms. Wright, do you have a moment?"

"Of course, Beth. Come in."

She stood uncertainly in front of my desk. "Did you hear? We got the Sprague Contract."

Without smile or cheerfulness, I said, "Yes, Beth. I heard."

She looked shyly down at her toes. When she spoke, it was real emotion this time, and not the feigned "come on" that she used on the men: "I've heard that the firm is going to be expanding. That there'll be new openings in the secretarial pool, in administration. Even in the creative divisions. Artists—copy writers."

I had a horrible, vicious thought: *Yes, Beth. Maybe a big step up for you. And best of all, this time it wasn't you who had to spread your legs to get it.*

Still staring at the floor, she continued, "I've heard that your artwork was a big factor in getting the contract. Everyone's talking about it. About the presentation dinner. About you."

God. Does everyone know?

She looked up and met my gaze.

"I know how much you did for us. How important it was. I know—"

It was there, in her eyes: Genuine compassion, and shared pain.

Understanding.

Suddenly, I was so ashamed. I had been wrong about Beth. Terribly wrong.

I started to think about the night before last, but shied away from the memory. Kevin Sprague had violated me. But it had been the violation of a schoolyard bully terrorizing a weaker child. Though Kevin didn't know it, and would never know it, he had raped an illusion. He hadn't really touched me. Not the *real* me.

At least not physically.

When I'd finally made it home, I was able to strip off Pamela and toss her in a corner.

But what did Beth do when she got home at night?

I remembered Emma Huddleston's words about choices and "playing The Game." Perhaps Beth had made a bad choice. Did that give me the right to scorn her? To feel so superior to her? Had all my choices of late turned out the way I'd planned?

And worst of all, if it had been Peter working here instead of Pamela, and if Beth had offered herself, would I have been quick to turn her down?

Or would I have used her too?

How different am I from Kevin Sprague?

She turned to go, but paused at the door. "I just wanted to say thank you. That's all. Thank you, Ms. Wright."

"You're welcome, Beth. Thank *you*."

****

The final irony played itself out that very afternoon.

All the senior staff was called into Old Man North's office at two o'clock. Chairs had been set out for all of us, and I noticed that Josh took a seat as far away from mine as possible.

I was puzzling over that when Mr. North called the meeting to order—

"As you all know, I'm moving toward retirement. It is true to say that the acquisition of the Sprague Contract has opened a new door for our fine firm. A door into a shining, promising future that is paved, I hope, with success for all of us. Sadly though, it is a future in which I will not be taking an active part."

There were polite murmurs of feigned sadness at the Old Man's pending departure.

He finally stilled them with a raised hand. "Now, now. This is as it should be. 'The old makes way for the new.' It is 'the new' that I've called you together to discuss. We are moving forward into the future. But to steer our course, we will need young, strong hands at the helm. We will need leadership that can benefit from the wisdom of the past, but that also has the vision to move in daring new directions. It is time for our fine firm to waken from the slumber I know we've fallen into, and sail boldly into this new millennium."

You could feel people lean forward in their chairs. We all knew where this was leading.

North paused, scanned the faces, and then sat very erect in his chair.

"It is therefore my great pleasure to announce to you today, the addition of a new General Partner to the firm. A person who is the very embodiment of this bold new thinking, this exciting new direction. A person without whom the fundament of our new future could not have been laid."

North looked directly at me—

—*and smiled.*

"Lady and Gentlemen, I give you the firm of Whitman, North—"

I sucked in a breath.

"—and Arjer."

****

The days have passed.

Pamela Wright still comes to work every day, to her office at Whitman, North, and Arjer. The charade is impossible to escape, for obvious reasons.

I could quit, I suppose, but then what would be the point of all that has gone before? Quit, and I'll be back where I started—an unemployed artist. I won't even be able to claim Pamela's success. How could I explain?

Considering what it took to land this job, I don't relish the prospect of what it might take to land the next!

If I sound bitter, I want to say that truly I'm not.

Well—not really.

I live in my own apartment now. I can afford it.

It isn't out of anger with Josh that I moved out. He'd never been anything less than honest with me. I remember my first night as Pamela, sitting at the table over burgers and beers. I remember the distant look in Josh's eyes as he'd said, "Don't worry Bro, you'll pay me back—and you'll be doing all the work."

That he might have foreseen everything that's happened, or perhaps even have planned it—that's a thought I leave untouched.

Josh may sometimes be manipulative, but he isn't an evil person. He truly isn't. Greedy? Yes. Power hungry? Yes. But he has his good side too. For two years he put a roof over my head, and never even considered asking for anything in return.

Josh Arjer, my brother. He'd give you the coat off his back—after he'd checked the pockets for loose change.

I moved out because sometimes a girl just needs her own space.

I can honestly say I'm happy.

I'm doing the job I've wanted to do all my life, the job I love: creating art. If part of that "art" is the constant creation of the illusion of woman, well, so be it. It's not such a great price to pay.

We all have "faces" we choose to show to the world. Mine just takes a little more hot water than yours.

Does my acceptance of my situation seem strange to you? Why?

After all, lots of people have to "get dressed" to go to work.

PART 2
The New Model

Chapter 2-1
The New, New Girl

In a Los Angeles office

"You're insane!" an upset male voice said.

His sibling's reply: "I'm telling you, bro, it's meant to happen. We both know what he wants. We have the means to provide it. Nobody else is available—"

"It will never work! Nobody's going to believe I'm a woman. They sure as hell aren't going to believe me as some kind of fashion model!"

I grinned at Josh. "I think I can solve *that* little problem," I said.

My grin was genuine. Oh, how I was enjoying watching Josh squirm and sweat!

****

Everybody calls me "PJ." Just what those initials stand for, depends on the time of day and the day of the week. After 6 p.m. and on most weekends, it stands for *Peter James*. But from nine to five on weekdays, it stands for *Pamela Jane*.

This rather odd set of circumstances arose out of a desperate attempt to land a job as a graphic artist with my brother Josh's advertising firm. At that time, his firm (Whitman, North, and Arjer; or "WN&A") was only hiring women. Using a marvelous bit of technology called a "NuGen Transgender Appliance, Model I-2000S," I was able to fool the powers-that-be into believing I was a young, upcoming, *female* graphic artist; and thereby to land the graphic-artist job.

To be sure, there were a series of misadventures along the way, but over the past few months, I think I've settled into my new professional persona quite well. The job is challenging and very rewarding, and it's a job I truly love. All my life, I've wanted to be a professional artist, so I've never felt that the sacrifice of masquerading as a woman on a daily basis has been too much of a price to pay.

Times are good down at WN&A. My first work for the firm involved landing a prestigious major client. Close on the heels of that success, WN&A went from a sleepy little ad agency that was quietly fading into the mists of obscurity, to a very sought-after company. Offers from other high-class clients started to flow in.

We were on the way up. The sky seemed to be the limit.

Then the eccentric but fabulously successful fashion designer "Giancarlo of Venice" contracted us to promote his new line of lingerie.

And for a period of three weeks, it seemed like my whole world had gone nuts.

****

It began on a hopeful, fairly innocent note.

I was sitting in my studio one Thursday morning, lost in artistic reverie, twirling a lock of my fake golden mane around a shapely, well-manicured finger.

Well, actually I was trying to figure out what kind of a scam I was going to pull today, down at the water cooler, when the Football Pool gathered to debate this weekend's pro games.

It's like this: WN&A had taken some steps recently to overhaul their horribly outmoded—and very sexist—hiring policies. But there were still quite a few Neanderthal "knuckle draggers" lurking in dark back offices. A good selection of the most "macho" of these throwbacks congregated at the water cooler every mid-morning, to thump their chests and debate the latest athletic exploits of their favorite teams. It was a foregone conclusion that a betting pool should form.

I was walking by one morning (*en femme*, of course) just as the debate grew rather heated concerning the Patriots' chances against Pittsburgh in next Sunday's game. As I passed, I casually observed that I rather liked the "Pat's" chances.

I'll wager you could have heard the bellows of male indignity for a hundred yards.

What did I—*a lowly female*—know about the noble, intricate, *masculine* art-form that was professional football? How dare I voice an opinion to these sage experts on this ancient and hallowed diversion?

Okay, so maybe I'm exaggerating. But not that much. In any event, I got jeered at, and put down, and—

Something snapped.

You have to understand that I like pro football. I follow it closely. I could have engaged these jerks on their own terms, and held my own. But I guess I was getting tired of being patronized.

Petite Pamela gazed through her long lashes at the assembled hairy apes and, in a dreamy voice, cooed that any team whose quarterback had as cute a butt as the challenger's was bound to win.

Howls of injured male pride. What a senseless, illogical, *female* opinion! Would I care to lose some money on a bet based on that outrageous claim?

The following Monday I was $32 ahead, and the "War of the Gridiron" was fairly joined.

So, anyway, there I was, sitting at my desk, playing with my hair and weighing the odds on this Sunday's Seattle-Denver contest. Denver was a perennial favorite, but I thought Seattle had a really good shot this week, provided they could keep their quarterback healthy.

(Let me digress for a moment and, for the record, state that my preference for a Seattle team does not make me a traitor to the Golden State. At least not in my opinion. When it's the Raiders or the 49ers playing anyone else but Seattle, I root for the home team with genuine gusto. It's just that—I don't know. There's something about Seattle's perennial ability to alternately snatch defeat from the jaws of victory on one weekend and then pull off an "against all odds" miracle the next weekend, that resonates with me.)

In any event, and with respect to the Seattle/Denver match-up, my money was squarely on Seattle. The question, as I say, was how to get the most "bang for the buck" with respect to that money, and the wager I'd be making with it.

Maybe I could scam a five-point spread on Seattle by playing moody and absent-minded, and letting word get around that it was because it was "that time of the month" for Pamela.

At the moment I was thinking this, my secretary Carl stuck his head in my door.

(Yes, I have a male secretary, the only one in the whole firm. I think it's a little joke by Emma Huddleston, WN&A's personnel manager; and the only other one in the firm besides my brother who's in on Pamela's secret.)

Carl said, "Mr. Arjer wants to see you in his office in ten minutes, Ms. Wright."

"Did he say why?"

"No, Ma'am. Just to tell you to, and I quote, 'Get your little ass up here most pronto.' "

"Okay. Thanks, Carl. Oh, Carl, who do you like in the Seattle-Denver game this Sunday?"

"Denver all the way."

"Why?"

" 'Cuz Seattle can't stop the run to save their lives. Denver will pick 'em apart."

"You're nuts! Look at Seattle's stats on first-down defense against the run! Why, in the last four games they've—"

But Carl, knowing my penchant for running on about my favorite topic, had wisely remembered some typing, and had already disappeared back to his desk.

****

Josh Arjer is my half-brother by my late mother's remarriage. Nobody in the firm knows about our relationship. (Except for Mrs. Huddleston, that is.)

Josh had been made a full partner in the firm based on "his" work in landing that prestigious client I mentioned. Now he had his own suite of offices on one corner of our floor, and his own secretarial staff to attend to his every whim. Before the events that I'm about to describe, I'd been a bit jealous and angry with him for his success on the shoulders of my work. That's all changed—my jealousy and anger, I mean.

But I'm getting ahead of myself.

At the appointed hour, I arrived in the waiting room of Josh's office. His bubble-headed blonde bimbo of a secretary deigned to notice me, and to trouble herself to point to one of the couches against the wall.

"Mr. Arjer has an important phone call. He'll be with you in a minute."

I sat on the couch, primly crossed my legs, and wondered what our mother would think about Josh's taste in women if she were alive to see it.

At that moment, the outer door opened and Beth DiAngelo, our newest copywriter, walked in and was directed to the same couch that I currently occupied.

Once more, I felt that little stab of shame that I sometimes felt when Beth was around. When I'd first come to work at WN&A, I'd only seen Beth as a scheming little wench who was trying to use sex to get ahead in the company. I've subsequently come to know her a lot better, and to appreciate the lengths to which she had been forced in her attempt to get ahead in this still very male-dominated world of business. I'd badly misjudged her, but I'm pleased to say that I've subsequently mended my ways. Beth is now one of my best friends and my only "gal pal" down here at WN&A.

Beth glanced at the door to Josh's office, then sighed and looked around for something to occupy herself, while we waited to be allowed into "The Presence."

"So, Pam, whom do you like in this Sunday's games?"

Which served as a welcome reminder that Beth likes football too, and suddenly there was an interesting way to pass the time.

"I'm taking Chicago, Miami, Washington, Oakland, Carolina, and Seattle."

"Seattle? You're crazy! Denver will push them all over the field."

I sputtered, "What do you mean? They've got a good chance—"

"Girlfriend, I've had two-dollar pantyhose that was better at stopping runs!"

I was saved by the door to Josh's office opening, and Josh's imperious, "Get in here, both of you."

****

Josh was pacing back and forth in front of his massive desk when Beth and I entered. "Sit down, you two. I just got off the phone with New Accounts, and we've been handed what I'm given to understand is a golden opportunity. Have either of you ever heard of some fashion designer named Gian—"

Second try: "Gian—"

Josh stopped pacing and glanced down at his notepad. "Giancarlo 'of Venice,' no less?"

A little squeak of surprise confirmed that Beth certainly had. I glanced over at her, and saw her eyes had gotten as big as dinner plates. "You mean, *the* Giancarlo? Giancarlo *himself?*"

Josh raised an eyebrow. "Yes, 'the Giancarlo himself.' I don't imagine there's more than one fashion fairy with a name like that."

Beth's hands had flown to her mouth. "Are you saying— Mr. Arjer, you want us—you want *me*, oh god, to work on an account for *Giancarlo of Venice?*"

Josh's eyebrows had just about crawled off the top of his head. "Well, Beth, it's either *you*, or we take Silverman off the Ever-Roll Tire account. Somehow, I think you're a bit more familiar with what we're going to be advertising than Silverman is. At least, I certainly hope you are."

Beth dissolved into soft, panicky *ohmigod, ohmigod*s.

I'd heard of Giancarlo. (You couldn't read a woman's magazine these days and *not* hear of Giancarlo. And I read a lot of woman's magazines. Call it "professional development.") So we had a shot at an account for a big-name fashion designer? Certainly that was exciting news.

But like Josh, I was a bit put off by Beth's near-hysteria. To divert my brother's increasingly obvious ire, I asked, "Just what are we going to be advertising, Mr. Arjer? What product line? Evening wear? Sports clothes?"

Josh tore his eyes off the floundering Beth, and for a moment I caught that evil little glint that I knew so well. "*Lingerie*, Ms. Wright. We're going to be introducing Giancarlo's new line of lingerie to the world. And since you and Ms. DiAngelo are going to be singing its praises, I've made arrangements for several of the signature items to be delivered to your homes tomorrow. I want you to become 'intimately' familiar with them for our first meeting with Giancarlo next Thursday."

Beth was hyperventilating. Josh was leering. And I was wondering if my karma had finally caught up with me.

(And speaking of karma, the final score was Denver 28, Seattle 3.)

Chapter 2-2
Inspired

The next day (Friday) turned out to be a very *bizarre* day at WN&A. Word had gotten out about Giancarlo's new line of lingerie, and all the secretaries were acting like the Second Coming had been announced. There were dozens of little knots of women speaking in whispered tones, comparing notes about their choices for updating their "unmentionables" drawers, and accomplishing very little else. It was a relief to leave the office at five.

When I arrived home, all I wanted was to draw a hot bath and slip out of Pamela. I'd tossed my keys and purse on the kitchen counter, had kicked off my heels, and was unbuttoning my blouse when the doorbell rang. Muttering curses and rebuttoning my blouse, I padded stocking-footed to the door and flung it open.

"What?" I demanded.

A team of uniformed, *armed* couriers stood on my doorstep, their leader holding a huge box.

"Ms. Pamela Wright?"

I swallowed my surprise and nodded.

The leader looked me up and down in a businesslike way, and then asked, "Do you have identification, ma'am?"

Again, I could only nod mutely, and head to my purse for my Visa credit card. (All Pamela's photo I.D. consisted of credit cards, the kind with your picture and signature on the face. I've got a whole stack of them.)

The courier examined the card, then examined me, then nodded to one of his partners, who handed me a clipboard. "Sign on line seven, please."

I complied, the leader handed me the box, tipped his uniform cap, and wished me a pleasant evening, before the platoon of them closed ranks and trooped away.

****

I stood there in my stocking feet, hefting the box, and wondering what national-security information I'd just been handed. Then I remembered.

Giancarlo's lingerie.

Taking the box into my kitchen, and using a pair of scissors to *very* carefully cut the tape on the top, I was soon looking into a box containing some of the sexiest underwear I've ever seen.

So this was what all the fuss was about. I lifted out the top item, which proved to be a full-length peignoir, and turned it front and back in my hands. It was nice, there was no question of that. Part beautiful rose-colored silk, part sheer bodice and lots of lace, the peignoir was lovely.

But it hardly took my breath away.

Shrugging, I decided that the best thing was to get this over with, and try on the various items.

Taking the box, I trudged off to my bedroom. I slipped out of my work clothes and underwear, then I slid the peignoir over my head, letting the spaghetti straps fall naturally over my shoulders. I fluffed out my hair, and turned to examine the effect in the full-length mirror that I kept in the corner.

I don't think I have the words for what I saw in that mirror.

The hem of the peignoir rode just high enough to reveal a pair of dainty feet. The gown ascended in shimmering rose colored perfection to the gentle swell of hips, then curved back in a graceful arc to accentuate a narrow waist. The silk climbed for a few more inches, only to melt into swirls and flows of delicate lace. Lace that invited the eye higher, till finally that eye was drawn, naturally, to two breasts that were lovingly caressed within sheer, glimmering fabric, their nipples concealed by delicate lace roses and vines. Those lace roses and vines themselves trailed upward perfectly into the two slender straps that rose over my reflection's smooth shoulders.

Pamela Jane Wright has always been either a rather "neuter" creature (when I'm not thinking about sexuality), or a rather sleazy "sex kitten" (when I am.)

But now? That woman in the mirror?

Not wanton.

But certainly not neuter!

I remember a tightness in my chest as I gaped at the bewitching angel gazing back at me from the mirror, her eyes large and shimmering in wonder (and, perhaps if I was truly blessed, with desire of her own?) I wanted to shelter that vision of delicate beauty in strong masculine arms. I wanted to protect it, and cherish it. I wanted to possess it.

I have never felt at once both so masculine and so feminine.

I suddenly understood just what the fuss was all about. There was no denying it: Giancarlo was a certifiable genius.

****

I called in to the office the next morning. For the first time, I'd slept *en femme*, plus wearing the peignoir and a pair of matching silk panties.

I have no idea what Pamela dreamt that night, but I awoke refreshed, with my imagination more fired and insistent then I've ever experienced. I've converted my spare bedroom into a small studio, and I told the folks at the office that I'd be working at home today.

A rather worried Josh came on the line and hissed, "What are you up to?"

I chuckled—well, giggled actually (I'd had to change my normal baritone into Pamela's contralto to call in, this morning)—and assured Josh that everything was fine. I told him I was "on a roll," and that I'd have some dynamite stuff for him by Thursday.

This seemed to reassure him, and he told me to stay home as long as I thought necessary.

I fell into one of those "artistic fugues" you hear about. I lost all track of time. I ate when the grumbling in my stomach grew distracting. I slept when I couldn't hold my eyes open anymore, and awoke charged with new visions.

And through it all, I wore that marvelous, magical lingerie. If my creativity ever flagged, I needed only to look into the mirror (which I'd dragged in from the bedroom), and my paints and pencils seemed to fly of their own volition.

It was late Tuesday evening when I finally set my pencil down, capped my paints, and took stock of my work.

I've never done better.

And these were only rough, presentation graphics.

With no small measure of regret, I slipped out of the satin teddy I was wearing, and went into the bathroom to draw the hot water for my transformation back into Peter.

I was exhausted, drained. I needed sleep. I do remember my dreams of that night. Wild. Erotic. How I envied a woman who could wear one of Giancarlo's magical gowns to her lover's bed! And oh, how I envied the man who could romance such a woman!

Chapter 2-3
The One, the Only...

I'm often struck by how, in so many cases, the world's greatest geniuses have also been the world's greatest eccentrics. Think about it: da Vinci, Tesla, Einstein—I'm sure you can add more names to the list.

Be sure to add Giancarlo of Venice.

Thursday rolled around and the whole staff was in early that morning. I guess it could be due, in part, to that fact that we'd never had a real celebrity in the office. And Giancarlo was a celebrity. Even Josh, whose awareness of high fashion extended to the ability to (occasionally) coordinate his ties, was a bit more keyed-up than usual. That explained the air of excitement from the males. And the females? Well—

Okay—Under my conservative business suit I was wearing those same French-cut panties and an absolutely "to die for" silk full slip that had come in the box of Giancarlo's lingerie. If the "magic" could work on me—a male (no matter outward appearance), I think the feeling of giddy anticipation circulating in the secretarial pool was understandable.

Giancarlo's arrival was scheduled for 10 a.m. At 9:30, a stretch limo pulled up at the curb, and "The Maestro's" advance team disembarked. We met them in the large conference room.

There were six of them, evenly divided into a rather strange mixture of professional business assistants and "camp followers."

The former consisted of a middle-aged and very distinguished looking woman named Nina, a late middle-aged man named Angelo, and an early thirtyish fellow named Anthony.

The camp-follower group consisted of Alberto, (Giancarlo's "autobiographer"), Madame Lafarge (a wacko old woman who served, so she claimed, as Giancarlo's spiritual advisor), and Petrov (whose official function I never did figure out, though I suspect bodyguard was at least part of the job description. He was a huge, mustachioed hulk who just loomed in a corner, scowling at everyone and everything.)

After introductions, Nina managed to foist Alberto and Madame Lafarge off on Angelo, on the pretext of touring the rest of the firm's facilities. (Angelo seemed to take it with an admirable resignation. Apparently, care of the "looneys" was his job description.) That left Nina, Anthony, Petrov, Josh, Beth, and me waiting for Giancarlo's imminent arrival.

I was very quickly impressed by Nina and Anthony's cool professionalism. Being a commercial artist myself, I knew only too well that creative genius mattered little without the business sense to market your art. Apparently Giancarlo had learned this lesson too, since he employed folks like Nina and Anthony to handle the financial matters. Within ten minutes of meeting, and once the pleasantries of introductions and small talk were out of the way, Nina and Josh were fully engaged in business matters.

I've always said that Josh was a "natural businessman." In Nina, he'd found a perfect foil—it was fun to watch them fence back and forth, all under the cover of pleasant conversation.

As Nina and Josh jousted, I became aware that Anthony had also gone quiet. I glanced over at him just as his eyes wandered in my direction. Our gazes locked for a brief instant. I smiled politely. He smiled politely.

Anthony was a handsome fellow. He was of obvious northern-Italian stock, with ice-blue eyes and well-trimmed white-blonde hair. A high clear brow rose above well-defined aristocratic Roman features. He was just under six feet, well proportioned, and athlete-trim.

For the briefest moment, I had memories of a very bad experience I'd had with another handsome businessman, but the thought vanished almost before it formed. Anthony was no Kevin Sprague. You could tell in just a moment that this was a true gentleman. His smile was easy, open, and genuinely friendly. I found that mine was too.

Again I thought it a shame that under this lovely woman disguise lurked Peter Wright. It seemed a waste somehow. I'd wager that if Pamela were the "genuine article," she and Anthony could generate a few sparks—and have a lot of fun in the doing.

Little did I know.

My reverie was shattered when the conference room door flew open, and in strode "il Maestro" himself. The one—the only—Giancarlo of Venice.

You could tell it was him as easily as if he'd been wearing a sign around his neck reading "Fashion Genius." He was wearing a silk suit, silk cravat, and had a camel-hair coat thrown over his shoulders. Dark aviator glasses shielded his eyes from the flash of the paparazzi's cameras. (A pity there weren't any paparazzi around at the moment. It rather ruined the effect.) That Giancarlo himself was a rather rotund, late-middle-aged, dark-visaged little gnome didn't help the overall effect either.

He stopped in the door, effectively blocking the entrance of the dozen or so "groupies" that followed in his wake, and swept the room with a disdainful gaze.

"Where is-a she? Where is-a *l'Artista?*"

Josh rose to his feet. "Signore Giancarlo, on behalf of the firm of Whitman, North, and—"

Giancarlo waved him to silence with a preemptory flick of his hand. "Sì, sì—you are hon-or-ed. Everyone is. Now, where is-a she?"

Josh spluttered to a halt, then shifted gears. " 'She', signore? Which 'she'?"

But Giancarlo had stopped paying attention to Josh, and was sweeping majestically in my direction, arms flung wide. "Ah! This is-a she! Here is *l'Artista!*"

Before I could get my feet beneath me and stand, Giancarlo had my right hand in his, and was raising it to his lips! It was all I could do to keep from snatching it back in my surprise.

I managed to stammer, "It's a great honor to meet you Signore Giancarlo."

He continued to fondle my hand and cooed, "Ah! *Bella—bellissima!*"

Without taking his eyes off me—I could see his eyes glimmering behind the dark glasses—he spoke to Nina and Anthony. "Do you see? In her eyes—*il fuoco, la passione*—this is the one! This is *l'Artista!* Giancarlo knew it the moment he first-a see this angel's work!"

Well. He is a definite "flake." But he apparently knows artistic talent when he sees it.

I let my hand relax a bit, raised my chin an inch, and gave him that well-rehearsed smile I'd once used on Josh. (So long ago now, it seemed, on a sidewalk during the first day of another life.) "Oh, *Maestro, grazie.*"

He finally surrendered my hand, and then lowered himself into one of the chairs. "So, *bella donna,* you have-a something to show Giancarlo, sì?"

That one brought me up short till I realized he was asking to see my proposed artwork. "Ah, yes, *signore.*"

I rose and—with a little added sway to my hips, I couldn't help it—walked over to the covered easel that held my sketches.

For the next twenty minutes, I displayed my concept, described the effect I was aiming for, talked about form and color, and generally did my graphic-artist song-and-dance.

It was several minutes into the presentation before I realized that Giancarlo had gone completely silent. Rattled, I kept plugging away, doggedly staring at the sketches. If I'd bombed out, if I'd blown this, Josh would skin me, and hang Pamela's "hide" from the flagpole atop our building.

I finally reached the final panel, then stuttered to a halt.

Dead silence.

Then Giancarlo was on his feet applauding wildly. "BRAVA! SÌ! SÌ! This is-a what Giancarlo wanted! This-a is-a *perfeccione!* Giancarlo himself could-a no have-a done better!"

Thank God once again to the folks at NuGen. I must have been sweating like a horse at this point, but Pamela maintained the vision of *l'Artista,* and inclined her angel's face in acknowledgment of *il Maestro's* praise. "*Grazie, signore—molto grazie.*" (And thank you, Beth DiAngelo, for your "Fawning in Italian" quickie-course.)

Giancarlo was rubbing his hands with glee. "*Buono.* Now-a then. You have-a make arrangements for-a the models, sì'? Show them-a to me."

Josh's smile of victory froze in place. "Models, *Maestro?* Um, it was my impression that this was to be an 'artwork,' rather than a photographic, ad campaign."

Slowly Giancarlo turned to face Josh, and with one finger pulled the dark glasses down onto the bridge of his nose, so he could peer over them. " 'Your impression'? And since-a when did-a your impression matter, eh?"

Before Josh could answer, Giancarlo was back to me. "No, no—ask-a *l'Artista*. She will tell-a you. We must-a have the *realtà* of-a woman for-a to create *la fantasia*, sì?"

And you know what? He was dead right. It hadn't even occurred to me till he said it, but my sketches *were* the blueprints upon which to base a photo shoot of live models. Drawings wouldn't work. By God—a flake Giancarlo might be, but an artistic genius he certainly was!

I gave Josh a superior, smug little smile, and simply nodded.

The look I got in return probably would have melted case-hardened steel. "Ah. Well—forgive me, Maestro. I've obviously misunderstood. Of course we can obtain the services of any modeling agency you'd care to specify."

Giancarlo sank back into his chair and shook his head in sadness. "No, no. Professional models? No. I have-a models and models. *Bella donna,* surely you know that a professional model won't-a work. Why have-a you no tell this"—a vague wave in Josh's direction—"this *persona* that-a you require a new face, a new woman for this new *fantasia*?"

Right again. It was so obvious, once Giancarlo said it: The concept that ran through all my art was the "discovery," the "exploration" of femininity. A professional model wouldn't work. A professional model had already discovered all there was to discover about her femininity. It was her stock and trade. If we used such a model in our ads, she'd look sleek and glossy and perfect. Which would make her *all wrong* for the ads.

I must have been speaking out loud. Giancarlo's fist slammed down on the table, and he smiled hugely. "*Esatto!*" Exactly!

I glanced over at Josh, and the predatory grin on his face would have frozen that melted case-hardened steel in the blink of an eye. Josh purred, "Well, the solution seems to be obvious. If a professional model won't work, we'll simply get a novice. And since Ms. Wright is intimately familiar with the concept, it seems only natural that *she* should be that model."

I was about to shriek a denial, but Giancarlo beat me to it. *Thank God!*

"No, no—oh, no. You understand-a nothing—*nothing!* Have-a you no art in you at all?"

He made a gallant little gesture toward me: "The artist can no be-a the art too!"

A rather vaguely rude gesture toward Josh: "What were-a you a-think, eh? You, you ... *bookkeeper!*"

Josh was framing an answer, but apparently the audience was over. While Josh stammered, Giancarlo rose from his chair, swept over to me who was still standing beside the easel, again kissed my hand, then turned and strode for the door. His entourage scrambled to follow.

At the door, Giancarlo paused, turned back on Josh, and in a voice that would have made any Roman emperor proud, commanded, "You will have-a the model ready for-a my approval within-a two week."

And he was gone.

Chapter 2-4
Soldier of Fashion

I wasn't being difficult. I swear to God I wasn't.

For the next week, the entire art staff pored over model's photos, contacted talent agencies, drafted ads for newspapers—hell, we even got some college yearbooks from nearby colleges. Nothing was right.

I vetoed every candidate. It got to the point where some of the staff wouldn't speak to me.

I'd become infected with Giancarlo's vision. I knew what was required: A beautiful woman who didn't know she was beautiful; an adult female for whom femininity was a new discovery. Of course, it took me the better part of that week to realize that the answer was, literally, right under my nose.

Well, *covering* it, actually. And covering my face, and my shoulders, and my legs.

All we needed to get what I instinctively knew would be the perfect model, was to place an order with the geniuses at NuGen for a new I-2000S built to my specifications.

And then find the right man to stick inside the suit.

I *ran* down the hall to Josh's suite, and barged right by his blonde bimb—er—receptionist—

She managed an outraged "Hey, you can't just—"

—and then I was through the door, which I slammed shut behind myself.

Josh was on the phone; but one look at my face and he mumbled, "I'll call you back, something's come up."

He hung up, then raised an eyebrow at me.

I panted, "I've got it! I've figured it out!"

"What?"

"Where we get the model for Giancarlo. It's so obvious!"

Josh perked up. "Yeah? Which girl did you decide on?"

I made sure the door was shut, then said quietly, "Not a *girl* at all. We let *technology* solve the problem."

Josh leaned back, and considered what I was proposing. "Ooh, PJ, I don't know. That is risky. Do you really think this is the 'girl' you want?"

I nodded. "Damn straight. It'll be absolutely perfect. It's just the effect I'm shooting for. Swear to God, bro, I'm right! I know I am!"

Josh held up a hand to still further protest. After a lifetime together, we knew each other's strengths and weakness. When it came to business matters, I trusted Josh implicitly. And he knew that when it came to things artistic, my hunches usually proved correct.

"Okay, okay. This is gonna be awfully tricky though. We gotta get just the right person for this. And I don't mean, in terms of looks. Have you stopped and thought what a hold the person whom we'd get, would have over us?"

I came up short. "What do you mean; 'hold'?"

I got the disgusted 'you naïve artist' stare that Josh reserved for when I was being particularly dense. "PJ, think about it: We get some guy to pose as Giancarlo's dream model, right? Then for some reason, our fake female later gets pissed off at us, and takes the story to the press. Can you imagine the headlines? It'd be the end of us as a firm. Who'd ever hire an agency that pulled something like that on a client?"

That finally brought me back to earth. Of course I hadn't thought of that. I started to suggest that maybe we could just explain it to Giancarlo beforehand.

Yeah, right.

Yet deep in my gut I was absolutely, positively convinced that this *was* the answer. The only answer. This would be the ideal "girl" for the ads. Thinking that, I replied, "Okay. We just have to be careful about the person we get, that's all."

Josh shook his head, leaned back and folded his hands behind his neck. "It's got to be somebody we can absolutely trust. I mean absolutely and forever. I can't think of anybody like that. Can you?"

I looked at Josh sitting there, and got my second inspiration for the day.

Actually, yes, I *could* think of somebody. I gave Josh a sly smile.

****

We must have gone around and around in Josh's office for the better part of two hours.

He was adamant about it: He wouldn't do it. No way, no how. It wouldn't work. Nobody would believe it. I was crazy. I was just trying to get even for the whole Pamela deal. On and on.

I let him vent. I was right; I knew it; Josh would just have to see it my way.

After two hours, Josh had run out of arguments. He'd run out of counterproposals. He was forced to acknowledge that this was the only way out for us.

Glaring daggers at me, he called Accounting and got me a purchase order made out to NuGen, Inc.

We charged it against "Supplies."

****

The idea had occurred to me on the Friday morning of the week before the deadline. By mid-morning, Josh had finally surrendered to the inevitable. I spent what was left of the morning, and all of the afternoon, closeted in my studio working through sketches of what I thought the ideal physical appearance for our "girl" would be. I then used my desktop computer to contact NuGen's web site. I submitted my "specs" and requested two-day air delivery.

Josh phoned me from his home, right on schedule on the Monday before our Thursday deadline.

"It's here. You better come over," was all he said.

"On my way."

I don't think I've ever seen Josh as edgy as when I arrived at his place.

He was holding a beer when he met me at his door. I'd be willing to bet he'd already polished off another, between when he got home and now. Just to be sociable, I rummaged in his fridge for a cold one of my own, then clapped my hands together and rubbed them in anticipation.

Josh just about jumped out of his skin at the sudden noise. He was nervous as a cat.

"Come on, Josh. It doesn't hurt. Well—not much." (Oh, it was going to be hard over the next few hours not to remember all the childhood injuries and abuse I'd taken from him.)

He just looked at me, stricken.

I relented. "Really, Josh. It's not bad. Hell, I do it every morning."

"But you're used to it. It doesn't seem to bother you to pretend you're—hell, sometimes I think you enjoy it."

There was a long moment's silence.

"Just what's that supposed to mean, brother mine?"

Josh waved a hand in quick dismissal. "Oh, hey. Not that I think you're queer or anything. *You* know that *I* know you're not. It's just that I think sometimes you get into the role a little too much, you know?"

I set my beer down. When I spoke, even I was surprised by the quiet intensity of my words: "Are you insinuating that there's something 'wrong' with me? That I enjoy being a woman?"

Josh started to splutter a denial—

—but I cut him off. "And what if I do? Hm? Does that mean it's time we started considering counseling?"

Josh's eyes were getting big, and he was waving his hands in front of himself, trying to ward off my words. "Hey, PJ, come on. I—"

I cut him off again. "Well, sport. I got a flash for you. Pamela was a desperate measure for a desperate situation. But over time—you're right—*I have begun to enjoy it.*"

Josh's eyes were a big as saucers.

"But not for a sexual thrill. Well, not only for that. I enjoy it because of all the new experiences it's opened for me. Does my getting a thrill out of exploring my femininity make me a transvestite—a 'queer'? Maybe it does. Maybe it doesn't. And you know what, Josh? *I don't think I care one way or the other!* Does that rock your comfortable little boat?"

Josh just stared at me, slack-jawed. I plowed ahead.

"What is it about cross-dressing that is so God-awful terrible, huh? The tone in your voice just a moment ago— Why do 'normal' people get so bent out of shape by it? Who does it hurt? If I don't set out to really injure somebody by the deception, and you know I never have, where's the harm?"

I picked up the box from NuGen. "You know what, dear brother? This little invention has opened my eyes. With it, I've found out a lot about myself—myself as a person, not just a gender."

I shoved the box at him, and he caught it. I said, "I think, if you're lucky, you might just learn a little something about yourself. I think maybe you need to."

I turned on my heel and stalked off and, to his credit, Josh silently followed. We trudged up the stairs toward the bathroom where Pamela had first "appeared."

I was seething, and Josh looked like he was being led off to the gallows.

We weren't getting off to the best of starts.

****

I managed to calm down a little as we were filling the tub. Josh just shifted from one foot to the other, looking miserable. I finally sent him back downstairs for the meat thermometer.

I was skilled enough now that I could pretty well judge whether the water was the correct temperature to activate the suit, just by sticking my wrist into the tub. But Josh's anxiety was getting on my nerves, and I wanted to give him something to do.

After he'd left, I opened the box, took a quick look at the manual to ensure that there weren't any new features or instructions that I needed to be aware of (there weren't), and finally pulled out "The Suit."

Like Pamela, the "new girl" (we'd have to come up with a name for her) was sealed in a clear plastic envelope. Holding it, I had a pleasantly nostalgic memory of my first impression of Pamela. The suit was just a flesh-colored slab, its only features being a bunch of nondescript folds and a thatch of fur at one end.

This time, there was a difference in the fur. Per my specification, "the new girl" would be a dark redhead with long, curly tresses. Looking at the rust-colored patch of fuzz, I was again struck by just how marvelous was the technology I was holding in my hand.

The last of my anger evaporated. This was going to be an exciting new chapter in the exploration I'd mentioned. And this time, I got to be the spectator rather than the daring explorer.

I was trying to open the plastic envelope with my teeth when Josh returned with the thermometer.

He said, "Is that it? Is that what it's supposed to look like?"

I managed to tear one of the corners off the packaging, and nodded. "Uh-huh. Not too impressive yet, but wait!"

I pulled the suit out, and set it gently into the now half-full tub.

Josh watched it sink; and I couldn't help but snicker at his raised-eyebrow look of disapproval. He asked, "You sure it's supposed to do that?"

Again I nodded. "Trust me, everything's okay."

"Hummph. Okay, now what?"

I thought about that for a second. "Well, it's supposed to soak for a few minutes. In the meantime, we can skip ahead a few steps and take care of your voice."

Josh tensed up. Here it was: the first concrete step in his "transformation." He said, "Um, what do I have to do?"

I'd already spotted the Styrofoam packing for the bottle of chemical spray that tightened the user's vocal cords. I pulled it out, and spotted the boutique-style box underneath. I wondered just what kind of outfit this suit came with. Well, one thing at a time.

I took the "convenient spray bottle" out of the packing. "All you have to do is trust me, bro."

Now both eyebrows shot up on Josh's forehead.

I said, "Open wide."

He did, though you'd think I was holding a dental drill rather than a spray bottle.

I said, "Now, when I say, take a deep breath in through your mouth. Ready?"

He nodded, mouth hanging wide.

He should have worried about my big grin as I said, "Okay—*Now!*" I gave him a healthy spritz.

He spluttered and gagged for a second, then looked at me accusingly. "You could have warned me before you did that. And you could have said it tasted like shi—Hey, my voice hasn't changed!"

I grinned. "It takes a few minutes to 'kick in.' And, uh, you're right: I really should warn you about some of the stuff that goes on. I promise that I'll be good from now on. And to that end, I told you this doesn't hurt 'much.' Uh, this is one of the parts that does hurt just a—"

The sudden furrow on Josh's brow, and the fact that both his hands were now wrapped around his throat, indicated that the formula was indeed "kicking in."

"Swallow a few times, Josh. It'll stop in just a second. I promise."

He glared at me, and I saw his Adam's apple bob several times.

I waited a moment. "Better?"

He finally nodded, glaring at me. "Yeah, but listen, you son-of-a—"

What a beautiful, lilting soprano! *As Pamela, I just might have to be a little jealous!*

Josh's mouth snapped shut, and both his hands slapped together over his lips.

I grinned. "Kind of surprising, isn't it?"

He just nodded, his eyes large and round. He moved his hands away, still ready to grab whatever it was he thought was lurking in his throat. "This goes—wow—this goes away after a while, right?"

"Yep. Eight hours from now, I'll be back to hearing that annoying nasal bray you call a voice."

"PJ! This isn't funny!"

"You wanna bet?"

Chuckling, I glanced at my wristwatch, then into the bathtub. *Ah! Now the fun really starts.*

Josh joined me looking into the tub. "Holy—" The note of surprise changed to a female growl. "Hey, wait a second. That doesn't look anything like a real—"

"Patience, all right? Would you have believed that you could get that dynamite voice out of a bottle? Have a little faith in the technology."

I suppose I could understand Josh's confusion. The various plastics that compose an I-2000S are temperature/moisture activated. They go through three "phases," depending on the suit's temperature. When dry, and/or at temperatures below 80 degrees, the suit enters what NuGen calls its "dormant" state: that nondescript slab of flesh-colored plastic. Saturate the suit and raise its temperature to 110-plus degrees, and it enters its "neutral" or "donning" state: this rather disappointing facsimile of a woman that was currently floating face-down in the tub. It is between the temperatures of 90 to 104 degrees that the memory plastic of the suit activates, and magic happens.

I motioned to Josh. "Help me get 'her' out of the tub."

Josh reached out, his fingers touched the "flesh" of "her" shoulder, and he recoiled.

"Come on, Josh. It's only plastic, no matter what it feels like."

"I'm not scared. It's just that it's—it's hot! Yeah, hot!"

"Whatever. Just give me a hand."

He pitched in with a will, just to prove that his initial contact with his new alter-ego hadn't rattled him.

I've never had too much trouble handling "Pamela," but the "new girl" was a bit awkward, mostly due to the long, wet mop of chestnut hair. That hair was beautiful, even soaking wet. I couldn't wait to see "her" when we finally got Josh decked out. I could already tell, perhaps from my experience with Pamela, that "she" had a *lot* of potential.

Apparently Josh didn't share my optimism. He muttered (in that gorgeous voice), "It's gotta be broken. This doesn't look anywhere near as good as you do when you're Pamela."

"Will you have a little faith, please?"

"All right, all right. Now what?"

I couldn't help it: I started to chuckle. "Show time, bro. *Strip!*"

"Oh, man—do I have to?"

I just held the suit up by its shoulders and grinned.

"Oh, man—"

Reluctantly, Josh pulled off his shirt and tie, kicked off his shoes—he really was rattled; my anal-retentive brother didn't even untie them first—unbuckled his belt, and slid off his slacks. Then he looked at me expectantly.

"Boxers too, Josh."

"Oh, man—"

Finally my dear brother stood there, blushing furiously and trying not to look too embarrassed.

"Okay." I handed him the suit, which he looked at dubiously. "Just like a pair of coveralls—make sure you get your toes into the right toes on the suit and—"

"I can figure it out, thank you. Would you mind turning your back, please?"

"Ooh, excuse me! What *am* I thinking of? Standing here gawking at a woman getting dressed."

"Screw you, all right?"

Laughing, I turned my back. I heard Josh struggling quietly for a moment.

"Hey, PJ, what's this . . . pocket thing . . . for?"

"Just what you think it's for, bro."

"Oh, maaaaan—"

After a brief pause, there was the sound of more struggling. Finally I heard, "What do I do with the head?"

"Just pull it over your own head, like a hood. Don't worry, it'll stretch."

Then I realized: I'd forgotten to warn Josh about—

"MUMMMMPHHHH!"

"Hey, relax man—stop flailing—don't—OUCH! WILL YOU QUIT? The mouth and eyes are *supposed to be* closed. Just give it a second!"

Josh finally calmed down enough for me to get a look at him. He looked like—

He looked—

He looked like a man wearing a plastic suit that was failing completely to disguise him as a woman.

He looked awful, freaky, and ridiculous.

Just as when I'd first seen Pamela, the individual parts far exceeded the whole. The hair still looked nice. A pair of perky little breasts bobbed about on this apparition's chest—the skin had a lovely "peaches and cream" complexion—but everything was out of both proportion and position. Worse, it was all attached to a very masculine form. No matter how good the parts, the whole was horribly, embarrassingly artificial.

Lord! Is this what Pamela looks like when I first put her on, every workday? Remind me never to "dress" in front of anyone!

Josh stood there, forlorn. He mumbled something that I had to make him repeat twice, before I finally got it: "Now what?"

"Ah! Okay. Now I gotta warn you: As soon as the suit cools down to body temperature, the memory threads are gonna activate."

"Mummph?"

"The threads are gonna activate, and you're gonna feel a little—"

"Mummph?"

"—a little squeeze."

"MummPH?!"

"It's not bad, it's just a little—uh, oh—"

"MUMMMPHHHH!!!"

What happened next was simply astonishing. It was like watching one of those science-fiction movies where one thing "morphs" into another. Except this was happening in the real world! Before my eyes, Josh *changed*. Things *shifted*. His waist suddenly contracted, as his hips swelled. His square shoulders rounded out. Those silly-looking breasts shifted into a much more natural position, and suddenly didn't look silly at all! And down at Josh's groin—

Oh, my!

My suspicion about "her" potential had been correct. Josh was gone. I stood there, slack-jawed, staring at the woman of my most private fantasies.

Where Pamela has full pouting breasts, this woman's were a bit smaller, and upturned in the most delightful fashion. Her long hair, though still wet, was already beginning to show curl and body, and a deep lustrous mahogany sheen. Her figure was trim, almost lean—but deeply, arousingly feminine. I felt a stir of embarrassment when my eyes passed quickly over her womanhood. *Hey, This is Josh, remember?* Her face was narrow and aristocratic—and would have been rather cold, but for a bewitchingly child-like spatter of freckles across the bridge of her nose, perfectly matching a second band of spots above her gorgeous bosom.

With a distinct popping sound, her eyes and mouth opened.

This fantasy-come-true glared at me in stern disapproval. "Well, shithead, any other surprises for me?"

I could only stare, wide-eyed and dry-mouthed.

"What? What are you gawking at? Oh hell, did something go wrong?"

I dumbly shook my head.

"Then what?"

Josh started to turn to the mirror over the sink behind him, but I grabbed his wrist. *God, is this what Pamela's skin feels like? This satiny smoothness?*

I said, "Wait. Have you thought about what you want to call yourself? A girl's name, I mean."

Delicate eyebrows rose above deep hazel pools. Josh was trying to decide if I'd gone completely off the deep end. "Yeah. I thought we'd—God, this voice!—I thought we'd go the same route as we did with you, and try for a name close to mine. Something I'd respond-to naturally."

"What did you pick?"

"I thought—this is so embarrassing!—I thought I'd go with *Jessica*, and shorten it to *Jess*. It's close to *Josh*, see?"

I nodded, released "Jessica's" wrist, and motioned to the mirror. "Well, all I've got to say is: Heeeeere's Jessie!"

I'll never forget the look on "her" face when she first saw "herself" in the mirror. Or how, even though the outward appearance was so undeniably a stunningly beautiful woman, my brother Josh proved beyond doubt that it was still him behind that beguiling disguise.

Her jaw dropped almost to her chest, and in an awed, little-girl whisper, "Jessica" gasped:

"Fuck me!"

****

Josh simply wouldn't get into his new role.

"Look. It works, okay? Now can I take this thing off?"

We were still in Josh's apartment, sitting in my old bedroom, which Josh had converted into a home office. He was perched nervously on a stool, his beautiful new body making it almost impossible for me to concentrate on anything else for more than a few seconds.

"Josh—Jess—what the hell is wrong with you? Don't be in such a rush! You need to get much more used to it if this scheme is going to work."

"Please don't call me 'Jess.' "

"Damn it! I'm going to call you 'Jess' till you answer to it without thinking. Will you stop being such an ass, and try to get into this?"

"I don't *want* to get into it. Can't you understand that? I'm going along with this out of necessity. That doesn't mean I have to enjoy it, or do it any longer than I absolutely have to. Understand?"

"No. I don't. What's the problem with you?"

"*I feel like a god-damn idiot, sitting here!* That's what's wrong!"

"Josh—Jess. You don't need to feel like an idiot. You sure as hell don't look like one! You've seen yourself. You know how good you look."

"That's the point! It's wrong! I'm a guy! You shouldn't be sitting there looking at me the way you are. Bad enough that *anybody* look at me that way, but my own brother?"

I forced myself to look away. "And that's why I want you to put on some clothes."

There was a long, pregnant pause.

Then, in a soft, pleading voice—a voice that made the man in me want to gather Jess into my strong arms and protect her (a voice that I struggled to remember, still belonged to my conniving brother)—Jess murmured, "Please, PJ—please don't make me. I—I can't."

"Why not?"

She looked down at the slender hands folded in her lap, the satin veil of her hair hiding her face. (If she started to cry, I'd be in big trouble!) "Because if I put on woman's clothing—"

"What? You afraid you might *like* it?"

Jess (Josh!) looked into my eyes, and I melted. "PJ—please. I'm sorry about earlier. I really am. I didn't mean anything by it. You're right. There are lots of things I should be more sensitive about. I know I can be a real schmuck. I don't mean to be. Sometimes, it's just the way I am."

I summoned the last of my willpower: "The only way you're going to learn to be more sensitive is to see how other folks live. Seems to me that this is a golden opportunity."

With a small nod and a ragged sigh that made me feel like ten kinds of monster—*It's Josh, you moron! He's pulling another scam!*—Jessica finally agreed. "Okay. What do I do?"

I tossed her (him!) the boutique box. "It's not rocket science. I'm sure you can figure it out."

She (he!) fielded the box, and nodded in resignation.

I looked over her shoulder as she opened it and was a bit disappointed to see a familiar dark-blue floral print.

Apparently all the suits came with the same outfit. I made a mental note to remember that dress, and to be very cautious about hitting-on any "woman" whom I might encounter wearing it in the future.

Jess pulled out the dress, set it aside, and then bit her lower lip, looking at the antique-white lingerie.

I pointed. "Start with the panties, please."

She pulled them out, held them at arm's length in front of her delicious breasts, and looked at them for a moment. "Which is the front and which is the back?"

I sighed in exasperation. "Lace on the front, tag in the back. Jeeze, Jess! It's not that hard!"

She nodded, her hair again concealing her face. In a small voice, she murmured, "I'm sorry, PJ. Please don't be angry. I'm doing my best." She stepped into the briefs and slid them up her shapely legs, then over the curve of her hips.

Thank goodness! One less distraction to deal with.

"Bra next, please."

Jess started to slip the straps over her shoulders.

I thought I'd be a nice guy, and spare her all the trouble of my first encounter with that devious device: "Jess, wait. Don't put your arms through yet. Spin it around so you can see the fasteners, clip them together, spin it back around, then put your arms through the straps."

"Like that?"

Oh, wow.

I had to swallow before I could speak: "Dress next. Just pull it over your head like a sweater, and let the skirt fall naturally."

The dress slithered over Jessica's slender form, and swirled around her knees for a moment.

How could strippers have gotten it so backwards?

Jess fumbled for a moment, trying to reach the zipper, while holding her long chestnut hair out of the way. "PJ—I can't reach—help me."

"Wait." I stood up, and she turned her back to me, hair still held over her shoulder, neck bowed in submission. Were my fingers actually trembling a little as I zipped her up? God, she was so beautiful!

We both sat back down, she again perched on the stool, legs demurely pressed together, hands folded delicately in her lap, hair cascading down over her shoulders and falling like a wave over the beguiling freckles above the deep cleft of her bosom.

Again there was a hitch in my voice: "Um, let's forget about the stockings for now. Plenty of time for you to practice that on your own, later. Just, uh—just put the sandals on."

She nodded, retrieved the sandals, and slid one on each foot, using her free hand to hold back the fall of her hair, so she could see what she was doing. Then she returned to the same position, perched on the stool. Again she looked meek, demure, and submissive. "Anything else, PJ?"

"Um, no. I think that's enough for now. See? That's not so bad, is it?"

Still staring at her folded hands, she gave me another of those ragged sighs and a small nod.

"Aw, Jess. Please, don't be this way. What's wrong? I do this every workday!"

She looked up, meeting my eyes through her long lashes, the anguish on her face making me want to find a hole to crawl into. "It's okay, PJ. It's just that wearing this dress, I'm remembering your first day as Pamela."

"What do you mean?"

"You know—out on the sidewalk."

Then my brother couldn't hold that fake submissive expression anymore; the corners of his lips curled into that wicked, scheming grin that I knew so well. "Jessica" said:

"So, what do you say, PJ? Turnabout's fair play. Wanna go down the hall and fuck?"

****

Josh and I called-in, Tuesday morning, and warned the office that neither of us would be in for the next two days. We gave as our excuse that Josh and Pamela had found the model, and we needed the two days to prep her.

Actually, this wasn't a lie. With Pamela's help, Josh had the "look"; now he needed everything else that went into being a woman.

Two days to make a woman. Do other people face situations as outrageous as this?

By mid-Tuesday morning, the distraction of working with lovely Jessica had proven more than I could stand. We tried not changing Josh's voice to see that would help me concentrate on the task at hand. It didn't. The first time Josh's nasal voice came out of Jessica's lovely semi-naked form, it just about blew my mind. We finally settled on something that made giving demonstrations easier and, oddly, reduced my own distraction.

Man. I wish either Josh or I owned a video camera. Imagine two full days of Pamela and Jessica, practicing feminine gesture and mannerisms—walking, sitting, dressing and undressing. I'd keep one copy of the video for myself (and never need another "girly" magazine); and sell the other to some porno channel for a million bucks.

Josh never did "get into it," but he is a quick study, and by late Wednesday night, I thought he had enough of the fundamentals to "pass." Besides, she was so drop-dead gorgeous that folks might think Jessica a bit "tomboyish," but someone would have to be a mind-reader to suspect the real situation.

I worked with Josh/Jessica for most of Tuesday, and all of Wednesday. Then Thursday morning came.

Ready or not, it was time for "Jessica" to meet Giancarlo.

Chapter 2-5
On Distant Shores

Thursday

Josh had called in "sick," and informed everyone at work that I (Pamela) would take care of the meet with Giancarlo.

It was a bit of an anticlimax.

The entourage swirled into the office at just a bit after 11:00. Giancarlo was at the center of his courtiers, his right hand giving what I call the "*il Duce* Wave"—fingers together and moving slightly, back of the hand toward the "adoring throngs." If he wasn't such a genius, he'd be laughable.

We met in the conference room. Giancarlo swept in, nodded to me, took one look at Jessica—

—and stopped dead in his tracks, his jaw hanging open.

There was a moment's pregnant silence. Poor Josh, he didn't get it. Too new to the role, I guess. But I'd been around long enough as Pamela to know that look on a man's face.

Dear God! It's "lust at first sight."

Finally Giancarlo managed to tear his eyes off the object of his desire. To me, he said, "*Bellissima Artista*—you have find—find—" A dreamy little sigh. "Botticelli had-a his-a Venus. Da Vinci had-a Mona Lisa. And I, Giancarlo, have-a—a—"

He snapped his fingers after a moment, and looked expectantly at Jessica.

The penny finally dropped; and Josh, in the best "shy virgin" manner that I could teach him, lowered his eyes and cooed, "I'm Jessica, *maestro*. I don't know how to tell you how happy I am that you think I'm right for your ads."

Yikes! What a come-on, albeit unintentional.

And it was working. Giancarlo was beginning to perspire. How was I supposed to know that he and I shared a common erotic-fantasy woman?

There was another long moment's silence, then Giancarlo turned to Anthony (that good-looking assistant from last time) and commanded, "Have-a the jet ready. We leave tonight. Pamela and—*bella, bella* Jessica shall wake tomorrow on-a my island!"

Then he was gone, and the court followers were scrambling to follow. Except for Anthony. He just stood aside and watched, with a bemused expression, as the tide of humanity receded toward the bank of elevators.

I finally managed to catch his eye. "Island?"

He turned those amazing ice-blue eyes on me and smiled. "Indeed. *Il Maestro* owns a small island. He likes to do his 'creating' there."

"Oh. How interesting." Trapped alone on an island with Giancarlo while he was "creating"? This could be very interesting! "I guess I should take Jessica home and start packing."

Anthony waved a hand in dismissal. "No need. There is a rule. On *il Maestro's* island, women wear Giancarlo's clothing—or they wear nothing at all."

He gave me a harmless little leer that, coming from him, robbed that statement of most of its threat. Still—

"I see. So, where is this island? East Coast? West Coast? Gulf Coast?"

Anthony's lips curled into a charmingly boyish grin. "Mediterranean Coast, actually."

****

We flew out just as the sun was setting. "The jet" turned out to be a Grumman Gulfstream II. One of those largish multi-engine business jets that show the world you're so big that you had to trade in the Learjet for more space.

The passenger cabin was an exercise in "I'm filthy rich and I can flaunt it." If it wasn't Corinthian leather, it was genuine teak, or ivory, or velvet—or whatever was needlessly expensive. I claimed a leather "captain's chair" over one wing, Anthony grabbed the other, and poor Jessica wound up in a huge crescent-shaped sofa that was set against the back wall—with Giancarlo sprawled right beside her.

He petted, he praised, he cooed. And then, a little over an hour into the flight, he mercifully fell asleep and spent the rest of the trip snoring; while Jessica sat and looked perplexed, and I bit my lip to keep from laughing.

The jet began its descent to "Isla Giancarlo," just as the sun was rising out of the cerulean waters of the Aegean.

By mid-morning of our first day, we'd pretty well settled in. Giancarlo had disappeared to arrange for delivery of the lingerie that we would be using in the photo shoots, and to get a photographer that he knew of. I got a room on the west wing of the second floor of the Byzantine castle that someone had built here a few odd-hundred years ago. As promised, the closet was filled with clothing: everything from sundresses to evening gowns. And all in Pamela's size. I wonder how they'd figured that out. Somebody was very efficient.

I took my toilet case containing my one vital personal item (NuGen's voice spray), gave myself a good spritz, and then put the bottle away in a drawer in the bathroom. Then I slipped out of my business suit (which I'd been wearing since yesterday morning) and donned a mid-calf length, white-cotton sundress and sandals. I felt it went very well with my new "Grecian" surroundings.

I spent several hours getting the "grand tour" from Anthony. "Isla Giancarlo" was one of the Cyclades Islands, off the southeast coast of Greece. Technically a part of that country, the Greek authorities pretty much left Giancarlo alone, so long as he didn't do anything too outrageous. This explained how we'd managed to avoid the (in Jessica's and my cases) embarrassing details of obtaining passports.

The mansion had belonged to some Austro-Hungarian monarch at the turn of the last century. As Anthony told it, the potentate had a nubile young daughter who had a bit of trouble "keeping her knees together" when handsome young gentlemen were around. I guess in those days, princesses could be ugly as mud fences and still attract boys. But by all reports, this princess was as lovely as she was horny; so you can imagine what kind of trouble Daddy was having. He solved the problem by building her this gilded cage till he could arrange a suitable marriage to some prince, at which point it would all become someone else's problem.

The villa was an imposing heap in classic Byzantine style, three stories tall, and right out of the "Arabian Nights." It also overlooked one of the most beautiful white-sand beaches I've ever seen.

The shoot was scheduled to begin the next morning, so I had the rest of the day to myself to explore. I wandered the halls of Giancarlo's villa for the better part of the morning, but by 11 a.m., the warm temptation of the beach became too much to bear.

Of course, whoever was in charge of my wardrobe had foreseen the inevitable attraction. In the bottom drawer of my dresser was an elegantly simple white-maillot swimsuit that fit me like a glove. There was also a terry-cloth beach robe and a large, floppy straw hat. I donned them all, paused to wink at the sizzling little beach bunny who smiled back saucily from my full-length mirror, and headed off for a well-earned afternoon of lounging on the crystalline sand.

It was heaven. I lay in the sun, listening to the gentle susurration of waves caressing the shore, and the distant cry of the gulls. All my cares drifted away. I was dozing off when a shadow fell across me.

Dressed in trunks and a terry-cloth robe of his own, Anthony was smiling down at me.

"Anthony, what a pleasant surprise! What are you doing here?"

He raised a finger to his lips, and grinned. "Shh! I am playing truant. What is the American word?"

I giggled. "*Hookey*. It's called *playing hookey*."

A delightfully bemused expression crossed his face. "*Hookey*? This means—?"

I shrugged, and leaned back on my elbows. "Darned if I know. It's just a word."

He matched my smile. "*Hookey* then. *Il Maestro* has been called to Rome on some matter concerning the new spring line. He will be back tomorrow evening. In his absence, I've been left with instructions to see that you and *Signorina* Jessica are well cared for. The *signorina* has retired to her room for an afternoon nap. That leaves me with no concerns but you."

It's hard not to play the part my disguise allows me.

I laid the fingertips of my left hand over my well-displayed cleavage, and assayed a "southern belle" drawl. "Why, goodness, Signore. Such a handsome gentleman—and all to myself!"

He laughed, enjoying the byplay, and suddenly his mild Italian accent grew much broader: "Ah. Handsome?" He made an elegantly Romanesque shrug. "I do not-a know about that. But a lucky fellow surely—to find a nymph of-a the sea washed up on his humble beach!"

****

That afternoon I spent with Anthony was delightful.

He was charming. A good conversationalist. He had lots of stories about growing up in Genoa. Like many Italians, he came from a large, extended family. And like many Italians, he loved to talk about them. I laughed till my sides ached over tales of mad uncle Giuseppe and his never-ending schemes to export olive oil to Germany, while avoiding the import duties. Of his brother Marco's adventures at University, which seemed to encompass everything *but* learning—at least, learning anything that could be taught in a classroom. And of cousin Sophia and the thousand-and-one suitors.

Before we knew it, the sun was sinking in fire, and the high mare's-tail clouds were gilded in rose and peach.

"Ah, Signorina Pamela. We must go in. Dinner will be ready soon, and Chef will have our hides if we delay service of the first course."

We parted on the second floor to dress for dinner. I quickly showered, fortified my voice with another shot of spray—just in case—then found an exquisite off-the-shoulder cream-colored gown (with Giancarlo's label, of course), as well as a simple linen tie for my hair, all laid out on my bed.

The formal dining room, big enough to seat an infantry platoon, was set for three. It turned out that we'd be dining intimately tonight: just Anthony, "Jessica," and myself. I felt a girlish thrill when Anthony held my chair, inclining his head in a formal bow. It's nice to be pampered.

Josh of course quickly jerked out his own chair and seated himself before Anthony could attend him.

Josh still refused to play along with the charade, and it was truly a pity. He was wearing a low-cut black velvet gown and a string of pearls that perfectly accented his complexion (and his fake freckles). His luxurious cinnamon mane tumbled in casual abandon over his bare shoulders, looking wild and sensual. I wondered how he'd managed to achieve that carelessly-elegant effect; then realized he probably had achieved it by shaking his head when he came out of the shower, and then ignoring it completely.

The dinner was superb. Lamb and a wild-rice dish. I wouldn't care to guess what a dinner of this quality, in such surroundings, would cost. I knew it was probably still beyond my recently elevated bank account.

Anthony was the perfect host. If anything, he was even more charming than he'd been on the beach. He chatted brightly and intelligently on almost any subject that came up. He even managed to draw Josh out for a few minutes with a discussion of the Italian stock market.

Suddenly, Josh realized how free he was being (and in fairness, how out of character), and he quickly clammed back up.

Anthony seemed a bit nonplused, but I managed to distract him with a request for more stories of his family.

Josh excused himself and retreated to the safety of his room, as soon after dessert as was polite. This left Anthony and me giggling and chatting over brandy.

Sometime around midnight, Anthony announced that since we were working tomorrow, it was probably time to retire. I agreed (reluctantly—I can't remember when I've had such a good time at dinner), and we headed upstairs. Anthony paused with me outside my door, and we fell silent for a moment before saying goodnight.

I don't know why what happened next, happened. Maybe I'd had too much wine with dinner, or maybe I shouldn't have mixed the wine and the brandy.

Maybe that's just a rationalization.

Suddenly, Anthony's lips were pressed against mine.

I remember that little sermon to Josh about my uncertainty concerning my sexual orientation. But, in truth,

I'm quite secure in my heterosexuality. I'm simply not sexually attracted to men.

The urgency of Anthony's passion passed like electricity through me, and I discovered that there's a difference between sexuality and romance.

My arms, almost of their own volition, wrapped around Anthony's neck, drawing him close. In a moment, we were in my room. In another moment, we were tight in each other's arms upon the huge four-poster bed.

****

The morning dawned cool and bright, with a soft breeze that smelled of sand and salt and Asia across the bay.

I-as-Pamela stood on the balcony of my room, letting the breeze caress my flowing blonde hair, and letting the breeze mold the silk of my peignoir against my warm, womanly body.

I had but one regret, and it had nothing to do with the night that had gone before. Anthony and I had shared something magical and beautiful. It was nothing of a lie, or a deception, for I had truly given myself to him, as he had given himself to me.

The need to be needed, to be cherished—that's not a thing of gender. It is a thing of spirit, basic to humanity. Last night Anthony and I had surrendered to that need, with the understanding that it was both the first and the last time for us together.

I make no apology for it.

I feel no shame.

Standing here, the gentle breeze pressing against me, my only regret was that I couldn't feel its warmth against my own skin.

****

The jet arrived at about 9:30. Giancarlo was still in Rome. He'd be back this evening. Aboard the jet was Giancarlo's chosen photographer: a fellow by the name of Billy Cotterwood from London. I knew of his work, and agreed with Giancarlo's choice.

Anthony introduced me to Billy, and we spent an hour or so in my room going over my presentation graphics. Billy was very attentive, and asked some excellent questions about lighting and posing. He did have one annoying habit: He constantly chewed on a toothpick, which he occasionally used as a pointer. But he was more than professional enough that I allowed him that one eccentricity.

We trooped around the villa and the surrounding grounds, looking for locations. By noon we were ready to begin shooting.

Billy had set up in a ground-floor salon for the first of the shoots. The furnishings were elegantly rococo and "fantastic," just the mood I was looking for. The centerpiece of the room was a huge gilded mirror. I had a little plan that I thought would aid in the first few shots. I'd made sure that Jessica didn't have access to a mirror while she was dressing in the first item that she was going to model: her copy of that peignoir that had first inflamed my own imagination. Billy set up his cameras and light reflectors, and indicated he was ready. I went and fetched Jessica.

I can't begin to describe how she looked in that peignoir, other than to say she was *perfect*.

Quietly, almost reverently, I brought her into the room. I made sure that she didn't see the mirror, but was standing with her back to it.

The toothpick fell out of Billy's mouth and he whispered, "Blimey!"

I motioned to Billy, he raised the camera, and Jessica looked from the lens to me. I nodded my encouragement and smiled. "Turn around, hun."

Jessica did. She saw herself in the mirror.

I confess: Part of my motivation in making Josh agree to the deception was my desire to get a little payback, to make him feel a bit of what it was to pretend to be something he wasn't. Hell, to be able for the rest of our lives to say, "Hey, remember Jessica and the lingerie?"

But now I just stood, hands at my sides, and watched Jessica discover the miracle of femininity as Billy's camera clicked. All thoughts of payback and gloating evaporated. The genuine wonder of what was happening before my eyes made any of that kind of thought impossible.

The actual shoot took six hours. It, too, was *perfect*. My vision was more than vindicated.

Chapter 2-6
Suicide Mission

My half-brother and I were sitting in Jessica's room when the climax of this morality play occurred.

Once again, Jess was wearing that peignoir. We'd come full circle through Giancarlo's new catalogue. We'd ended where we'd begun: with the peignoir, because we wanted to get the effect of the setting sun against that shimmering rose silk.

I'll always remember that last picture: Jessica, standing on a small bluff above the shimmering Aegean, arms angled behind her, head tilted back, letting the gentle breeze caress her sorrel locks as she gazed out over the water, aching for her lover's return from the sea.

What an image!

"Jess" was sprawled in an overstuffed chair, legs spread wide, wine glass in hand. "Thank God that's over."

I took a sip of wine. "Come on, Josh. I saw you looking in the mirror. You can't deny you felt a little of the magic."

He gave me a sexy leer with Jessica's face that instantly raised my blood pressure a few notches. "Oh, hey, I'm not dead yet. I gotta admit, I've had a woody all day that Paul Bunyan would have trouble felling."

I favored him with a knowing grin. "You know that's not what I mean."

There was a long silence as Jess stared into the depths of her wine glass. "PJ, I've been thinking about what you said to me. When we were in the kitchen, the night that I first put on this"—a little gesture to the body that lay encased in the luscious silk. "I just want to say, I may have been—"

I didn't find out just what Josh may have been, because at that moment, the door to the room flew open and in raced Giancarlo.

Jess had just enough time to draw herself up in the chair, and to regain her modesty by closing her legs, before Giancarlo was on his knees in adoration before her.

"Ah—*carissima*—the pictures! I have seen them!"

He grabbed a hand and began showering it with kisses. "You are (kiss)—you make (kiss)—"

He was beginning to work his way up her arm. "Never in my life—such beauty (kiss)—such passion (kiss, on her upper arm by now)—Oh! (Kiss on the shoulder)—"

The expression of alarm on Jess's face was priceless. *Where is Billy and his camera when you need him?*

Jess said, "Uh—uh—Signore Giancarlo—uh—thank you, I—" A look of pleading in my direction.

By now, Giancarlo's hands were on Jess's waist, and his expression was one of absolute religious transport. "You make-a the fire in me burn bright. You make-a the man in me roar with desire."

This was getting serious, but it was also too comical for words. When Kevin Sprague had violated me, it had been a viscous, animal attack. But this little gnome slobbering over Jessica? This was comic opera, not crime drama. I started to giggle, I couldn't help it.

Jess's look of pleading turned to one of incipient anger. A look that vanished, as she felt the material of her skirt start to slide up her legs.

"Whoa! Now wait just a second! If you think—"

There was a little squeak from Jessica, right when I saw Giancarlo's tongue on her knee—her thigh—

"Oh . . I must-a have you. I must-a—oooh!"

Giancarlo's head was between Jessica's thighs. Jessica had both hands up beside her head, waving them in mortal dread at what was about to occur. I was gagging on suppressed laughter, biting my lower lip for all I was worth.

Then *it* happened.

****

To the Wonderful Folks at NuGen,

Your magical suits are everything you've ever claimed. The illusion of femininity that they create is <u>art</u> *in the truest sense of the word: their lovely curves; their soft, silky skin and satiny hair; the honey music of their voices. Truly, you work a miracle every time you create one of these sorceresses.*

But gentlemen, there are five senses, not three. You have artfully catered to sight, touch, and hearing.

But what of smell? What of taste?

****

Suddenly, Giancarlo reared back from Jessica's "secret garden," licked his lips—

—*and in the broadest "Joisey" accent I've ever heard, exclaimed,* "What da foick?"

You could have cut the sudden stillness with a knife. Jessica was the first to shatter the tableaux.

She stabbed an accusing finger at Giancarlo and shrieked, "You're not Italian!"

Giancarlo leveled his own finger at Jessica's crotch and shouted, "And you ain't—you ain't—I don't know what you ain't!"

The true story finally emerged over the next few minutes, but not without a lot of shouting, shrieking (from both genders), and recriminations and accusations.

Giancarlo was in fact one Joey Carletti, native son of that most exotic of cities: Hoboken, New Jersey. He had been, until twenty-eight years ago, apprentice clothing-buyer for his father's small-time men's store. It was at that time that Joey had finally done something about his belief that he had a talent for designing clothes. His submission of designs to a cut-rate men's-clothing maker, and those designs' quick acceptance, had vindicated his belief. The die was cast for his eventual meteoric rise to fame, and his eventual adoption of a more "suitable" pseudonym.

As for Jessica—well, it was impossible to continue the charade. The fatal flaw of the I-2000S had reared its ugly head (so to speak). Though Josh made a valiant attempt to regroup and to continue the deception, it was eventually for naught. He was too rattled.

Besides, it wasn't necessary.

I let them both flail for a moment, then I told the *whole* truth.

"Youse guys are *both* guys?" was Giancarlo's response.

Josh uttered a shriek of dismay, but I stilled him with an upraised hand. I calmly pointed out that each of us was guarding a hidden truth, and it was in all of our best interests to keep each other's secrets. After all, if word got out that WN&A had pulled this stunt, it would be our ruin. And if word got out that the deception *had actually worked* on Giancarlo—*née Joey Carletti*—who would be served?

It took a while, but finally Giancarlo saw the wisdom of my suggestion. He pledged secrecy—in exchange for Josh's mutual promise, *plus* a significant decrease in our fees.

Josh gave the latter willingly. From the first, it had been more about prestige than about profit. (Profit that would eventually follow the prestige anyway.) And

Giancarlo had to admit, even with the deception, the photos were exactly what was needed for the ad campaign. We parted on this uneasy truce.

My last sight of Giancarlo of Venice was his suspicious, uncertain frown as he stalked out of Jessica's bedroom.

****

It was several weeks later, when I was sitting in my studio reading one of my women's magazines, that the door opened and Josh quietly entered.

We'd long since consigned Jessica to a dark corner of Josh's closet. I had a slightly melancholy idea that I'd never see that lovely woman "in the flesh" again. Life can be very cruel sometimes.

Josh closed the door behind himself, and perched on the corner of my desk. He sat there for a moment, head down on his chest, lost in his thoughts.

I silently allowed him to gather those thoughts. I've catalogued his faults elsewhere, and I see no need to repeat them here. He's a good man, for all of those faults. He's my brother, and I love him. In his own way, I think Josh loves me too.

"PJ—I've been thinking."

"About what, Josh?"

"About that conversation we had that night when I first—you know—when you told me about your feelings about—"

"Josh. I didn't mean everything I said. I was just—"

He held up a hand, but still wouldn't look in my eyes. "Look, his isn't easy for me, okay? I just wanted to tell you: When I was Jessica—remember that day we took the pictures? I guess—"

Finally he met my eyes. "I don't pretend to understand it all, PJ. But you were right about something, at least."

"And that is—?"

"That you can always learn something new about yourself. If you're willing to try."

Then he grinned, and shook his fist at me. "And if you ever tell *anyone* about any of this—even this conversation—I'll beat the crap out of you. And you know I can!"

We shared a smile, and then he was gone.

I sighed happily, and went back to my magazine. Josh had nothing to worry about; I would never breathe a word to anyone.

I didn't need to.

There on page 36 of one of the largest women's journals, Jessica stood on a small bluff overlooking the Aegean, hungry for her lover's embrace, as the warm sea breeze fanned her passion. The caption extolled the virtue of Giancarlo of Venice, and his glorious lingerie.

As they say: "A picture is worth a thousand words."

PART 3
Much Ado...

Chapter 3-1
Life Is But An Actor...

So there I was, in a beauty parlor in a small town in the Deep South, with a roomful a women looking at me.

As "Pamela Jane," I'm used to being looked at. Big breasts, long and blond hair, hourglass figure, great butt, shapely legs—by now, I'm used to men desiring me and women envying me.

But that isn't why these particular women were looking at me.

"Well?" Dori asked, while tapping her foot. Dori was a local woman whose real breasts were bigger than my NuGen breasts.

I took a breath, swallowed, and said, "But soft, what light through yonder window breaks?"

The room went silent. Not because all the women realized I was quoting Romeo instead of Juliet. Nope, the silence was because—

I was speaking in Peter James' baritone, not Pamela Jane's contralto.

Like I said, there was dead silence from everyone. Then Dori said something that maybe-was, maybe-wasn't insulting.

To which Norma Jo Sivley replied, "You hush your mouth, Dori! Pamela, sweetie, you're perfect!"

Hm, maybe I need to back up and explain how I got myself into all this.

****

My name is PJ Wright. As you've probably heard by now, on weekends and after six on weekdays, the *PJ* stands for *Peter James*. During working hours, it's *Pamela Jane*. How this all came about is too long a story to relate here. Suffice it to say: With the aid of the folks at NuGen Transgender Appliances, Inc., the fellow born as Peter makes his living as Pamela, the female graphic artist.

I love the work. As time passes, I'm growing more comfortable with the fact that I spend most of my waking hours as a woman. That the NuGen I-2000S that I use to transform myself, creates the perfect illusion not just of a woman, but of a lovely, sexy, young woman—well, that's just a little side benefit.

The firm I work for, Whitman, North, and Arjer, is currently riding a tidal wave of success. We're a *hot* agency. We've "arrived." We can pick-and-choose our clients.

The good times have translated into a very healthy bank account for yours truly. The days of living on "Cup o' Noodles," and wondering where I'm gonna find money for this month's water bill are over. When a hefty bonus for my work on the Giancarlo lingerie campaign raised my savings-account balance comfortably into six digits, I decided it was time to buy myself a toy.

It was love at first sight, my candy-apple-red passion. I knew it was meant to be the moment I walked into the Adagio Motors showroom. She was a new model, just introduced this year. They called her a *"Bufera di Vento,"* a lyrically Romanesque (to my ear, anyway) rendering of *Windstorm*. I named her "Buffy," and drove her out the door just as the sun was firing the clouds on the western horizon.

After large purchases, I've heard you're supposed to experience something called "buyer's remorse"—the nagging feeling that the purchase has all been a mistake somehow. Well not me, not this time. Sitting behind the wheel, as the wind flowed through the open convertible top, I was sure this was PJ Wright in his natural environment: an Italian sports car.

****

Buffy and I began the adventure that I'm about to relate when Josh—Josh Arjer, my half-brother and the managing partner of the firm—finally surrendered and assigned me to meet with a new client out in Virginia. It was a pretty straightforward account, something that one of our new stable of artists could have handled easily. But the weather had just turned to warm spring, the skies were depthless and crystal blue, so it was perfect weather for a road trip in a brand new candy-apple-red sports car—

As I say, Josh finally surrendered and gave me the account.

****

I allowed myself two weeks for the whole expedition. I figured five days to drive from the west coast to Virginia, two days to meet with the client, and five days to drive back. That should allow for a leisurely pace and a good two-day slack for sightseeing. I thought I was being overly cautious, that I was allowing way too much time.

As it turned out—

Buffy is a sports car; and as such, she doesn't have the largest of trunks. I did some judicious packing, and managed to fit everything into two suitcases, which barely fit into Buffy's "boot." It was a bit of a problem packing—since I needed clothes for two weeks for *two* people.

See, there's a rub when it comes to Buffy and Pamela. Pamela doesn't have a driver's license. I've never figured out a good way to get one for my female alter-ego. I've heard that you can go down to the DMV *en femme* and ask them to use that picture on your license, and they'll do it. But your personal information doesn't change. There's still that huge black letter 'M' in the box labeled *Sex*. And you can only have one license at a time; they check on things like that. The problems were just too great, the results of embarrassing discoveries too terrible to consider—so no driver's license for Pamela.

Pamela still relies on her "picture credit cards" for her ID, and rides the bus to work every day.

This being the case, Peter would be doing the driving this trip. Pamela would appear, once we were safely in the motel in Norfolk to conduct her meetings, then it was back to Peter and the open road home.

At least, that was the plan.

In retrospect, I knew I wasn't even thinking that way when I did the packing. But it was subconscious. I'm sure it was. At the time I didn't even stop to wonder why I was packing some of Pamela's more *playful* garments that it would be wildly inappropriate for me to wear in front of the client.

Yeah. I'm getting way ahead of myself.

****

The ride east was everything I'd hoped it would be. The weather was beautiful.

And the scenery? Uniformly spectacular. The sere, desolate beauty of Utah's high desert. The Colorado Rockies gleaming snow white in the moonlight. The endless emerald fields of the Great Plains, vibrant with new spring life. The wide Mississippi sparkling in the afternoon sun. The Smoky Mountains, dozing hazy blue and dreaming of ancient legends.

The shriek of gulls on the Chesapeake, and the wide Atlantic curving over the edge of the world.

****

The meeting was the slam dunk that I thought it would be. The new clients were very happy with the proposals. We closed after only three hours of meetings, with their eager assurance that they'd contact our sales department that very afternoon.

I headed back to the motel for a quick bath, a quick change, and a leisurely start on the return trip.

Looking back, I realize that this is where the adventure all started: in the bathroom of my motel room.

I'd shed Pamela's conservative business suit and was standing in the bathroom with the bathtub running, starting to slide her slip up over her head, when Pamela—that bawdy little minx—caught my eye in the mirror.

She gave me that pleading, pouting, wanton look that she does so well—at least in private with me. Biting her lower lip, and batting those huge, round, starving-orphan eyes, she begged, "Come on Peter, let me drive for a while. Think how *hot* we'd look. Pamela's blonde hair flying in the wind, with us wearing that little pink sundress that you know you brought along just for this. I won't speed, or get into trouble, or *anything*. Pretty *pleeeeease?*"

What can I say? She's got me wrapped around her little finger, and she knows it.

Okay, okay, I'm rationalizing again. But damn! Pamela would look incredible flying down the Interstate in Buffy. My black aviator sunglasses perched so "butch" on her aristocratic nose. An arrogantly haughty sneer on her full lips, for all the poor "huddled masses" in their blah little commuter-mobiles, as she blazes by. The object of passion and envy of everyone she encounters.

Gawd, I'm such a slut. I didn't even wear any underwear. Just that little pink sundress and the old reliable white sandals. With the bags in the trunk and with Peter's "shades" on her nose, Pamela roared out of the motel parking lot just as the sun hit high noon.

****

I headed south on I-95. I was going to take the "southern route" on the return trip. I'd never seen the Gulf Coast, and I was dying to absorb a little of that exotic Creole charm that I'd heard so much about. Besides, I think Pamela had always wanted to be a "southern belle." What better time than the present?

I swung down through the Carolinas, turned right into Georgia, and was well into—

Let me be polite here and not name names, out of class. Let's say, it was somewhere west of Georgia, and east of California, that the adventure *really* started.

Chapter 3-2
Not In Our Stars, But In Ourselves

I was gliding down I-10 in fairly light traffic, just after noon on the second morning. That little pink sundress had been just too perfect a match for Buffy; and I was still wearing it, still too daring to bother with underwear.

I was feeling so *alive*. My life was going well, after so many years of struggling. I'm not so prepossessed that I don't know I've had more than my share of luck. But I've worked for what I've gotten too. I was happy with myself, happy with my life, and happy with my car; and I was feeling wicked, wonderful, and free.

I'd just pulled around an eighteen-wheeler, and was accelerating past the cab, when I realized that the trucker was staring down at me from his perch behind the wheel. I glanced up, slid my dark glasses down with one hand while I steered with the other and locked eyes with him. I knew what he was grinning at: an impossibly beautiful woman, wearing a skimpy little dress and driving a sexy sports car.

I slid the glasses back up; blew him a "If you can catch me, you can have me" kiss; flicked my skirt up around my hips, granting him a glimpse of what he so desperately wanted to see—and then stomped on the accelerator and blazed away, to a lusty fanfare of air-horns.

I'm so bad!

****

Sometimes, when I get this way, it's like salted peanuts. I just can't stop. I wanted more admiration. I wanted more men panting for me. I wanted to be the object of unattainable desire.

I wanted a cup of coffee.

There was a truck stop ahead, and I wheeled Buffy in. This little pit stop turned out to be both my salvation and my curse.

****

I parked in a spot near the entrance, opened the door, and slid out with a delightfully feline grace.

I'd already found out that you can get out of a sports car one of two ways. You can either just try to climb out, in which case you look awkward, no matter how naturally graceful you are. Or you can make a big production out of it. Men have to slowly uncoil and stick one leg out, while levering themselves into a tall, commanding stance as they survey their conquests. Women need to swing both legs out, (letting one stick out straight a bit longer, while the other first makes contact with the pavement), then uncurl themselves with catlike languor as they stand—maybe brushing back their hair from their temple as they do it.

I sauntered up to the door, swinging my hips in that flirty little dress as I went. I deigned to allow a burly trucker to hold the door open for me. I swept past with a little smile, and a little extra wiggle, and a little extra spring in my step to get those luscious C-cup breasts into action. Poor helpless schmuck, I know what you'll be dreaming about tonight up there in the sleeper.

Man, I wasn't just swinging my hips anymore, I was positively strutting.

I picked a stool right in the middle of the counter; and tried not to look too smug when conversation ground to a halt for a good minute, while all the males tried to tear their eyes off me, and the women tried to convince themselves I hadn't just blown all of them out of the water without even lifting a finger.

A puffy waitress long past her prime finally wandered over, and we both sharpened our claws while she took my order for a cup of coffee and an order of toast.

After a few moments, conversation stuttered back into motion. I sipped my coffee and let my mind wander.

I heard a man say, "So they been there all day? They don't usually do that."

Another man replied, "Yep. I guess they's gonna make sure they get ever-one t'day."

"Pfft. You'd think Smokey had som'tin' better ta do than ta jest sit out there, checking licenses."

The coffee that I'd been sipping, I snorted it back out my nose.

I swung around on the stool, trying to locate the two speakers. They were a pair of middle-aged men sitting at a booth behind me. One of them was wearing a "Peterbilt" baseball cap; the other favored a stained and battered cowboy hat. I quickly stood and scurried over, forgetting all about my sexy "sashay."

"Excuse me, I couldn't help overhearing. Did you say that the police were out checking driver's licenses? Did you mean that they were stopping all the trucks, perhaps?"

The two truckers eyed me appreciatively (which suddenly had lost all its charm), and "Peterbilt" finally grinned. "Nope, ma'am. They's stoppin' ever-one. They do it sometimes. Make sure ever-body's got valid licenses, got proof of insurance"—they exchanged a knowing look—"they's make sure nobody's up to no good."

Oh, gawd! "Um, where are they set up? Which direction?"

"Well, ma'am. That depends. You're kinda in the middle of the whole shebang. If'n you go west, you'll meet up with the roadblock about four miles from here. If'n you go east, they's set up at the rest area at milepost 132."

"You mean, they're on *both* sides of us? We're *surrounded?*"

The truckers made another exchanged glance. "Yep. Either way you go, you're gonna be talkin' to Smokey 'fore the day gets much older."

My mind was swirling. Of course, you can see there was an easy solution: sit here and wait for the check to end. But I wasn't thinking that way.

I was panicking with visions of trying to explain to a sweaty, small-town southern sheriff why my driver's license was for a Peter Wright; and visions of the county judge peering at me over the top of his glasses, while he slammed down the gavel and sentenced me to six weeks on the chain gang for being some kind of communist pervert—

All I could think was: *I'm trapped, and I've got to get out of here!*

Maybe I could shed Pamela and then everything would be fine. A bathtub—I needed a bathtub filled with hot water. I think the panic was starting to show in my voice. "Please— is there a motel around here? I mean real close by?"

That didn't get the reaction I'd intended.

Both my informants sat up a bit straighter, and this time there was definite calculation in their smiles. "Well, there's the Motel 6 over in Crosbyville. That's just fifteen miles west."

I almost shrieked with frustration. "What I mean is, Is there someplace that I can get to without crossing the police checkpoint?"

Peterbilt rubbed his stubbled chin and thought about it. "No, ma'am." Pause. "Course, you don't actually need to go through the checkpoint if'n you're westbound."

Cowboy Hat piped up: "Tha's right. If'n you don't mind a little side-road detour."

Salvation!

I smiled with relief. "I can take a side road and avoid the checkpoint?"

"Yes'm. You just go back out on to the highway, go about two miles, and then watch for the Horraceburg Road on your right. You take that road—go right through Horraceburg for about another six miles—then take a left on County Road 1108. That'll fetch you right back to I-10 about seven miles past the checkpoint. Nothin' to it."

I was so rattled that I actually shook both their hands. "Thank you, guys. You're real lifesavers!"

I threw a five on the counter to pay for the coffee, and made a bee-line for Buffy, barely noticing all the perplexed stares I'd left in my wake.

****

For the next five minutes, I was in a state of utter, unreasoning panic. I kept looking down at the odometer, convinced that I'd already gone more than the recommended two miles. I began to wonder if I'd missed the turn, if those two yahoos had been lying to me, if I was about to run into the checkpoint, full tilt.

Maybe they'd seen through my disguise? Maybe everyone had? Maybe that's the reason they'd all been staring at me?

Would I be spending the night in the county lock-up?

What would I tell all my friends back home when the news hit the national papers?

Dear God, get me out of this. Let me find the turnoff. Let me get past the cops, and find a motel with a bathtub and some hot water. Let me ditch Pamela and go back to being Peter, like I should have in the first place. I promise

I'll never tease anyone again. I'll just stick to business and be proper and prim and never put evil thoughts in folks' heads. I swear, I'll start going back to church, and—

The white lettering on the green sign read "Horraceburg, Exit 1/2 mile". I could see the turnoff. I couldn't yet see the police checkpoint.

I'd made it.

Instantly abandoning all my promises—*Hey, they were made under duress. I'm sure nobody expects me to keep them.*—I slowed, and with a huge sigh of relief veered gracefully off the perilous freeway onto the two-lane country blacktop.

Slowly my heart returned to a normal rhythm, and my fingers loosened their death grip on Buffy's steering wheel. The cool spring breeze washed across my face, and the trees formed a sheltering canopy over my head.

My problems are over, I can relax—

Buffy's motor started to simultaneously thump and screech. A pair of warning lights glowed red on the dash: "Check Oil" and "Stop Engine."

Perhaps I'd been too hasty in dismissing those promises to God. *Um, is it too late to reconsider?*

Buffy's engine faltered, then abruptly died—

—leaving me to coast to a stop on the side of the road.

I guess it is.

****

I hopped out. (No pretense at feline grace this time. In fact, anybody standing by the side of the road would have gotten a real show as I just sprawled sideways in the seat and levered myself into a standing position.)

I fumbled for a second, getting the hood open, and then peered inside.

I'm nobody's idea of a mechanic. I knew vaguely that the round thing on the top was the air cleaner; that all the belt-things should be in one piece (they were); and that the wires should all be connected. (They seemed to be, but I didn't want to fiddle with them. I liked Pam's hairdo just the way it was; I had no interest in obtaining a do-it-yourself "Bride of Frankenstein" electric frizz.)

And then I saw poor Buffy's "mortal injury": There was oil leaking in a fairly steady flow from a kind of electric motor-looking thing that was bolted on to one side of the engine block, and that was connected to one of the belts.

Hm, could that be the oil pump? I knew that cars had oil pumps. I also knew that pumps shouldn't be spewing oil all over the ground.

Oh, fine. Dead in the water, on a country side-road in the middle of nowhere.

Do I start walking? Which way? Back toward the interstate? What if I run into some of the cops from the roadblock? Don't they ask for ID, just as a matter of course?

That was out.

How about toward that town that's supposed to be up ahead? What was its name again? How far did those two good-ole-boys say it was from the turnoff? I remember the distance was stated in miles. Lovely—a little stroll in the country, wearing flimsy sandals and a skimpy sundress.

Or did I just stay by the car and wait for the auto club? I looked up and down the road. This didn't seem to be the heaviest-traveled thoroughfare in the whole world.

What do I do?

Ultimately, I was saved the decision by the appearance of a rather battered-looking pickup that was coming from the direction of the interstate.

I smoothed out my skirt, smoothed out my hair, and tried to look fetching (not difficult for Pamela) and helpless (not difficult for Peter, the world-class auto *not*-mechanic).

I'd just flashed on a mental image of getting pounced on by the driver of the pickup, and dragged off to some backwoods cabin as a mate for his half-human son, when the pickup pulled off on the shoulder and a middle-aged and very *well-endowed* woman got out. (Was I in dairy country?)

"Hey there, hon, you havin' car trouble?"

No, you moron. I always park by the side of the road in the middle of nowhere, with the hood up. It's a hobby. "Golly, I sure am. Thanks for stopping. I don't know *what* could be wrong. It's a brand-new car."

"And a right pretty one! Let's take a look see." My savior walked around to the front, peered for no more than a second into the engine compartment, and then announced: "Well, there's yer problem right thar! You got a blowed-up oil pump!"

"I was afraid of that. Oh, dear. Now what? Is there a garage in the town up ahead? I really need to get this fixed and be on my way."

The woman dusted her hands off on her jeans and then turned and examined me. "Normally, hon, I'd jest say ta take it inta Floyd. But these ain't normal times."

"I don't understand."

My benefactor folded her arms and looked at the ground. "Well, see, it's kinda complicated. Just yer bad luck ta be a girl in trouble around here. If'n you was another no-account *man*, why then them boys'd be happy to—"

And then she stopped talking, and flashed me a sidelong gaze. Something had occurred to her. She was having some kind of brainstorm. A plan was forming.

I didn't know what was going on. Suddenly, I suspected I didn't want to.

For the second time today, I was the object of a rather uncomfortable scrutiny. She "sized me up" for a good two minutes, without saying a word.

It finally got uncomfortable enough that I had to do something: "Excuse me, Ms.—"

"Oh, where are my manners?" She stuck out a hand. "I'm Doris Ploughwright, but ever-body jest calls me *Dori*."

I took the offered hand. "I'm Pamela, Pamela Wright. 'PJ' to my friends and roadside saviors. Um, Dori, is there something wrong?"

She got a not-entirely-reassuring smile on her face. "PJ, everything might jest be finer'n frog's hair. How'd you like a chance to get yer car fixed, where 'twouldn't otherwise be possible, and do the ladies of Horraceburg a real service in the process?"

I thought about the wording of that offer for a minute. What did she mean by *'twouldn't otherwise be possible*? That didn't sound good.

"I, uh—"

She took my arm, and began hustling me toward the idling pickup. "Here, let's get you back to town so's you can meet the other womenfolk, and we can work out how we're gonna do this. PJ, this might be our lucky day!"

Why did I suddenly doubt that?

****

The story came out after Dori had smuggled me in through the back door of the Horraceburg Beauty Parlor. The beauty parlor had been chosen as the headquarters for the female contingent, in the ongoing war-of-the-sexes that currently raged in this little hamlet.

Yep, the cold war that had smoldered between the genders since the Garden of Eden had burst into a shooting war (so to speak) here in Horraceburg.

And I was just in time to get drafted into the cause.

Dori introduced me to the assembled women. They were gathered to plan strategy for their next campaign. It was down to trench-warfare at this point, and both sides seemed pretty well stalemated.

Um, maybe I should back up a bit, and give you some history as to just what was going on here.

Chapter 3-3
What Fools These
Mortals Be!

It all came down to Bobbi Mae Whitley's apple pie.

Bobbi Mae was currently sitting in the back corner of the beauty parlor. She was a pretty little thing. Somewhere around seventeen or eighteen, I'd guess; with an open, well-featured face and a petite, feminine-without-being-showy figure. She was what you picture when you think of "the girl next door."

And evidently, that's just what she'd been for one Billy Ray Whitley. He was the hometown hero, the quarterback of the local high-school team, Horraceburg's favorite son and the natural choice to marry the homecoming queen: Bobbi Mae Gentry.

And so it had turned out.

Their storybook wedding had taken place three months ago, with the whole county in attendance.

At first, things had gone just the way they were supposed to. Proud, handsome husband; blushing, beautiful bride; a marriage made in Heaven. And Billy and Bobbi were in love—*so very much in love.*

One look at poor little Bobbi Mae sitting forlorn in the corner, staring far-away-eyed out the window, and you knew just what—or rather *who*—she was thinking about.

So, what had gone wrong?

As I say, it all came down to apple pie.

A new batch of beautiful red apples had come in to Mr. Granger's General Store last week, and Bobbi Mae had decided that it was high time she made one her mother's special secret-recipe pies. Nothing was too good for Billy Ray, and Bobbi apparently pulled out all the stops that afternoon in the kitchen.

Now if you're expecting me to tell you that Bobbi Mae was one of those cliché new brides who couldn't cook, you're in for a disappointment. By all accounts, Mama Gentry walked away with the blue ribbon for baking at every County Fair she cared to enter. And Mama Gentry had made very sure to pass down every one of the old family recipes and cooking skills to her little girl.

No, sir—thar weren't *nothin'* wrong with *that* apple pie.

Billy Ray came home from a hard day in the field. His adoring wife met him at the door with a hug and a kiss, and the aroma of Billy's favorites (fried chicken and mashed potatoes) wafting out of the kitchen. They laughed and talked and gazed into each other's eyes over dinner, just like newlyweds are supposed to do. Billy finally pushed his plate away, and told his young bride that she was probably the best cook in the whole county, if not the whole state.

Bobbi beamed at this sincere praise from the person who meant more to her than anyone else in the world, and then brought out the piece de résistance: a great big slice of Mama Gentry's Secret Recipe Apple Pie À La Mode!

Billy tucked in. He swirled the first bite around in his mouth, and then smiled like a man for whom the Pearly Gates have just swung wide.

Bobbi grinned and asked, "So, honey, ain't that about the best pie you ever ate?"

Billy swallowed that delicious bite and nodded. "*Yes'm!* Why, that's near as good as my own Mama's!"

Lightning flickered on the rosy horizon of Bobbi's and Billy's little world.

"Hon, what do you mean, *'near as good'? That's my Mama's secret recipe,* ya know."

Maybe Billy saw the danger, maybe he didn't. It was probably too late, anyway.

"Well, baby, I don't mean nothin'. It's jest—well—when my Mama makes apple pie, she uses a bit more brown sugar. Makes the pie sweeter, you know. This is *fine* pie. Nothin' wrong with it at all! It's jest a bit more tart than I'm used to, tha's all."

Bobbi had slaved all afternoon on that pie. She pushed back from the table and folded her arms. "Oh, your Mama's pie, huh? That same pie that comes in *second* every year to *my* Mama's at the Fair? That the pie you're talkin' about?"

The bite of pie that Billy was just now swallowing, kind of caught in his throat. "I suppose if I was wantin' to eat a blue ribbon, that'd mean somethin'. Turn's out I'd rather eat my own Mama's apple pie."

Tears welled up in Bobbi's china-blue eyes. "Billy Ray Whitley! You take that back!"

"I won't, neither! You take it back first!"

War had come to Eden.

****

It might have been all right if Billy and Bobbi had just thrashed it out there at home. It was inevitable that eventually there'd be a squabble. I've heard that if you can fight with your spouse, and then make up—learn to forgive, and to forget, and to listen—that you grow thereby.

Billy and Bobbi had everything going for them. They were in love. They were meant for each other.

If they'd only just shouted for a while, there in the dining room—

If Billy had only had the chance to really see those tears in Bobbi's eyes—

If Bobbi had only really seen that hurt on Billy's face—

Ten minutes, tops. The fight couldn't have lasted for more than ten minutes. Then one of them, probably both of them in unison, would have said, "Oh, baby. What are we doing? We're fighting over *pie*! It ain't worth it! I love you too much to be fighting over something so silly." And they would have kissed, and hugged, and Billy would have told Bobbi that her pie would beat out both their mamas' pies at this year's fair, and Bobbi would have admitted that a little pinch of brown sugar was just the thing that recipe needed.

That's what would have happened—if Billy hadn't grabbed his coat and stormed out the door, heading for the Dew Drop Inn, leaving Billy Mae sobbing and wringing her napkin in her fingers, and reaching for the telephone to her Mama.

****

Remember, Billy and Bobbi were the town's favorite children.

When Billy made it to the Dew Drop Inn, the regulars— males one and all—were there. Billy cried in his beer and told the sordid tale. The men all gathered around and patted his shoulder, and told one another how silly and wrong-headed womenfolk were. How unfair it was to treat your man like Bobbi had treated Billy, after he'd come home from a hard day in the field, sweating to put bread on her table and a roof over her head. I mean—to talk bad about a man's Mama *to his face*! There were some things that you just didn't do!

And as the beer flowed, and the tongues wagged, each man there began to think about all the little wrongs and slights that his own mate had heaped on his head.

Bobbi couldn't reach Mama at home. So she fled the house and headed for the one female sanctuary in Horraceburg: this very same beauty parlor. The sewing circle was there, digesting all the day's news. When poor

Bobbi burst through the door, sniffling and looking for her Mama—well, you can imagine the effect that had on the conversation. What a horrible thing for a man to do to his new bride! What an unfeeling monster! After Bobbi, out of the goodness of her heart and with no other thought than to make him happy; after she'd spent the whole afternoon working on that pie—*to have him insult her that way*! Men were such callous, unfeeling *brutes!*

And as the tongues wagged, each woman there began to think about all the little wrongs and slights that her own mate had heaped on her head.

And so the battle lines were drawn.

Chapter 3-4
Twelfth Night

And that pretty much brings us up to the present. The sexes had divided into two camps. Neither side would give an inch.

If the women wanted to be all flighty and unreasonable and take Bobbi's part, well, that was just fine! Let them do all the heavy chores and such. Let them fix the washing machine when it broke, and change the fuse when it blew. Let them tote the firewood and mend the flat tires.

If the men wanted to be so pig-headed and side with Billy, well, that suited the women to a tee! Let those hairy apes get their own food, and wash their own clothes. Let them fetch and carry. Let them balance the checkbook and pay the bills on time.

Of course, standing on the sidelines looking in, it's obvious that both sides were right—

—and both sides were wrong.

And it's equally obvious therefore, this was doomed to be a stalemate from the outset.

But how do you get someone to see reason, when so much of their ego has gone into their position?

More to the point, how do you get some small-town southern mechanic to fix your car, when he isn't interested in giving a woman the time of day—and you're standing here in a too-short sundress that's hugging every one of your traffic-stopping curves; as your long, blonde hair is falling down around your Hollywood-starlet breasts?

You agree to Dori Ploughwright's hare-brained scheme, *that's* what you do. Because it's the only thing that you can think of.

****

I arrived at the beauty parlor at a little after 2 p.m.

There were currently five ladies present, including Dori. (Six if you count me—you might as well.)

The town's womenfolk were taking turns to "keep Bobbi company." As I later found out, there was an ulterior motive other than solicitude. They wanted to make sure that Bobbi didn't have a sudden change of heart, and go running back to Billy Ray. Now, since you can't keep a person prisoner in the beauty parlor for twenty four hours a day, one of them would always take Bobbi home with her at night, so Bobbi would have "a friendly place to stay"; as opposed to "that cold, lonely house."

And there was no end of discussion in Bobbi's presence about how mean Billy Ray was being to her—

How if he really loved her, he'd have come by and apologized by now—

Of how he must not be such a wonderful boy after all—

—all psychological warfare at its finest.

Now, I don't think that there was a conscious attempt to warp Bobbi's mind, or to really harm her in any way. I do believe that the women had Bobbi's best interests at heart. It's just that they believed that it wasn't in Bobbi's best interest to get back with Billy Ray until the men caved in.

They understood that in this battle, the first side to "blink" would be the loser. Both camps were as strong as their weakest member. In the women's case, that person was obviously Bobbi Mae.

Anyway, Dori dragged me into the beauty parlor through the back room. Here's what I saw when we first walked in—

An older woman, Mrs. Mavis Horsey, was sitting in a chair, having her hair frosted. The town's beautician,

Norma Jo Sivley, was plying her spray bottle—and holding forth about her second husband's penchant for going on a "toot," and "lighting out fer weeks at a time with the closest skirt" sitting near the barstool upon which he happened to conducting his bender. A portly middle-aged woman, Elizabeth Shoee, was blinking and nodding, and throwing in an occasional "Ain't that jest the way of it?"

And of course, poor little Bobbi Mae was sitting in a corner, gazing out the window at the Dew Drop Inn, three blocks down Main Street.

Dori called out, "Ladies! Lookie here. I want all of you to meet PJ Wright."

Conversation halted, and I was suddenly the center of attention. I said, "Um, hello everybody."

Dori pushed me into the center of the room. "I found PJ out by the turn off to the Meeses' place. Seems like she's havin' a bit of car trouble."

Mrs. Horsey made a clicking sound with her tongue, and in a voice loud enough to carry to Bobbi's corner, exclaimed, "Oh, now that's a shame, sure 'nuff ! To be a woman broke down in a town full of no-account men who don't have a good word to say to a woman, much less—"

Dori broke in: "Yes, Mavis, I've told PJ all about it."

Norma Jo gave Mavis another spritz. "I guess there's nothing for it but to let the poor woman use the phone and see if'n she can't get a wrecker to come out from Crosbyville and give her a tow."

Dori began pushing me in the direction of an empty chair near Bobbi Mae. "Well, that was my first thought. But then I kinda had a—here, PJ, set yourself down here next to Bobbi and keep her company—I had a idea as to how we might jest get a leg up on those no-account men. That is, if we can convince PJ to be a real dear and help us out."

There was an expectant silence, as everyone looked from Dori, to me, and back to Dori.

This went on for at least two minutes, till I decided to take the bull by the horns. "Of course I'd be willing to listen to any plan that you might have, Dori. But I don't know if I'd be willing—"

Dori took the fact that I didn't reject the possibility outright to be the cue to take the center stage and launch into the details of her plan.

"Oh, that's just fine! Now then, we all know that the onlyest reason that this whole thing started in the first place is 'cuz Billy Ray was bein' mulish. And we also know that as soon as he admits that he was wrong to poor Bobbi, and he asks her fergivness—why, the rest of them jackasses will have to admit that they's bein' wrong too. So, the question is: How do we get Billy Ray to see reason?"

Mavis chimed in. "I can't see why he hasn't seen reason already. We all know that he's basically a good boy—even if he does have his pappy's stubborn streak."

Dori nodded her head emphatically. "Uh-huh. I 'spect it's 'cuz he really hasn't taken time to think on it. He's over to that bar—hasn't set foot out of it. And he's surrounded by those no-account loafers what always hangs around in there. And you can bet they've been fillin' his head and pourin' the beers down his throat."

Dori laid a hand on Bobbi's shoulder. "But I bet, if someone would just get him to thinkin' about how he's done so bad by Bobbi Mae—why, before you know it, he'd be over here on his knees beggin' her pardon. Jest like he shoulda done two days ago!"

Norma Jo gave Mavis another spritz. "Well. Seem's to me that that's the problem right thar'. You can bet none o' them men are gonna start tellin' Billy Ray that he oughten to make up. And none o' us womenfolk can get anywheres near that old bar to make him see reason. So I guess we're back where we started."

Dori smiled large, and folded her arms. "That's right, Jo. None o' us women can get near that bar. But what if one o' us was to get in there, and none o' them old fools knew it were a woman?"

There was a thoughtful silence. Then all the eyes turned back to me—and for the *third* time today, I was the object of a close, uncomfortable scrutiny.

"PJ, hon," Dori said, "how deep can you pitch yer voice?"

****

It was a screwy plan—bound to fail.

But I had to admit, there was a certain symmetry to it. A woman couldn't get her car fixed in this town. A woman couldn't get near the men. But if that woman were to disguise herself as a man, and go to the bar where all the other men were, and if "he" was to just happened to strike up a conversation with Billy Ray, while the mechanic was tending to "his" car—

"Dori? Ladies? Look. It's not that I'm unsympathetic to your situation. If I thought I could pull this off—"

"Does that mean you won't even try? I mean, how do you know it won't work?"

This was so outrageous. Not the plan, so much, though that was certainly silly, and it had about a snowball's chance in hell—even with a person of my "unique qualifications" trying to run the scam.

What was so weird was: If I had had access to a bathtub, and if Peter didn't look so much different from Pamela that the sudden transformation would be too noticeable, I'd be the perfect person, in the perfect place, to help these ladies out.

But as it was, it was just too far a stretch. I decided it was time to cut my losses, and call for the Crosbyville wrecker. I tried out my best diplomatic smile. "Dori, I just— I don't think—"

My throat is tickling. Oh, shit.

I'd gotten up at five this morning—I don't sleep too well in motels—and I had gone about making the change into Pamela. The "conversion" had been complete by 6 a.m. It was then that I'd last used the chemical spray to change my voice.

The clock on the beauty-parlor wall chimed to announce 2:30 p.m., just a little over eight and a half hours since the change—

—And a familiar little tickle in my throat was telling me that I was about to start doing a very convincing impersonation of a man's voice—

—Whether I wanted to or not.

And better yet: My bottle of voice-altering spray was three miles back down the road, snug and secure in my suitcase, which was locked in Buffy's trunk.

****

Meanwhile, a good deal of the warmth had gone out of Dori's smile. "PJ, I really do wish you'd reconsider. This seems like such a good opportunity. I don't know when we'll get another stranger in town; and you do need help with your car; and poor little Bobbi Mae—"

I had a quick thought about what had brought me to this predicament in the first place: my attempted escape from the police checkpoint. *Talk about leaping out of the frying pan!* My mind was racing. I don't know, maybe there was some other solution, but the tickle in my throat was starting to turn into a burning. From experience, I knew I had a minute left, at most, of Pamela's contralto.

Still speaking contralto, I said, "I suppose I have nothing to lose by at least seeing if there's a chance."

Dori's broad smile was back. The rest of the women, excluding Bobbi Mae (who seemed disinterested), leaned forward and stared at me expectantly.

I cleared my throat.

Still speaking contralto, I said, "I once played a male role in my school play. Let's see if—"

Another clearing of my throat. The burning was becoming pronounced.

"Let's see if I remember—"

My voice was starting to crack. I counted to three in my mind—

"But soft, what light through yonder window breaks?" All spoken in baritone.

Dead silence. Even Bobbi Mae was staring at me, wide-eyed.

Dori finally broke the silence: "PJ, that is—that is *scary!*"

Norma Jo Sivley replied, "You hush your mouth, Dori! Pamela, sweetie, you're perfect for this!"

I nodded and smiled, and tried to make sure that all my feminine charms were still very evident for everyone to see. "Anyway, this is how I got the part."

The women exchanged puzzled glances—which slowly changed into puzzled smiles—which slowly changed into calculating grins.

****

By a little after five, Dori was ready to set her grand scheme into motion, and I was again having doubts as to whether my own planned double-cross had any chance of working.

Plans within plans—"Oh what a tangled web we weave—"

It had been a *very* strange four hours.

Being stuck with the Peter-voice, I'd managed to convince everyone that it would probably be a good idea to just keep talking this way. I claimed that I wasn't quite positive I could just switch back and forth between my "normal" voice and this "assumed" one. Since I had this voice working "correctly," I suggested that I not mess with a good thing, and just keep it up.

The ladies had all agreed that this was probably a very wise precaution. I still caught the odd sidelong glance out of the corner of my eye though.

Mavis had quickly vacated the chair, and I had come under Norma Jo's talented hand. She fussed with my over-the-shoulder-length blonde hair for a few minutes, but it rapidly became obvious that there was just no way to style those long tresses into anything even remotely masculine.

Hey, I'd specifically ordered that hair that way! Why pay several thousand dollars for something that looked even vaguely masculine? Wasn't that contrary to the object of the whole exercise in the first place?

Norma Jo finally set down her brush in disgust. "I can't do nothin' with this."

Dori delicately cleared her throat. "Uh, PJ, I don't suppose you'd be willin' to get a little length taken offen that lovely hair?"

Norma Jo chimed in. "They do say that short hair is gonna be 'The Thing' this season. I could just trim a few—"

"*Don't even think about it!*" Pamela was marvelous technology, but even the folks at NuGen hadn't figured out a way to make her hair grow out after some backwoods beautician had whacked off a couple of feet.

That preemptive bark in Peter's rather commanding baritone had the desired effect. Dori quickly waved her hand in dismissal. "You're right, you're right. That's askin' too much, I grant."

Norma Jo spoke up again. "Wait a sec—I've got some old wigs in the back room. Shoot, we can shorten them up or do anythin' we want with them."

Just under an hour later, blonde Pamela was gone. In her place was a neuter-appearing brunette with a very short, very masculine haircut. I also had a set of sideburns that were right out of the Seventies.

The person staring out of the mirror reminded me a great deal of that comedienne, the one with the androgynous character whose true gender, nobody could figure out. At least until you proceeded downwards from my new face, that is. Then the substantial cleavage and the long slender legs that were sticking out of that pesky-short skirt removed any doubt.

We all studied the effect in the mirror for a while, but nobody there believed that I'd ever pass as a man. Then Norma Jo came up with the idea of making a mustache out of all the trimmings on the floor. We used false-eyelash adhesive to glue it in place.

Believe it or not, I looked passable, if certainly not macho.

Dori detailed Mavis and Elizabeth to go round up some of the other ladyfolks, and make sure that Buffy got moved off the road and placed in such a way as to not be easily observed. We'd decided that my "entrée" into town would be arranged by letting word get back to the men that one of their fellow males was having car trouble out on the road. Theoretically, Floyd would then be dispatched to my rescue, and I'd have my "in."

Dori and Norma Jo headed off to Norma's house to get some of Norma's third husband's clothes. Norma's third mate had worked out about as well as the first two. Apparently he had been a fairly slender fellow, of my approximate build. And he'd left some clothes behind.

Now there was nobody in the beauty parlor. Well, nobody but Bobbi Mae and me.

****

Bobbi Mae and I sat there, alone in the beauty parlor, in silence for a few uncomfortable minutes.

"Miz Wright. I—well, first off, I want to thank you for goin' along with this fool stunt."

"Please, call me PJ. And hey, anything for the cause of love."

Bobbi stared at her feet for a second, then she turned those big, innocent eyes full on me. "Miz Wri—PJ—I got no right to even think o' asking you this, but—I need a favor of you."

"What's that, Bobbi?"

"Don't go through with this. Just get your car fixed somehow, and then—"

I arched an eyebrow and stared at her.

"—and then—oh, I don't care where you're goin', or how far you want to take me, but please, take me with you when you go."

I couldn't have heard her correctly.

"Bobbi—I—"

Then I just threw my hand in the air. I was out of my depth. This made no sense. I said, "I don't understand. Don't you want to get things back to normal? To get back to your husband?"

Then the worst possible thing happened—or, in retrospect, the best.

Bobbi's lower lip began to quiver, her eyes finally overflowed, and in a lost, anguished voice she wailed, "Oh Miz Wright, I don't know what I want anymore."

I quickly sat beside her and patted her arm, and tried to comfort her. "What's wrong, honey? You can tell me."

She sniffled a bit, and wiped her eyes and then nodded. "I expect you're about the only woman around here I can tell. I don't know what to do. I thought Billy loved me. I thought I loved him. But ever-body keeps tellin' me that if he really loved me, he'd a-come for me by now. And I gotta think that maybe they's right. PJ, if'n a man loves you, shouldn't he show it? Shouldn't he stick by you?"

"Yes, I suppose so—"

Then the tears started to really fall, and her words came out between the hiccupping sobs: "Then why ain't he stood by me? *Why's he left me alone for two whole days*? Please, PJ—*please*—I cain't stay here no more. I cain't listen to Mama and the women no more, and just wait and wait and—Please take me away. I got no one else to turn to."

I squeezed her shoulders, and let her cry on mine, and tried to maintain a maternal posture, and made little comforting noises in Peter's voice—

And then, in a flash of clarity, I saw the answer.

Best of all, *It's so simple, it might even work!*

I took her shoulders in my hands, and held her out at arm's length. I said with assurance, "Well, maybe that's what's needed, Bobbi Mae. Maybe you just need to get away for a while, and think about things. And I'll help you. Now, here's what I want you to do—"

****

Dori and Norma Jo returned in about half an hour with my "new" male clothes. They'd given it some thought, and I guess I was supposed to be some kind of traveling businessman. They'd selected a polyester business suit in a rather bizarre shade of blue, a light-blue shirt, and a print necktie whose width very nicely matched my sideburns. A pair of brown penny loafers completed my ensemble.

We stepped into the back room for a bit of privacy. Dori reached into her bag and pulled out a large "Ace bandage." "I guess the first thing we need to do is take care of some o' them curves of yours, hon."

I unzipped the sundress, and let it fall around my ankles so as not to mess up my haircut/facial hair.

My lack of underwear raised several eyebrows. "Um, Norma, why don't you hand me them boxer shorts."

I was pleased to notice that my borrowed undershorts had been recently laundered. I slipped into them and then Dori began to wield that bandage.

Objectively, I could imagine that, for a woman, having your bosom squeezed tight against your chest had to be a bit of an uncomfortable operation. I'd been prepared to fake a bit of discomfort. I had no need to fake anything. True, those breasts had no sensory nerve endings. As I'm so fond of saying: They were just two largish lumps of plastic. But the chest beneath the suit was very real. And all that mass had to go somewhere. I gasped, and wheezed, and tried to draw a breath, and felt generally like I was trying to fit back into the sweater I'd worn in third grade.

Dori made sympathetic noises, and assured me that everything was all right—and went on wrapping that bandage tighter and tighter.

Finally she finished. I could breathe—sort of.

The effect was what we'd desired. Pamela's bountiful bouncing breasts were suddenly no more than a slight rounding of my upper torso.

I donned the shirt (which was a bit too large) and the slacks (which were a bit too tight, particularly in the

posterior), then Dori handed me the necktie. I fumbled
with it a bit, lending a nice (if unintentional—I don't often
wear neckties) touch to my masquerade as Pamela. Add
the penny loafers and the suit's wide-lapelled jacket, and I
was dressed.

After making sure that there were no men out on the
street to observe the "goings-on," I got a quick trip out into
the main room to check out the overall effect in the mirrors.

Well, my baritone voice would be the selling point. The
"fellow" staring out of the mirror was a real wimpy-looking
wuss—but believably male. Barely.

Then we got around to making the disguise "work."

Dori finished primping and straightening my jacket,
then commanded me to "Walk around a bit, hon. Let's
make sure you can do that as well as you can talk."

At least here was something I could do. I usually didn't
spend a lot of effort trying to "walk like a girl" when I was
Pamela—at least, not unless I was showing off. Usually, I
just remembered to take somewhat smaller, quicker steps
than I normally would; and to try to place one foot directly
in front of the other. I think it was actually a case of:
Pamela's appearance was so obviously that of a woman that
I probably could have goose-stepped and folks would have
thought, *Boy, she's pretty, but she sure walks funny.*

In any event, I just dropped trying to take small steps
and to put one foot in front of the other, and took a quick
"turn" around the room.

The women all stood, considering, and then Dori shook
her head. "Nope, hon. You walk like that and the boys are
gonna think you ought ta be carryin' a purse. Can't you put
a little more 'macho' inta it?"

"What the heck was wrong with that?"

"Well, goodness, girl, you was swingin' yer hips and
wigglin' yer butt.—"

I thought, *When I was expressly trying not to?*

"—Ya gotta put more *stride* inta it. Like this—"

And Dori promptly stomped around the room for a few minutes, like a lumberjack struggling in deep mud.

Norma Jo chimed in: "Oh heavens, Dori! You look like yer wallerin' in pig slop. You don't need to stomp, jest throw yer feet out. Like this."

Okay, maybe it did look odd when a woman goose-stepped.

Mavis giggled and said, "If'n the three of you don't make a sight. Why, there ain't nothin' to it. Ya jest gotta roll yer hips, 'stead of swingin' em. Lookie here—"

That one beggared description.

In the end, after much discussion and practicing, we finally had a masculine walk for me. Watching myself in the mirror striding around the shop, all I could think was: *So this is what it would have looked like if John Wayne did an ad for Preparation H.*

Eventually everyone was satisfied with the "whole picture." The women smiled and nodded, and congratulated each other on the fine job of disguise. Then they hustled me out the back door to Dori's waiting pickup.

I made eyes with Bobbi one last time, and she gave me a subtle nod. Then I was on the floor of the pickup's cab, and we were heading back to Buffy.

****

Several of the town's women were waiting near where I'd been forced to abandon Buffy. They'd pushed her off the highway and a few yards down a private road, to prevent her premature discovery by any passing male.

We went through a few more minutes of "Ooh, what a wonderful disguise!" and then, with me lending a hand, we pushed Buffy back out on to the road. I got a last bit of encouragement and compliment on my appearance, and then the ladies were in Dori's pickup, disappearing back down the road toward town.

We'd figured I had at least twenty or thirty minutes till word of the "stranded male" could reach the bar in a believably roundabout fashion; and then another half-hour or so for Floyd to fire up the wrecker and get out here to my assistance.

I stood around for a while, trying to adjust the bandage that still made breathing hard enough to give me a bit of a light-headed buzz. Then a thought occurred to me, and I rummaged in the trunk for a while till I found the bottle of voice-altering spray, which I tucked in the pocket of my jacket.

I wanted to be able to create at least one wholly convincing illusion as a fallback position. I figured that Pamela would be my ultimate refuge. The women already believed in Pamela's reality. If the men penetrated this rather obvious faux male exterior, I wanted to be able to retreat to Pamela in convincing style. I had to believe that though the men might be angry, they were still southern gentlemen—weren't they? They wouldn't beat up some poor, defenseless woman for pulling this stunt on them.

Would they?

How to get the spray into my mouth? Well, I'd cross that bridge when I came to it.

About an hour after I'd arrived, right on time, a battered old wrecker came rattling down the road from the direction of town.

Chapter 3-5
Reason And Love

Floyd was a laconic fellow in greasy coveralls and a welder's cap. He climbed down from the wrecker and sauntered over to me, who was standing at Buffy's front fender. He stopped about five paces away and proceeded to look me up and down, his left eyebrow raised in obvious disapproval at what he saw.

That made *four* times today that I'd been sized up like an unattractive cut of meat.

"Y'all havin' car trouble?"

I suppressed the comments that struggled for release, and nodded. "Yep. She just quit on me. I think it's the oil pump."

Floyd slouched over. "Is it the lines, or the pump housin'—or is it just a gasket?"

I shrugged. "Beats me. I'm not much of a mechanic."

That got me another disgusted frown. Wasn't every "real" man able to diagnose and fix an internal-combustion engine from the time he could stand on his own hind legs and walk?

He peered under the hood for no more than ten seconds, and then straightened up. "Well, it's pretty obvious—y'all got a blowed gasket."

"Um, is that serious?"

Floyd looked to heaven. "It'll take me 'bout an hour ta fix. That is, if'n I got a metric gasket that'll fit this here Eye-talian gear. I guess yer trying ta get somewheres. I don't think I'd be far off the mark if'n I was ta say you ain't from around here."

"Oh no. No, I'm on a business trip. I'm heading back home to California."

That seemed to confirm Floyd's suspicion, and to explain a lot. "Thought so. Well, let's get her hooked up and drag her back to town. I'll get her fixed. It ain't like I got anywhere's ta go tonight."

I tried to make some light-hearted chat. You know, get a little male-bonding going: "Dull night tonight? You got no big plans?"

"Shoot, no. Not with all the womenfolk holed up in that old froo-froo parlor. I swear, if'n somethin' don't give soon, I'm gonna just bust. It's been two whole days now."

I played dumb. "Two days since what?"

Floyd was trying to unreel the towing hook and make small talk at the same time. "Oh, it's nothin'. It's them damn women. You know how they can be, sometimes."

Then he paused and gave me a sidelong look. His expression made his thoughts fairly clear: *At least men who have any interest in women, would know.*

And then his expression suddenly became thoughtful. He was having a brainstorm. A plan was forming.

Not again!

****

They say that "great minds think alike." I don't know about the *great* part, but the minds around here certainly did think alike.

Floyd hooked Buffy up, and towed her back to town. He maneuvered her into the repair bay of his seedy little garage/filling station, then insisted that we head over to the Dew Drop Inn.

I just followed meekly. I knew already where this was heading; or at least I had a very good suspicion.

There were about a dozen men in the bar by the time we arrived. I eventually got introduced around, but I can't remember the names. There were lots of Harleys and Franks and hyphenated Joe-Bobs and Jimmy-Lees. And sure enough, sitting alone in a seat near the window, staring down the now-rapidly-darkening street in the general direction of the beauty parlor, was Billy Ray.

Floyd was the obvious ringleader, though. The masculine version of Dori.

If I thought I was getting a bunch of raised eyebrows at my impersonation while I was with the women, it was *nothing* compared to the doubtful stares I got treated-to by the "boys." I don't know if it got better or worse when Floyd mentioned that I was on my way back home to California. Then the expressions changed from *What the heck kind of flower is this?* to *Oh, a pansy. That explains everything.*

I just smiled and nodded, and tried to accept it all with good grace.

Finally, after about ten minutes of small talk and introductions, Floyd got around to describing the brilliant plan he'd just come up with.

You've already heard the gist of it. It was just about a carbon copy of Dori's scheme. The boys figured that if they could smuggle somebody into the beauty parlor—plant a few words in Bobbi's ear—well, she'd be running down the street to Billy's arms before the night got much older.

Of course, to make it work, they needed just the right person. "Them women ain't stupid." The spy would have to be pretty convincing. Of course, none of the boys around here could get away with it. (One look around at this crew and I had to agree. Nobody in here could pass for a handsome man, much less any kind of woman.)

But if they could find a slender sort of fellow, one with kind of a "delicate" face—

Of course, they'd be just as grateful as could be, to such a noble gent. Why, he could pretty much name his reward. For example, and just as a what-if, mind you, if that person were to—for instance—have a *car problem* or some such. Why, Floyd would be just pleased as he could be, to fix ithe car for that fine fellow quicker'n spit! Free of charge!

Now, the boys didn't want me to get the idea that they were forcing anything on *me*. This was all hypothetical— "just supposing" kind of stuff. Floyd would get to fixing my car just as soon as he could get around to it. Of course, he had a lot on his mind right now. And them Eye-talian parts, why they could be *awful* "spendy." By the way, had Floyd mentioned that he only worked for cash on the barrelhead?

I let them twist my arm for a bit, just so it didn't look too easy. But I already knew I'd agree. Mainly because I was still working my "double cross," and I needed some time with Billy Ray. Plus, I intended to have a little fun at the boys' expense too. Just wait till they got a look at what a dynamite female impersonator I'd make; I could even do a spectacular voice! (I checked, just to make sure. Yeah, the spray bottle was still snug in my pocket.) After much hard-nosed persuasion, and with a great show of reluctance, I agreed—even going so far as to submit to shaving off my sideburns and moustache.

Gosh, the fellows all agreed, maybe I was a "regular Joe" after all. Maybe they'd been a bit hasty in their first judgments of me.

The first hurdle was a convincing "outfit" for me. Floyd sent all the men scurrying for items from their spouse's closet: dresses that the ladies hadn't worn for a while, and so might not recognize; and shoes that could fit me. "And Harley and Milt, don't yer missuses have wigs? Go and fetch 'em."

Some of the boys asked, with a distinct pink tinge to their cheeks, "What about, you know, 'flimsies' and such?" Floyd allowed as how he'd handle that.

Pretty soon, the bar was empty, except for me and a listless, disinterested Billy Ray.

****

I immediately stood up, picked up the third beer that I'd had foisted off on me, and walked over to meet Bobbi's "significant other."

He glanced up at me, and made an attempt at a smile. "Uh, I wanted ta say thank ya, Mr. Wright. Fer helpin' out, and all. It's a special kinda man what'd agree ta dress up like a girl for some stranger."

I let slide the rather ambiguous meaning of that "compliment." (At least, I chose to understand it as a compliment.) I said, "I'm pleased to help out, Billy Ray. It's for a good cause. We men have to stick together."

He sighed, and turned back to the window. "I suppose."

I set the untouched beer down in front of him. "You don't sound so sure of that."

He shrugged. "Oh, it's jest that I've been in here for goin' on two days now, and I kinda get the feelin' that it's stopped bein' so much about Bobbi and me as it is about all the other's problems, if ya take my meaning."

I nodded sympathetically. "Well, maybe it's just time to call it quits and head home to your Mrs."

He got the most touchingly wistful expression, as he looked down at the hands folded in his lap, and sighed. "I don't suppose there's much point in that no more, neither."

"What do you mean?"

"Bobbi's a good woman—true blue, sir. If I still meant anything to her at all, she'd-a been here by now."

"Maybe you need make the first move. Bending doesn't necessarily mean you're weak. Sometimes it takes more courage to be the first one to admit you're wrong."

He finally met my eyes, and there was such pain there. "Sir, I'd be happy ta be the one to admit I'm wrong. I was ready the first night I slept alone on this here bench, and all I could think about was to wonder where Bobbi was—if she was all right. Mr. Wright, you gotta believe, it ain't for orneriness that I'm doin' this. But it's all got so crazy and mixed up."

He indicated the now-empty bar. "They's all made it pretty clear that if I fold and let all them down—well—But I'd still go back—I would!—if I thought that Bobbi'd be waitin' for me."

We'd come down to it. Time to put my plan into operation.

"Billy Ray, may I make a suggestion?"

"If you've got any ideas, I'd surely love ta hear them, sir."

"Sometimes, people need to lose something before they really appreciate its value."

"Yes, sir?"

"What would happen if, once I was in disguise, I went over there to the beauty parlor and I just kind of mentioned what a handsome young fellow I'd met, before the menfolk threw me out of the bar? What if I said that he was such a lonely, unhappy boy that my heart just went out to him. What if I told all those women, especially Bobbi Mae, that I'd offered him a lift west—and he'd accepted?"

His eyes lit up as he considered the scheme—

—but then his face took on a hard set, and he shook his head. "I appreciate the thought, I surely do, and I thank you for it. But that'd be harder on Bobbi Mae than I think I want to be."

My brilliant plan is going down the tubes because Billy is too considerate? Oh no you don't!

"Billy Ray, I know you'd never do anything to really hurt Bobbi, and I admire you for it. But sometimes we need to be a little cruel to be kind, as the song says. It hurts to have a bad cut stitched up, but it's for the best in the long run. That's what I'm proposing. A *little* hurt now, to cure the *big* hurt before it really starts to fester. Before it really is too late to heal."

Billy was silent for a long moment, then he nodded. "You're right, sir. I'd be willin', I guess. But it won't work. Bobbi'd just think you were big-talkin', if I know her at all."

"I'm sure you know your wife, Billy Ray. So, we'll just have to make her believe it's true. She'd have to believe her own eyes, now wouldn't she?"

"I guess."

"So, we'll show her. Here's what I want you to do—"

I outlined the plan, Billy smiled (for the first time that day), and shook my hand.

And then the men started coming back, toting various grocery bags and boxes, and looking embarrassed and guilty as hell.

****

Horraceburg was a small town, no more than two hundred souls, all told. Now, it's not that Pamela is an odd size or shape. (She's actually a perfectly ordinary size 12; and can sometimes get down to size 10 in some things, when I don't stuff my face.)

The difficulty was: None of the other ladies of this fine town seemed to be a perfectly ordinary size 12. We pawed through the five or six dresses. (Nobody had thought to bring a pair of jeans, or even a nice baggy pair of shorts—

oh, no, say *women's clothing* to this crew, and that meant *dresses*. Period.)

After holding the dresses all up against my chest, we estimated that a rather dowdy cotton dress, with an unnecessarily busy polka-dot pattern, was probably the best candidate for a believable fit. Then we all stood around for an uncomfortable minute or two.

Floyd finally picked up his own Piggly Wiggly bag, and led me by the elbow to the men's room.

He stood there, looking for all the world like some commander sending one of his men off on a suicide mission. "I just want to say, and for the record, we surely do appreciate this, Mr. Wright. We surely do."

I squared my shoulders and tried to look brave.

"You got the dress, you got them shoes of George's— well, George's wife—and that red wig of Shirley Price's, I think that'll look good on you. Now, there's a razor, and some shavin' cream, in here." He indicated the bag. "And, uh, I got some of my wife's—uh, you know."

I nodded, though I was tempted to play dumb till he actually had to say *underwear*.

Then Floyd handed me the bag, and shook my hand, and went off to "tend to yer car—best as I know how!"

****

I closed and locked the bathroom door behind me. The first thing to go was my shirt and tie.

Then I clawed at that damnable Ace Bandage, till it unwound in a flurry of flesh-colored elastic. I stood there for a good two minutes, sucking one gloriously deep lungful after another into my abused chest.

A quick inspection in the mirror over the sink confirmed that Pamela's "charms" had suffered no permanent damage. I wonder how I'd explain the repair request to NuGen, if they had.

Shedding all the rest of my male accouterment, I then took a moment to peel off the moustache and sideburns, then shed the brown wig. I kept smiling at recurring mental images of the old "Mission Impossible" TV series.

In fairly short order, Pamela's familiar sexy nude body enticed me from the mirror. "Hi, Pam—you don't know how much I've missed you!"

I gathered her long, blonde hair up in a bunch on top of my head, and then wrestled with the woman's wig for a while. Counting the "male" wig I'd just discarded, this was only the second time I'd ever worn a wig. Pamela's blonde hair is permanently attached to her head and is "self-adjusting," as it were.

I think I primped and tugged and straightened that woman's wig for a good twenty minutes. In the end, it still looked like some ratty angora cat had crawled on top of my head to expire.

Well, with the Pamela-voice and the Pamela-figure, I guess the hair wouldn't be all that noticeable. And after all, if my "double cross" worked—and at this point, I had every reason to believe it would—I wouldn't have to fool any of the women anyway.

I was reaching for the bag for a pair of panties, or whatever Floyd believed a woman wore over her hips—

—when I was struck by an odd feeling of embarrassment.

I'd been dressing as Pamela every workday for almost a year. I'd been shopping for my own lingerie—what, six times now? Seven? It was to the point where I no longer even shopped for "sexy," I shopped for things that wouldn't "ride up" (yes, it was uncomfortable, even inside the suit), and wouldn't "dig in" to my shoulders, or that looked easy to care for. In short: Women's underwear was rapidly losing its mystery for me.

And then I realized: It was *Pamela's* underwear that had lost most of its mystery for me. But this wasn't Pamela's. This was intimate clothing belonging to some total stranger.

I stood there for a moment, looking at the bag. Had I met Floyd's wife today? What was Floyd's last name? I didn't believe I'd ever heard. Suddenly it was very important to me that I know just whose panties I was about to stick my legs into.

I was only guessing that this underwear belonged to Floyd's missus. But it seemed to me to be a fairly safe bet. After all, these were true Southern boys, one and all. Let's be polite and say *proper* (versus *repressed*), as these good ol' boys were, when it came to a woman's "flimsies"— especially the flimsies of another man's wife. It just seemed highly improbable that one man would be touching such things with a ten-foot pole, much less carrying a bag full of someone else's mate's around.

But I simply couldn't guess who of the women I'd met— if any of them—were married to Floyd.

Well, this was silly. I wasn't embarrassed when I'd put on Norma Jo's husband's suit. It was sexist of me to be feeling guilty about wearing this woman's clothes. I didn't intend any harm or insult. And it was for a good cause.

I reached into the bag. My hand first encountered what I immediately recognized as a bra, and I pulled it out. I studied it for a moment.

Oh.

Mystery solved: Floyd's last name was *Ploughwright*.

I couldn't help it. I started to giggle.

I own a few padded bras myself. Hey, every girl owns a few. Some outfits call for a little extra curve. There's nothing wrong with wearing one. It's not about vanity, just fashion. Or, at least—it isn't for most women.

Poor Dori. There could only be one woman in town who'd be as *voluptuous* as this bra would make its wearer, and that would be Dori.

But more than that: Judging from this bra, she had to be one of the most flat-chested women I've ever encountered. Maybe it was overcompensation on her part. This bra was obviously designed to add at least three "letters" to its wearer. And I'd guess Dori started out at the letter 'B' (as in *Boy*). Maybe. However, from the tag, I saw that she was a 36. I'm a "small" 38 (37, to be precise), so this shouldn't be too bad.

I spun the cups around behind me, and fastened the hooks. Then I spun it back around and began to pull it up over my breasts.

Thirty-seven into 36: no problem. *But* full C-cup into small B-cup (that was padded out to epic DD-cup)? No way!

I looked in the mirror and all I could think was *Nobody's built that way! Not even cows!* Between the extensive padding and Pamela's admirable bust—the result was: Even standing with my back straight, it still looked like I was falling forward.

Growing up as a teen boy, I never would have believed that there could be such a thing—but I'd just found out there was: I had too much tit!

I tucked and stuffed and poked and prodded. All for nothing. What I shoved in over here, just came bulging out over there.

After a while, I gave up and removed the bra. Going without a bra for long, however, was not an option, given Pamela's "attributes." You'd have to be blind not to realize that Pam was going braless. How "Mr. Wright" was managing that trick, would raise questions from the men that I just couldn't answer.

With a sigh, I picked up that infernal Ace Bandage and started wrapping.

****

The boys had gone through four more rounds of beer when the bathroom door opened, and conversation shuddered to a halt.

Their very own Mata Hari stepped into the center of the room and then stood there, inviting their inspection.

There was a long, expectant silence.

Then Floyd—who'd returned from fixing Buffy; the repair had taken him only an hour, just as he'd first said—broke the silence.

"It's a start, I guess."

I guess I'd expected no better. I'd tried—honestly, I had. And as I'd progressed, I'd started to become more and more desperate. I'd tried tinkering with the wig. I'd fluffed the dress and tried to adjust the unflattering neckline. I'd finally removed the "body shaper" brief that Floyd had provided, in order to try and minimize the "bubble butt" curve that it had grafted on to Pamela's firm little ass.

But nothing had really worked.

The best I'd managed was a fairly bland-featured woman suffering a terminally bad-hair day, with a bust that looked like a young explosion in a hydrogen-balloon factory, wearing a red-and-white polka-dot dress, thick opaque stockings (that somehow managed to remove most of the allure from my world-class legs), and four-inch heels, (that were already starting to make my ankles ache.)

"Sorry, guys. It's the best I could do. Do you think it will work?"

Nobody wanted to venture an opinion aloud.

Finally Floyd sighed, and decided to put the best face on things. (Somebody had to—I certainly wasn't having much luck trying!)

"Oh, I'm sure it'll all work out. It's not . . . all that bad. Is it, boys?"

A significant look from their leader got heads nodding, and voices muttering, "Oh no, it ain't bad."

Floyd continued, "Now, then. You are gonna have ta talk ta them women. I think we need to work on yer voice."

I glanced quickly at the clock. The timing should be just about right.

"Well, there I think you boys are in luck. I once played a woman's role in my platoon's Christmas play." (Okay, so the only "platoon" I've ever been in was my local Boy Scout Troupe—I was getting tired of all the "sissy stares" I was getting.) "Everyone said my voice was just unbelievable."

Skeptical stares. *Fine. Just you yahoos wait.* Another quick glance at the clock. The last thing I'd done before stepping out of the bathroom was to give myself a quick shot of the voice spray. It was just coming up on five minutes ago that I'd done it.

So where was the "tell-tale tickle"?

"Uh—yeah, I was a real hit all right."

Come on!

Floyd raised an eyebrow expectantly. "So let's hear it."

Ah! There was that familiar burning!

"Sure. Now, let's see—"

I cleared my throat.

I spoke slowly in baritone voice: "It went something like—"

One-thousand one, one-thousand two, one-thousand three, one-thousand four, one-thousand five. Go.

In contralto voice, I said, "Oh, Romeo, Romeo, wherefore art thou, Romeo?"

Stunned silence.

Floyd said, "Why, Pete—that's—that's—*scary!*"

****

I had to show off the voice for a while. And I used the same excuse for why I couldn't change back to my normal baritone. It worked as well this time as it had with the women. The boys began to believe that this might work, after all.

Then Floyd announced that it was getting late, and it was time for me to be heading over to the beauty parlor, before the women started going home for the night.

But first, we should work a little on my walk.

Let your imagination run wild. Just picture a dozen men prancing and swishing and wriggling, and you get the picture. I bit my lip and tried to keep from laughing. I just accepted the show as small payment for the indignity I was putting myself through.

Floyd ended the show by announcing, "Here's how you do it—watch, Pete. Ya gotta kinda clench yer butt and wiggle yer hips."

Imagine Marilyn Monroe advertising Preparation H.

I was finally prepared. The men shoved me out the door with hearty wishes of *Good luck* and *Go get 'em.*

I walked down the now-darkened street—

—till I was fairly sure I was out of sight.

Then I ducked into an alley, and made for Floyd's garage. The hour for my own plan to swing into action had arrived, and I wanted to be in there to see it in operation.

Chapter 3-6
A Mid-Summer Night's Dream

Small town America:

Floyd's garage was unlocked.

I quickly walked in, closing the door behind me. Buffy was gleaming in the darkness of the repair bay. There was a little note tucked under her driver's-side windshield wiper: "She's good as new. And she sure is pretty!"

I was debating whether or not I had time to get out of this ridiculous dress and wig *and to take this damn Ace Bandage off, once and for all*—when the door opened and in walked Billy Ray.

"Okay. I'm here, Mr. Wright. How long do you reckon it'll be before you come back from the beauty parlor and we can take that little drive past the window together?"

"Well, Billy—I guess it's time to come clean with you. I don't think we'll be taking that drive."

His eyes narrowed in suspicion. "Whaddaya mean? I thought that was the plan."

"Um, I haven't been entirely straightforward with you, son. Maybe it's time to tell you the whole truth."

I was reaching for that ratty red wig when the door again squeaked on rusty hinges, and Bobbi Mae stepped in, clutching a battered suitcase to her chest.

Billy and Bobbi's eyes met across the grease-stained floor.

****

Was it so very long ago?—

It seems like only yesterday.

—crisp fall mornings on the playground—

"My name's Billy Ray Whitley. You wanna play catch with me?"

—when everything was new, and frightening, and wonderful—

"Billy, look! Mama gave me a whole dollar for chores. You wanna go down to Mr. Granger's store after school and get us some ice creams?"

Cold winter nights—

"Bobbi Mae, it would make me about the happiest feller in the whole county if you would go to the Christmas mixer with me."

—close by the fire—

"See, Billy Ray? I told you so! You can so work those math problems! You just have to have a little faith in yourself, y'hear?"

Dark spring days when the clouds piled up, the thunder rolled—

"Don't you fret yourself, Billy. So what if you didn't get that dumb ol' scholarship? Who wants to go to some silly college about a million miles from home? Everybody knows you're the best man to ever grow up in this town. You don't need some piece of paper hangin' on the wall to prove it."

—and the rain fell—

"You go ahead and cry, Bobbi. You remember how much your Daddy loved you. You believe that just 'cuz he's passed on, it don't mean he's not still watchin' over you. Oh, Bobbi—hang on to me tight and we'll get through."

And a breathless summer night when a million stars glittered in an endless velvet sky—

"Bobbi Mae Gentry, will you marry me?"

—and a fairy-tale golden moon peeked over the old maple
tree—

"Yes, Billy. Yes, I will."

****

Now in Floyd's garage, quicker than a thought, they were in each other arms.

"Oh baby, I'm so sorry—"

"I was so wrong—"

"—don't know what I was thinking—"

"—didn't mean any of it—"

"—silly stupid pride—"

"—just want you back—"

"—miss you so much—"

"Please forgive me." "I'm so very sorry."

"I love you so much." "I love you, baby."

****

The rest of the story is anticlimax. Bobbi and Billy met the next morning, right out in the middle of Main Street. They kissed. They hugged. In voices that were loud enough for the whole town to hear, they told each other how wrong they'd been, how unimportant was whatever it was that had come between them. How the only thing that mattered was each other.

Then arm-in-arm, they went home.

Armistice. The war was over. Couples stared across the no-man's-land of Main Street at their other halves. Then, one at a time, then in twos, then in dozens, each side threw down their arms and met at the center of the street.

Old grudges were forgotten. Old loves were rekindled.

I wasn't there to see it, but I can picture it in my mind.

By that time, I was checking out of Crosbyville's Motel Six with Pamela safely stowed in my suitcase. I'd slipped out of Floyd's garage last night. Billy Ray and Bobbi Mae hadn't noticed my departure; and I'd had no intention of disturbing them with long goodbyes, either. They had enough on their minds at that moment.

The rest of the trip home went without incident. If Pamela objected to finishing the journey in the trunk, she never complained to me.

I wonder to this day, if the residents of Horraceburg have ever compared notes to the point that they suspect that their trusted spy wasn't everything s/he appeared to be. Or, if when the conversation turns to that silly feud, the men don't turn to the men, and the women don't turn to the women—and each gender perhaps shares a private wink and a smug little grin over how cleverly they pulled the wool over the other side's eyes.

If so, I'll just smile and nod.

And mention that "love conquers all"—

—and "all's well that ends well."

PART 4
Pas De Deux

Chapter 4-1
O, Brave New World...

Monday morning at WN&A

"ARRGH! You rotten pile of junk!"

The image on my desktop monitor mocked me with the accursed "Fatal Error detected in Module" message.

My work just sat there behind the error message, tantalizingly out of reach. It was gone, gone, gone.

Having struggled with this accursed computer for four weeks now, I knew that once that "Fatal Error" window appeared, I was in the same predicament as were the passengers of the *Titanic* when the lookout cried "Iceberg ahead!" Namely, I was irretrievably condemned to sink below an onrushing wave of the future.

The worst part was that the system forced *me* to click on that damned icon, thus consigning my work to some electronic bottomless pit! It was like being forced to pull the rope that dropped the guillotine on your own neck!

Screeching some of my favorite four-letter words, I slammed my fist against the side of the monitor. It landed with a satisfying thump. A thump that caused me to turn a guilty eye toward my open office door. Refined professional women didn't curse like longshoremen and didn't try to batter inanimate objects into submission.

It had been a little over a year now since I'd assumed the persona of "Pamela Wright, Female Graphic Artist." It was becoming more and more rare for me to "slip up" and let my masculine nature peek out of my otherwise-perfect feminine disguise.

Rare—but it still occasionally happened.

Like now.

Sure enough, a wide-eyed face peered around the corner of my open door. Carl, my secretary, tried to determine the cause of my latest outburst.

"Problems, Ms. Wright?"

"It's this damn computer again, Carl! The blasted thing just ate a whole morning's work."

"Did you save the work to disk? If you did, you can always go back to the last place that you saved it, uh . . ."

I guess the expression on my face was sufficiently thunderous to tell Carl that: a) I hadn't saved my work, and b) nobody likes to hear useful advice after it's too late to be of any use.

I glared at Carl for a moment, then turned back to my treacherous computer. Reluctantly, I pressed the "Terminate" icon, and watched four hours of work go down the drain. I stabbed a finger against the Power button and turned the diabolical machine off.

Then I stood and strode past Carl, shoulders set, face grim. "If anybody comes looking for me, I'll be in Mr. Arjer's office."

****

The vacuous blond who manned my half-brother Josh's receptionist's desk was filing her nails as I came stalking past her. As usual, she tried to protest my breaching of office protocol by simply barging into the Managing Partner's office. And as usual, I simply ignored her.

Josh had several file folders out on his desk when I barged in, slamming the door behind me. He looked up, took quick stock of my expression, and set the folder he was reading aside. "Now what?"

I rested my fists on his desk and leaned as close to his face as possible. "It's that damned computer system you installed last month. It just trashed a whole morning's work!"

"So? Can't you just redo it?"

"How'd you like me to redo your face? Damn it, Josh! This 'labor-saving intranet' that you blew all that money on has made my life a nightmare! I can't get anything done using it, and I can't go back to the old manual method, because none of the other departments will accept my 'non-media' submissions! And of course, on those few occasions when I actually can get something accomplished on the computer, whoever I try to send it to either can't receive it because *their* system is down, or if they do get it, they lose it, or they accidentally trash it, or—god, I hate it."

Josh held up his hands to ward off my assault. "Calm down, will you? I understand that we're having a little adjustment difficulty—"

" *'Adjustment difficulty'*? That's what you call it when I—"

Josh's voice rose above my own. "—so I've taken steps to get things sorted out."

I paused in my tirade, and glared at him suspiciously. "What kind of 'steps'? If you think I'm gonna spend my nights learning how to program a computer or—"

"No, no. Nothing like that. I've decided that we're a big enough firm, with complex enough needs, that we ought to hire a full-time professional staff to support our new technology."

" 'Professional staff'?"

Josh nodded, and indicated the folders on his desk. "Uh-huh. I've already started interviewing candidates for the position of Systems Manager for our intranet."

I was still dubious. "And when is this miracle-worker going to be available so I can finally get some work done?"

"As soon as I find the right person for the job. This is going to be a critical position, PJ. You don't just hire the first geek with a pocket protector to walk through the door."

Mollified, I straightened up, lifting my fists off Josh's desk, and placing them on my feminine hips. "All right. But let's expedite the procedure as much as possible, okay? I swear: If that Computer Chip From Hell fouls me up one more time, I'm gonna open my window and see if the damn thing's smart enough to fly!"

"Relax, okay? You'll see. This new technician is going to change your life."

Funny, I had no idea Josh was psychic.

Chapter 4-2
...That Has Such People In't

Three days later, Thursday noon

"God! Have you seen him yet? He's *gorgeous!*"

I carried my brown bag lunch and my diet soda over to where Beth DiAngelo and several of the girls from the secretarial pool were trying to find the time to both eat lunch and to share the latest company gossip.

I seated myself in the last vacant chair at the table, and began to rummage in my bag. Perhaps something more interesting than the weight-conscious lunch I'd packed this morning had appeared inside since then, but there was no such luck. My bag still held just the Tupperware container of celery/carrot sticks, the one rather dull tuna-fish sandwich (light on the mayo), and an orange. *Ah, the sacrifices we women make in the name of our figures.*

Judy (one of the girls from the secretarial pool) leaned forward and, with a conspiratorial smirk, murmured, "I don't know about you girls, but I think *I* am going to start having *lots* of problems with my word processor!"

I looked up from my disappointing culinary explorations. "Whom are we talking about?"

Beth was the first to answer: "The new computer technician. The one who's going to get the internet working right."

"Intra*net*."

She waved a hand in dismissal. "In*ter*, in*tra*—whatever. Just so long as he's 'inta' girls!"

That provoked a general round of giggling. I raised an eyebrow, and took a bite of my dry sandwich. "Good looking, is he?"

Judy took up the tale again. "Haven't you seen him yet? He's *soo*—He looks just like—"

Beth: "A cross between Mel Gibson and Fabio, with the best features of both."

Judy: "With the most gorgeous dark-brown hair—"

Carol (another of the "pool girls"): "And those eyes! He looked at me when he came by to survey the equipment. One gaze from those big brown eyes, and—ooh!"

Beth: "Best of all, he's got 'technician's hands.' Long and nimble. And you know what *that* means."

Another round of giggling.

I remembered the "female conventional wisdom" regarding a man's hands: Supposedly the length and size of a man's hands were directly proportional to—

I stole a surreptitious glance at my own small, slender hands. Hey, just because it was conventional wisdom, that didn't mean it was necessarily true!

Beth brought this particular topic to a conclusion by announcing, "Well, ladies, at this point I'm going to proclaim it's 'every woman for herself' as far as the new man is concerned. 'May the best woman win,' and all that. Unless that woman isn't me!"

More giggling. But this time I thought I detected just a bit of an edge to the mirth.

****

Friday morning

There was a soft tapping at my door.

"Yes?" I said.

"Ms. Wright? Hi, I'm Gene. I'm the new System Manager. Do you have a moment?"

Despite all the time I've spent living as a female, I still judge appearance based on my male perspective. Let's face it, sensibility is a matter of life experience. And with the exception of the last year, all my experience has been masculine. But that's not to say I don't know handsome when I see it.

The girls hadn't been exaggerating, and I could see what all the fuss was about. The fellow standing politely in my door was about 5′ 8″, with long legs, a trim waist, and broad (though not excessive) shoulders. He had an open, nicely featured face that was topped with wavy, dark-brown hair. And his eyes, they were a luminous, limpid brown. No wonder there was some mild friction starting to appear between a few of the office's best girlfriends.

I said, "Oh, sure. Come on in, Gene. You don't know how glad I am to meet you! Maybe you can finally get this damn idiot savant to start behaving."

I glared at the computer that was crouching on my desk, mocking me with its arcane superiority.

He chuckled, and stepped in carrying a small toolbag. "Do I have to give you the same speech I've been giving the other women? It's just a tool, you know. It doesn't have a personality, or intelligence. It can't form a grudge, or plot to overthrow the government, or anything like that. Once I've got the LAN connections sorted out, so long as you stay within some very simple protocols, pretty soon you'll wonder how you ever got along without it."

I raised a dubious eyebrow. "Well, I'm willing to give it one more chance. How's that?"

He favored me with a smile, and then began typing some command into the keyboard. I tried to follow what he was doing for a few moments, but he rapidly lost me as he began calling more and more mysteriously technical information up onto my monitor. I felt like a brand-new wizard's apprentice watching his master invoke subtle demons.

"So, Gene—where did you learn to do this kind of thing?"

He continued to work his magicks. With eyes still on the screen, he mumbled, "Six years as a Canoe Club ET."

"I beg your pardon?"

He stopped typing for a moment, and looked over at me with a shy grin. "Sorry. I get distracted when I'm working, and I sometimes slip back into the jargon. I was an Electronics Technician for six years in the Navy. I got out two years ago."

"Really? Gee, I bet you've seen some fascinating parts of the world. I've fantasized sometimes about sailing off to distant ports, seeing fabulous places, and 'meeting' exotic new people."

I give him my patented sultry smile. I was just trying to be friendly, mind you. If I'd been having this discussion in my masculine guise, a grin and a knowing wink would probably have replaced that smile. I wasn't making a pass or anything. Truly, I wasn't. I was just trying to be companionable and to break the ice. I swear.

I was surprised to get a forced smile and a quick view of his back, as he turned again to the keyboard. "Oh, I've made one or two port calls. Mostly in the Persian Gulf and India. I was in Desert Storm. But you have to be careful with 'exotic people' when you're a . . . stranger in a foreign port. There. That should take care of your connection problems for the moment. I'll be sending around a memo about protocols and the like. Thanks again for your time. It was a pleasure meeting you, Ms. Wright."

And then he abruptly was gone.

Was it something I said?

****

Tuesday noon

Judy: "Maybe he's gay."

Sarah: "Oh god, please no! Do you think?"

Lunchtime found me again sitting with the girls. I took a dainty bite of my peanut-butter-and-jelly sandwich. (I had to remember to go shopping today after work. I was out of tuna fish.)

I said, "I take it we're talking about Gene again?"

Beth: "Who else? Have you had any luck with him? I know he was up in your office last week."

"He was just checking out my equipment."

That provoked a round of giggles.

"My *computer* equipment, thank you. Goodness, don't you ladies have anything better to occupy your minds?"

My answer was a chorus of *no*s and more giggling.

Beth: "In any event, I'll take that as a 'no luck' from you too, PJ. Gee, maybe he *is* gay."

I'm still surprised occasionally by the insights that I'm able to obtain while living in my assumed gender. One of the greatest surprises for me was the similarity of conversational topics that came up when you gathered a bunch of women together, away from masculine influence. Before I'd lived among them, I'd always thought that women talked about clothes and makeup and exchanged recipes. That they discussed relationships in hushed, giggled tones.

That's how it worked when I was around in my Peter-persona. But put me among them in my Pamela disguise? Remove the necessity to conform to the prim-and-proper stereotype that society foisted on them, and things quickly changed. Though all those topics might come up, it just blew me away to discover that a common theme was a very open discussion of how much everyone was "getting," and by whom. It was all so similar in tone and tenor to the thousands of masculine conversations that I'd had over the years that it was sometimes difficult for me to stay "in character."

Also, for some reason, I found it a little embarrassing. "Just because he isn't interested in any of you, that doesn't necessarily mean he's gay. Maybe he just doesn't find any of you attractive."

The words were out of my mouth before I realized what I was saying.

I ate alone for the rest of the week.

****

Wednesday afternoon

"Gene, may I ask you something of a personal nature?"

Gene was once again in my office, making some kind of complex and incomprehensible adjustment to the cabling on the back of my computer. He paused for a moment and gazed up over the top of my desk, behind which he was kneeling.

"Sure, I suppose so." I could sense he was already becoming defensive.

"When you were up here last week, did I say something to offend you? If I did, I want to apologize."

He set his screwdriver down. "No, you didn't say anything. In fact, it's probably me who should apologize. I know I was a bit abrupt with you. It's just—"

I let him take his time.

He said, "Ms. Wright—"

"Pamela, please."

I expected a smile in exchange for that offer of intimacy, but I didn't get it. He just plowed ahead—

"It's just—Ever since I've been here, it seems that I can't turn around without some woman trying to—"

He quickly looked up, his eyes growing wide in embarrassment. "Oh, it's not like I thought *you* were trying to—I didn't—I—It's just that I'm getting a little paranoid, I guess, and when you started talking about—"

I raised a hand and chuckled. "It's alright, Gene. No offense taken. I eat lunch everyday with some of the girls, and I guess it'd be no surprise to you that you've been the main topic of discussion for these last few weeks."

He finally grinned sheepishly. "I just never expected to be a 'sex object.' I thought that only happened to *women* in the workplace."

"Oh, trust me. It does." *Heck, I'll let you in on a little "secret from behind the lines," my fellow male.* "But women have needs and interests too, you know. You might be surprised what we 'hens' cackle over when we're alone."

The grin became a bit rueful. "Yeah."

I was beginning to take a real liking to this poor beleaguered male. "Look, Gene. In the interests of inter-gender understanding and your sanity, let's make a pact. If you'll promise to keep your 'hunkness' to the absolute minimum, I promise to curb my raging hormones and refrain from trying to seduce you, except during alternate Fridays. How's that?"

That got me my first genuine, unguarded laugh from him. He stuck out his hand. "Deal!"

Chapter 4-3
Winter Wonderland

The following weeks

As Bogie said in *Casablanca*, it was the beginning of a beautiful friendship.

Gene was in fact a rather shy, private person. He didn't open up to just anyone, and even when he did, he didn't do it quickly. You had to take the time to get to know him. That perhaps was why none of the other women had had any luck. But I'd taken the time; or at least I had indicated that I was willing to get to know this interesting man before I turned back the covers and started patting the empty space beside me in bed.

In truth, I think my office became something of a refuge for Gene. He certainly started finding more and more reasons to work on my desktop computer.

After a while, it became kind of a game. He'd find some excuse to take the cover off my machine, and then he'd tinker for a few minutes while we chatted. At first, he tried to make his visits sound plausible. He'd describe some complex operation that needed immediate execution, as he removed the screws on the back of my unit. But by the second week, I began to suspect that he was just throwing together some jargon to justify his presence. Monday found him installing a software upgrade. Tuesday, he needed to reset the jumpers on my LAN connector. Wednesday, he stated a need to clean the power-supply fan. On Thursday, he explained that he'd come up to "empty the shift-register bit-bucket". By Friday, he was "greasing the logic gates" and I was beginning to giggle.

I started leaving him little doodle cartoons in his electronic mailbox. The first was a line drawing showing

"Gene, the Computer Missionary" in pith helmet and explorer's togs, standing in a jungle clearing, staring at a computer sitting on the ground. It was centered in a rope loop that trailed back to a bent-over tree. You know, that silly trap that Elmer Fudd is always using to try and catch Bugs Bunny. Peering over the bushes in the background were a bunch of female Amazons with bones through their noses, all smiling expectantly.

I followed that one up with two men in pith helmets who were sitting in a huge iron pot over a roaring fire. As the Amazons did a victory dance around them, the stranger was speaking to Gene the Computer Missionary, "I came to fix the copy machine. You?"

That earned me a little drawing of my own from Gene. It wasn't much more than a stick figure holding what I finally figured out was a tool kit in one hand and a bunch of cartoonish daisies in the other.

I was so careful when I saved it to disk. That disk is still sitting here, in the top drawer of my desk.

****

The Christmas holiday season was rapidly approaching. Josh, the inveterate party animal, had instituted a new corporate policy. Every year, in early December, he'd ordained that the senior staff would have a one-week "retreat" away from the offices. In public, it was stated that this was to be a chance for all the "movers and shakers" at WN&A to meet together and "develop synergy."

Nobody was fooled. Everyone knew it was just a way for the privileged few at the top of the corporate ladder to spend seven days living it up at some swanky resort, on the company's tab.

Being the artsy "bohemian," I was very torn about all this. On the one hand, I felt a natural outrage at this bourgeois decadence. On the other hand, I'd never been to

Sun Valley, Idaho. I'd heard it was absolutely beautiful, particularly in the winter.

In the end, my hedonism won out.

****

We flew in on Sunday night, aboard one of the regional air carriers. The WN&A contingent was large enough (twenty-three souls, all told) that we pretty much had the little turboprop all to ourselves. A pair of vans met us at Sun Valley's small air terminal and whisked us off to the "Bitter Root Lodge."

The building was—the best way to describe it was to say it was a three-story, 100-room, log cabin. That's not quite apt though, because it sounds very "Ma and Pa Kettle." Though the décor was definitely "frontier modern", it was also very swank. Josh's taste for the finer things was still intact. This was a world-class, four-star resort.

And as I'd heard, the setting was simply spectacular! Rugged, snow-covered mountains rose almost from the edge of the rear parking lot. There was also a series of natural hot springs and—"hot creeks"?—visible through the woods to the north. Apparently, the lodge had been built near enough to one of the springs for the boiling water to be piped directly to a large, Olympic-sized swimming pool, and to a smaller—it was kind of a cross between a wading pool and a hot tub. Big enough to seat at least a dozen folks in parboiled bliss.

I spent Sunday evening settling into my room and just drinking in the view outside my window. If the opportunity arose, I'd have to see if I could find an art-supply store in town. It had been a while since I'd done any drawing or painting just for the fun of it. I could have spent a whole year trying to capture the wonder that nature had provided just outside the door.

I don't know how much Josh was spending for this week, but I'm sure it was well into four figures for all of us. Not one dollar of which, qualified for an off-season discount. The lodge was at capacity, with skiers and other outdoors types.

As a result, we all had to share a room with another member of the WN&A staff. Since Beth DiAngelo was the only other female staff member who'd been invited along on this junket, guess who I wound up sharing a room with.

I was a little put off by this arrangement, at first. It was one thing to spend my days at work in my Pamela disguise. There I could always maintain a bit of personal space. My disguise was as perfect as technology could make it; and I've never been "made," as far as I can tell. But would the technology, as perfect as it was, hold up in the intimate confines of a small motel room? Would it continue to pass muster twenty-four hours a day, for a full week, in close proximity to a real woman?

More than that, I felt a bit uncomfortable for Beth. She was a good friend, and I would be taking advantage of her ignorance and trust regarding my real gender. I mean, we'd be undressing in the same room, and we'd be using the same bathroom.

We'd be sleeping together. (In the same room, that is! *Not* the same bed. Obviously.)

I don't really know what I was expecting. I had these weird visions of Beth parading around in her underwear. Or worse, Beth in the buff, doing wild, intimate things to herself while I looked on. I don't know why I imagined that that's what women did in the privacy of their motel rooms.

And of course, nothing like that occurred. Beth has a normally-developed sense of modesty. While we were still sharing the room, she'd dress in the bathroom. At least as far as lingerie, anyway. I never once caught a glimpse of her being completely nude; and frankly, even though Beth has a very attractive body, I was just as pleased that that was how things worked out.

I'm also pleased to report that for the period that we were sharing the room, I never once got even the slightest impression that Beth suspected anything was out of the ordinary. All in all, the experience was not that different from sharing a motel room with another male. (With the exception that Beth had the most annoying habit of using any of my makeup that I left lying around.)

You'll notice that twice I've said "while Beth and I were still sharing the room." On the Monday that we arrived, Josh scheduled a working breakfast. Over a fine omelet, he outlined the schedule of our "working groups." It was a very impressive, productive schedule that he proposed.

Of course, he then ruined the effect, by canceling the afternoon session right after he announced it. It was perfectly obvious to anyone who was paying even the least attention that the schedule was purely for show. This was playtime. There was no real expectation for anyone to actually attend the sessions.

As a result, as soon as the morning meeting broke up, the testosterone-laden males of our group promptly went off in search of suitable female companionship. As I've said, there was no shortage of skiers and outdoors types; and before dinner that evening there had been a rapid reshuffling of rooms. Even Beth had managed to attract the attention of a (I must admit) very handsome young orthodontist from Denver. Though Beth nominally continued to bed in our shared room, she made it very clear that I had no need to leave the light on for her every night.

While I was happy to have the room to myself, I must admit I felt a bit of perverse jealousy. Since I had no interest in seeking out "suitable male companionship," I was left as odd girl out. By the next morning, I was already searching for something to do. I even showed up for the morning briefing session.

As fate would have it, I didn't show up alone.

Gene walked through the door almost on my heels.

We sat around for a few minutes in rather stilted silence, waiting for someone—anyone—from WN&A to arrive.

But of course, nobody did.

Gene finally broke the silence: "It looks like we're not even going to get fed. Obviously the meeting is off. Would you like to go out and get something to eat? I'm famished."

And that was the beginning.

****

As it turned out, Gene hadn't found any "suitable companionship," either. Being the two oddballs, we just sort of gravitated together. We spent the rest of the day exploring the town of Sun Valley. I even managed to find a small art-supply store where I purchased a pair of artist's tablets and some charcoals and watercolors. Gene rose another notch in my estimation by indicating a genuine interest in my artistic endeavors. He asked if he could watch me at work sometime. That is, if it wouldn't be too great a distraction.

Again, the thought rose unbidden in my mind: It was really a shame that Pamela wasn't a genuine woman. In Gene, I think any real girl would have found a very attractive mate. The best I could hope for was a continuing friendship.

At least that's what I believed at the time.

Chapter 4-4
Karma

Around six o'clock, Gene mentioned that he was getting a bit hungry. Did I want to join him for dinner? We might even go bar-hopping afterward, if that was okay with me.

It sounded innocent and fun. Besides, it wasn't like I had other pressing plans.

When I think back today on how that evening turned out—whoa. I can only wonder about the mysterious workings of Fate.

****

We got back to the lodge from our first real "date" around midnight.

Gene parked the car far enough away from the entrance, and in a dark enough location, that I no longer had any doubts concerning the source of the tension that I'd sensed building for the last hour or so.

I'd felt that very same anxiety more times then I cared to remember, sitting in my father's car after a heavy date with my high-school sweetheart. I had the strangest little thought. *Did she ever feel the same anxiety?*

Now I can answer that question: She did.

As Gene's and my shared evening together had progressed, there had been more and more "meaningful moments." These next few moments—here, alone in the parking lot—had the potential for becoming a very personal encounter. It was only natural to feel apprehensive.

The question was: What did I do now?

Again, the memories of my awkward high school years returned. I remembered how unfair it felt, at the time, for the girl to always seem so much in control. How it was *she* who got to decide what was "right" and what was "going too far."

I was learning tonight what a misconception that belief had been!

You have to understand that while tonight may have been our first official date, and while Gene had never kissed me or gotten physically amorous with me, our relationship was already well established. We had already progressed past "just friends," and had moved to—

What, exactly?

At least to the point where a friendly little kiss, to close out the evening, was no longer sufficient expression of what it was that we felt for each other.

But what was?

We just sat there in the darkness, the tick of the rapidly-cooling engine the only sound in the car. Gene looked out his window. I looked out my window.

Again, what did I do now?

Was I ready to respond (as a woman should) to what I (as a man) would probably expect in this situation?

Or did I just smile, thank Gene for the lovely evening, and make a mad dash for my room?

There was a name for women who pulled that kind of stunt on men, and I didn't want that name applied to Pamela. Also, if I did that, it would probably be the end of my friendship with Gene. Nor would I blame him for it.

Oh, heavens. Was it really all that terrible? Tonight might just consist of a little "heavy petting." And even if it did go farther—well, I'd done that before, too. I'd lived through it. Heck, on one occasion I'd surrendered to the romance and even enjoyed it, in a detached, fantasy-dream kind of way.

Gene brought the matter to a decision point by leaning over and nuzzling my cheek.

What the hell? Maybe it would be just petting. If not, maybe I could recapture that fantasy-dream feeling.

This whole quandary was irrelevant anyway. Regardless of any feelings that I might have had (and I was still wrestling with just what those feelings were), I had a role to play, and a character to support. I might still be wrestling with my feelings, but Pamela had already committed herself. She turned her face to his and met his kiss, raising her hand to his cheek.

The kiss became more passionate.

Soon I felt one of his hands caressing my shoulder. Where was his other hand? Oh, there it was—on my thigh.

Time for Pamela to do her thing if this friendship with Gene was going to continue. I gave him a little moan of desire, and laid my left hand atop the one on my right shoulder, then guided it down onto my breast. I couldn't feel exactly what he was doing with the proffered treat, but there was sufficient pressure against my (real) chest that I figured he must be making the most of the offer. In my opinion, that called for another moan and a little more ardor in the continuing kiss. I supplied both.

Whoops! That hand on my thigh was now under my skirt, starting to work its way upward. This was rapidly progressing past the "petting" stage. It was getting both serious and somewhat uncomfortable—

Not for the intimacy (which wasn't great, but was certainly bearable), but because I was rapidly getting pressed uncomfortably against the doorframe in an awkward, bent-necked hunch. I tried to shift position, and only succeeding in bumping the back of my head against the seatbelt bracket. The small gasp of pain was genuine this time.

Gene, bless him for a gentleman, immediately removed his hand from my breast, and murmured a breathless little "Sorry."

Women are supposed to be moved by tenderness and consideration in their partners, and I figured that I should show a little appreciation. I brushed my lips against his, and quickly replaced his hand atop my fake boob, adding a little pressure of my own with the hand atop his. Then I whispered, "Don't stop. I want you to—"

Ah, well. We were "down to it." That hand on my thigh had reached my hip, and the fingers were beginning to slide under the lower hem of my panties.

How the heck did this work? I'd assumed we would probably be dancing tonight; and for that reason, I'd chosen a "dancing dress" that came with a matching bikini brief, the kind that you could "flash" without undue embarrassment when your skirt flared out. It was beneath these panties that Gene was trying to work his hand.

Unfortunately for Gene (and fortunately for me?) I'd donned those panties on top of a pair of sheer-to-the-waist pantyhose. Did he already know that there was still a layer of fabric between those probing fingers and his ultimate goal? If not, was I supposed to let Gene figure out the current situation? Or should I help him? Or. . . ?

What did a genuine woman do in this situation?

At the worst possible moment, that old joke about the couple screwing came back to me:

"Oh, darling, if I'd known you were a virgin, I'd have taken more time."

"Well, lover, if I'd known you had more time, I'd have taken off my pantyhose."

Apparently Gene had indeed figured out that he still had another obstacle to overcome, because the hand withdrew from beneath the panty, and began to try and work itself higher up under my skirt.

I tried to shift position a little lower—

Gene tried to move a bit higher, so as to be able to mount me better—

My right knee slammed against the gearshift lever—

By reflex, I bucked up and backwards—

Surprised, but aware of the cause of my sudden pained hiss, Gene tried to move up and off, to allow me to ease my discomfort—and succeeded in "braining" himself against the roof of the car—

By reflex, he dodged down and forward—

Our foreheads collided with a solid thump, and I saw stars.

By the time the sparkles cleared, Gene was off me and back sitting (awkwardly) behind the steering wheel, rubbing his forehead and muttering words that I couldn't make out.

So much for passion.

I tried to be a good sport. "Darling, it's all right. Maybe if we—"

He held up his left hand and continued to rub his forehead with his right. "No, no—it's my fault. We're both a bit too old to be fumbling around in a car. Let's go inside."

At the time, I remember thinking that was probably for the best.

****

What soon happened, happened because we were both distracted—and a little drunk—and the layout of the lodge was still unfamiliar.

Instead of walking the longer distance to the front entrance, we detoured around the corner of the building, making for the side door that led to the corridor to our rooms. We needed to skirt past the Olympic-sized swimming pool (the one heated by the natural hot spring), and then make our way down a short flight of steps to reach the door.

Steam was rising off the water of the pool in the below-freezing night air. I didn't think much of it. I was trying to map out a strategy for the least involved (read "shortest"), yet most satisfying sexual encounter I could contrive. We made it past the pool without incident. As my left foot hit the top of that short flight of stairs going down, I turned to look back at Gene, to offer him an encouraging come-hither gaze. (I actually felt a bit bad about the fiasco in the car.)

The steps were a sheet of glaze ice, formed when the steam from the pool condensed back out of the cold air.

My feet went out from under me, and I pitched butt-first down them. I bounced once, then slid on my side for a full two feet.

Then I landed in the smaller, "hot tub"-style, relaxing pool. The pool filled with *boiling* water direct from the hot spring.

I hit my left temple hard enough against the side of the pool that it stunned me.

Gallant Gene immediately jumped into the pool to rescue me.

A good thing, too: If Gene hadn't jumped in and lifted my head above the water, there's a very real chance that I might have drowned.

We flailed for a second, then I finally gathered my wits sufficiently to indicate to him that I was all right.

The water was *hot! Burning hot!* The strangest little thought flitted through my mind as I cuddled against Gene. *You'd think that after almost a year of parboiling myself every work-night as a prelude to freeing myself from Pamela, I'd be used to hot water by now.*

And then the significance of that fleeting thought struck me harder than ice-coated stairs against my artificially padded butt.

Hot water—

Plus Pamela—

Oh, dear God!

I started to flail in earnest, trying to extricate myself from the boiling water—when a sudden familiar relaxation of pressure against my skin, and a simultaneous gasp of surprise from Gene, informed me that it was too late.

My bodysuit had reverted to its "donning" state: that horribly artificial caricature of a woman. I turned to Gene, a half-formed explanation already starting to babble out of my mouth.

I caught sight of his face in the reflected light of the lodge—

His gasp hadn't been surprise at my sudden metamorphosis.

It had been at the sudden sick realization that <u>his</u> disguise was also in peril.

There, right next to me in the tub, was a horribly artificial caricature of a *man*, wearing Gene's clothes and staring wide-eyed, both at his predicament and my own.

Chapter 4-5
Getting to Know You

We struggled out of the pool, then just stood there staring at each other. The chill air quickly dropped the temperature of the suits back within the 90-104 degree temperature range, and our suits promptly assumed their "normal" mode. Pamela morphed back into Pamela; Gene morphed back into Gene. By the time we reached the side door of the lodge, the only cause for comment that any passerby would find, concerning our appearance, would be our soaking-wet clothing.

My room was closer, so it was there that "Gene" and I now went.

I unlocked the door though my fingers were now shaking from the cold.

Oddly, the thought that kept running through my mind at this moment was: *At least now I know that no matter how cold the air temperature, apparently it's my skin temperature that matters as far as the "mode" of the suit goes.* I'd always wondered what would happen if the surface temperature of the suit ever dropped below 90 degrees. Would it revert to its "dormant" state, trapping me in a walking, talking "papery feeling, vaguely feminine-shaped cut-out"?

Apparently not. I was freezing, but to all observers, it was a cold, shivering *woman* who fumbled with the key to her door, as her *male* companion chaffed his arms and danced from foot to foot.

We got inside. I shut and locked the door behind us, turned on the bathroom light, and grabbed every towel off the racks. "Gene" was already shedding his shirt and slacks. I followed suit.

There was no need for modesty at this point, both because of our previous shared intimacy—which now seemed not nearly so intimate—and because we both now knew that even when we'd shed every stitch of clothing, neither of us would be truly "in the buff."

It would just look that way.

Undressed, I tossed "him" a towel, and then proceeded to briskly rub myself down with the other.

It wasn't that I was trying to dry myself off. It didn't matter that much to me if "plastic Pamela" was wet or not. I was just trying to generate a little heat. Finally, because of the exertion of vigorously rubbing myself, the shivers subsided.

"Gene" seemed to be recovered as well.

An uncomfortable silence ensued while we both tried to look anywhere but at each other.

To his credit, it was Gene who first broke the silence.

"Well. I guess we have some things to tell each other."

"Yeah. I guess we do."

There was another uncomfortable silence. Still looking at my toes, I offered, "I suppose in your case, it has something to do with getting the job?"

He nodded. "Yeah. May I ask—?"

"The same—to get my current job."

"Small world."

Silence descended again. We just looked at each other.

Finally, I managed a vague gesture at "his" appearance. "I never knew that NuGen made a male version. I see they've maintained their high quality standards, and, uh"—I gestured again, at his groin—"the 'attention to detail.' It's quite, um, impressive."

He started to smile. "I thought, 'What the hell? If you're gonna do it, do it in a big way.' " I got a return gesture in my direction. "You're no 'small miracle' yourself."

I tried not to grin. "Thank you."

And then the spell broke and we were both laughing, though it was equal parts mirth and the release of tension. We eventually wound up sitting next to each other on the foot of the unused bed. The laughter subsided.

We sat there for a moment, then I turned and offered my dainty hand. "I'm Peter, by the way."

The figure next to me smiled shyly, and offered a big hand in return. "I really am Jean. But with a 'J', not a 'G'."

I suddenly realized that I wasn't absolutely sure, even now, of the true gender of the person sitting beside me. Gently shaking the offered hand I asked, "Is that *Jean* short for *Jeanette* or *Jeanelle*? Or . . . ?"

My companion's smile grew broader. "No. Not short for anything. It's just Jean. But my middle name is Marie. That should answer the question you're tap-dancing around."

I smiled in return. "It does. Thank you."

We sat for another moment's silence, though this time it was not nearly so uncomfortable. Rather, there was already a sense of camaraderie forming.

Then Jean turned to me, and in a soft voice, still masculine though now also beguiling, murmured, "I'd really like to meet you, Peter."

My lips curled into a mischievous grin. "Funny, I was just thinking the same thing about you."

****

The tub in the bathroom was not large enough for both of us to soak at the same time, and we couldn't decide who should "unmask" first. Finally, Jean left for her own room, and I quickly busied myself in the "de-conversion" process.

Twenty minutes later, I was simultaneously trying to towel my (genuine) light-brown hair and button the one "Peter shirt" that I'd brought with me, when there was a soft tapping at my door. I suddenly felt a case of butterflies, the like of which I hadn't felt since my dating days during high school.

Is Jean pretty?

I immediately berated myself for such a chauvinist thought. Wasn't I always bragging about how feminist-conscious I'd become, now that I'd lived in both worlds? It was the *person* who mattered. Beauty was only skin deep. (And who knew that better than I?) Jean and I would build a relationship based on our shared circumstance, and it would be an interesting, fulfilling friendship for that reason.

Sure. Just—*Please, don't let her be too ugly.*

I opened the door.

****

Ever since I first donned Pamela, my life seems to have been a wild roller-coaster ride of positive and negative happenstance, with each new outrageous predicament ultimately resolved by miraculous chance. Bad breaks seem to always balance out with lucky ones.

I guess I must have had one "bad break" outstanding on the ledger.

Standing at my door was a tall, attractive woman. Perhaps she'd never be a fashion model, but I bet she never lacked for a date if she wanted one. She had a soft, heart-shaped face that was framed in wavy, dark-brown hair that fell just above her shoulders. 'Gene's' limpid brown eyes searched my own cornflower-blue. Sensuously full lips, alluring even without any hint of lipstick, curled into a knowing, welcoming smile. Her figure was hard to determine, alas, as she was wearing fairly loose-fitting, unisex clothing.

(Now there was one distinct advantage "Gene" had over me. "He" didn't have to carry "clothes for two." A woman could wear loose-fitting male clothing, and still be considered "fun." If Peter ever tried to wear one of Pamela's dresses—first, it would be too tight; and second, he'd probably get hauled away.)

However, Jean's clothing was not so baggy that I couldn't get a suggestion of a very womanly body. *Please, let it be so.*

We stood there, looking at each other for a moment, and then in a very masculine baritone, Jean whispered, "Peter, please, let me in."

I offered a rueful little smile, by way of apology and stood aside. In Pamela's contralto (which wouldn't depart for a good five hours), I murmured, "I guess we aren't very 'conventional' yet, are we?"

****

We sat on the foot of the same unused bed and compared notes. Jean's story was almost a carbon copy of my own. She'd been trying for just less than two years to land a job for which her training made her eligible.

It turned out that her résumé wasn't all that fictional. She really had served six years in the Navy as an electronics technician. One of those years really had been spent as a combat sailor in the Persian Gulf, aboard an aircraft carrier. Upon her discharge, she'd headed out into "civvie land" (as she called it), ready to parley her impressive training and experience into a top-paying technical job.

And like my friend Beth DiAngelo, Jean had discovered that it was still a man's domain, out here in the dog-eat-dog world of commerce.

At every business where she applied, the senior technicians (men one and all) weren't ready yet to accept an "emotional, illogical, period-once-a-month female" into their fellowship. She'd drifted from one minimum-wage drone job to another.

Then she'd seen the ad announcing WN&A's need for a systems manager. It was a job tailor-made for someone with her expertise. She applied. Josh had turned her down flat.

(I didn't think this was the appropriate time for me to mention my relationship to Josh. I *did* think that it was time for me to have another long talk with him.)

Jean had finally seen the handwriting on the wall. She'd already encountered NuGen's web site while surfing; and using the last of her savings from her military pay, she'd acquired "Gene." When a "male" with Gene's qualifications had appeared in his office, Josh had jumped at the prospect.

(Yeah, I really had to have a *long* talk with Josh.)

I gave the précis of my own experiences, and then we lapsed back into that companionable silence.

After a moment, Jean laid a tentative hand on my thigh. "Peter—"

"Please, call me *PJ*. I prefer that my friends call me that."

That earned me a bewitching smile. "Okay, PJ, I like that." The smile shifted from bewitching to genuine contrition. "PJ, I'm sorry about earlier. When we were together. In the car. I thought—I mean—You can understand that I'm not very good at reading signals yet. I thought that you wanted me to—er, that is, that 'Pamela' wanted me, wanted Gene, to—"

A rueful little smile crossed my lips. "You're right. It's a 'small world.' I was having the same trouble, the same uncertainties about your signals."

She chuckled (which was so beguiling in that baritone), but the contrition remained. "It's important that you know that I didn't really mean to deceive—"

She looked away, down at the hand on my thigh. "No. That's not true. I *did* mean to deceive you."

Then she again met my eyes. "But please believe that I never meant to hurt you. I just wanted to—to be with you. To keep this, what we have—"

I smiled warmly and lay my hand atop hers. "No apology necessary. Particularly if you can believe that I wasn't trying to hurt you either, that I only wanted the same thing. Can we just say, 'No harm, no foul'?"

She nodded, and that bewitching smile returned. "Yes. Please."

More companionable silence.

This time it seemed so natural and effortless when I leaned over and gently laid my lips against hers.

Apparently she thought so too. Her hand rose to the back of my neck, to press our lips even closer together.

Chapter 4-6
How To Show A Lady A Good Time

Wednesday morning

Beth looked across the breakfast table with a smug little smile playing across her lips.

"I guess I don't need to ask," Beth said, continuing the smirk.

Pamela just buttered a slice of whole-wheat toast, and returned Beth's smirk with a pleasantly neutral smile. "What do you mean?"

Add a little note of frustrated curiosity to Beth's smirk: "Come on, girlfriend! You've got a nonstop grin this morning. If you haven't gotten laid in fine style, you just won a lottery somewhere. "

I just shrugged, and smiled that neutral smile, and ate my toast.

She gently beat her fists on the table and her feet on the floor. "Ooh—*Come on*! Give me the dirt!"

I raised an eyebrow. " 'Dirt'?"

"*Pamela!* Did you and he—Did Gene—?"

"Oh, that." I finished the toast, and then took a sip of coffee to prolong her agitation. Finally, I surrendered and gave her a full-blast grin. "Yes. We did—"

"—twice!"

****

Wednesday evening

Gene's masculine voice called out, "PJ, what size are you? I mean, what size is Pam?"

I stuck my head out of the bathroom where I was working on my makeup. We were going to try another night "on the town." Perhaps this time it would be a bit more fun, now that we were in on each other's secret. I was looking forward to it.

"Gene" was standing staring at the open suitcase sitting on the stand in the corner.

"Pamela is size 12. Why?"

"He" turned and looked at me. "What time does your voice spray wear off?"

"In about an hour. Thank you for reminding me; I'd better take a shot before we go."

"Wait! PJ, um—"

Again I stuck my head out of the bathroom, my lipstick half-applied, and looked more closely at "Gene." He was staring longingly into my suitcase.

I asked, "What's wrong?"

"I can sometimes fit into a size 12. I was thinking—"

"What?"

"Gene" gave me the cutest wide-eyed beseeching look, while biting one fingernail. "I really want to go dancing with *you*. I mean, with PJ. I mean—oh, you know what I mean."

I guess my grin showed my willingness, without my needing to say a word, because "his" face split into a grin.

I waved a hand in surrender. "Okay. But all I've got for Peter is a pair of jeans, a cotton shirt, and Nikes. Pretty casual. That kind of limits where we can go."

"I bet I've got some slacks and a blazer that would fit you. And you don't have big feet. I bet we could find shoes that would fit each other." Her excitement was contagious. "Please, let's try, okay?"

I finally nodded, unable to deny such enthusiasm. Still, I didn't want to seem too "easy," and therefore decided to add a condition: "Okay, you're the girl tonight. I'll hold the door for you, and pull out your chair—I'll even pick up the tab. But tomorrow night, it's my turn to be the lady."

"Gene" tried out a little pout that was spoiled both by his apparent gender, and by the fact that his eyes never lost their mirthful twinkle. "No fair! You've already had lots of chances to be the female."

I folded my arms and tried to look adamant (and probably succeeded as well as Gene and his pout). "None of that counts. We didn't know which game we were playing then."

My lover's pout dissolved into a giggle. "Deal!"

"Gene" clapped his hands, and then put them between his knees, giving his shoulders a little shake in the process. For Jean, that would have been a most fetching gesture. When "Gene" did it, it looked positively bizarre.

I chuckled, and pointed with my thumb at the door. "Go change, all right? I'll see you back here in half an hour."

****

Jean appeared at my door thirty minutes later, looking very "Annie Hall-ish" in navy-blue blazer and slacks, pale blue shirt, and subdued blue-knit tie.

I let her in. As soon as the door was closed, she promptly began to strip.

I just stood there in my bathrobe, with one eyebrow raised.

She must have felt my scrutiny, because she paused at struggling with the tie. The slacks and the blazer were off already, which revealed—

She wasn't wearing any underwear.

She followed my gaze (you can guess what I was staring at) and her cheeks took on a lovely pink tinge. But she smiled too. "Sorry. Navy manners. Spend enough time shoulder-to-shoulder with a hundred other women in ship's berthing, and you start to lose some of your modesty."

"Hey. No need to apologize. No need at all."

That got me what I deserved: Her self-conscious smile became three shades more sly. She finished undoing the tie. Very slowly and deliberately, she unbuttoned and then removed the shirt, turning it into a striptease as she did. Then she stood there, shameless, inviting my inspection.

Between Jean and Pamela, I think Pamela has the better body, all things considered. But it's not really fair to compare something "calculated" by using computer-aided design technique, with the random beauty of nature. And in Jean's case, it's a close contest anyway.

Jean looked me up and down, and finally her gaze locked on my—er—below my belt. A very knowing, very feminine smile crossed her lips. I didn't even need to look down to know what she was admiring.

As I say, conventional wisdom isn't always correct.

Now it was my turn to gain a little color in the cheeks.

I cleared my throat. "Let's call that one a draw, okay?"

She giggled, then scampered over to my open suitcase. She tossed me my one pair of male briefs, and then began to pick up and consider each item of Pamela's underwear.

As I slipped into the briefs, I said, "Look for black silk. I've got a pair of Giancarlo's designer panties and a matching bra in there."

She didn't look up, but instead began to dig faster. "Cool! Where'd you find them?"

I chuckled. "I'll tell you the whole story sometime."

She finally found what she was looking for, and held the panties aloft like a prize. "Oh PJ, they're beautiful!" She began to slip them on. "I hope they fit!"

They fit indeed. *Oh wow.* They were perhaps a little more snug than on me—or rather, on Pamela—but somehow, I didn't feel like criticizing.

Jean next found and donned the bra. I felt a moment's stab of envy when she reached behind herself and fastened the catch, without the slightest apparent difficulty.

I said, "How do you do that? I still can't do that without struggling."

She glanced over her shoulder and smiled. "You've been a woman for—what?—a year? I've been one for twenty-eight. It comes with practice. Put your clothes on. I want to get going."

She turned back to the suitcase, and I started to button "Gene's" shirt. I felt the oddest sensation as I did. I've heard that for some people, part of the thrill of cross-dressing is a feeling of guilty pleasure that comes of wearing someone else's clothing. But to feel that odd sexual tension while I, a man, was buttoning a man's shirt? Strange.

Jean was still rummaging in my suitcase. "Don't you have anything but pantyhose?"

"Why? What's wrong with pantyhose?"

She straightened up and turned to me, her luscious feminine charms barely concealed by *my* underwear. (I bet the next time I wanted to be "Pamela, Sex Kitten," I'd only have to wear that bra and panties under any outfit, and the memory of tonight would do the rest.)

Again I got that pouting expression (that worked just fine this time) as she placed her fists on her gorgeous hips.

When she spoke, it was in a pouty little-girl voice. "Pantyhose isn't sexy. I want something *hot*! I've got a good-looking man I'm going to seduce tonight. Don't you have a garter belt and stockings?"

I felt another little stab of embarrassment. But I guess if I was going to be the beneficiary, I could survive a little humiliation. "In the pocket on the lid."

"Ooh, Pamela, you little vixen! I can see why you don't keep *these* out in plain sight. These *are* hot!" In repayment for my embarrassment, Jean fastened the garter belt around her hips, then made quite a show of sitting on the edge of my bed, meticulously rolling each stocking in her fingers and then carefully sliding them up her legs.

At this point I didn't care if we went out tonight or not; and I said so.

But Jean would have none of that. "You promised!"

I went back to putting on the rest of "Gene's" suit, and Jean browsed my wardrobe till she found a little red dress that came to slightly above my—Pamela's—knees. Since Jean is slightly taller than me, it came to mid-thigh on her. It was barely long enough to make modesty with the tops of her stockings not too big a problem. (But still something of a concern. Which again, I found delightfully sexy.)

With the dress on, she again invited my inspection, even turning once—just fast enough that the skirt flared out sufficiently to grant me a peek at my own lingerie.

I nodded my approval as I finished knotting the tie.

She spent a seemingly endless twenty minutes using my cosmetics to "fix her face" (women!), and then we were on our way.

****

On balance, it was a wonderful evening. That it got off to a bit of a rocky start was, I first thought, my fault.

We went to a nice little "burger and beer" restaurant down the road from the lodge. We both played our roles. I made sure to be very macho and masculine: always opening doors, holding coats, pulling out chairs. Jean reciprocated by being coquettish and flirty. I paid close attention to her. I hoped she wouldn't notice that I had an ulterior motive for my attentiveness; but halfway through dinner, she set her fork down and gazed into my eyes.

"PJ, are you having fun?"

"Sure! Aren't you?"

"Well—you seem—I don't know, I'd say 'a bit distracted,' but you never seem to take your eyes off me."

"Can you blame me?"

She gave me a pleased smile at the compliment, but refused to be sidetracked. "No, seriously. Is something on your mind?"

I lowered my eyes to the table and added a sheepish grin to my blush. "Okay, you caught me. I haven't been out on a date in a while, certainly not since I've had Pamela. I confess: This is the first time I've ever had both the interest and the opportunity to—you might say I've been 'taking notes' for my own deportment, when I'm playing my alter ego."

Her hand flew to her mouth to try and stifle the giggle, but she failed. Then she blushed too, looked down at the table, and whispered. "Ditto."

After that, the night was glorious. Both of us began playing our roles to the hilt. She flirted and vamped, and made very good on her threatened seduction. For my part, I strutted and postured and basically behaved like somebody suffering from testosterone poisoning. Anybody watching must have thought we were right out of a bad romance novel or something. But we both knew what the other was doing, and it added a delightful "gamesmanship" element to the whole evening.

We didn't get home till after the bars closed at 2 a.m.

We spent the night in Jean's room. I couldn't say whose seduction worked better, since each of us spent the rest of the night in bed "having our way" with the other.

****

Wednesday night

So far in my career as Pamela, I've had sexual intercourse in my feminine guise twice. The first of those occasions, being raped by Kevin Sprague, had been unpleasant. In the extreme. The second time (with Anthony, on Giancarlo's private island) had been magical, but entirely unplanned and with such a dream-like quality. And that fumbling attempt with Gene in the car? It certainly could be improved upon.

Tonight, "just because I could," I was determined to see what it was like for a woman to plan and execute the satisfaction of her carnal needs. Deliberately and methodically, and completely for her own pleasure.

I determined that the first step would be to get myself into the proper frame of mind. To "get into character," as the actors say.

That would require some imagination on my part. But I *am* an artist, after all. I make my living off my vivid imagination.

****

She is charged with excitement.

Her long, blonde hair cascades over her smooth shoulders, and laps against the rose circles of areola. She examines herself critically in the mirror over the desk of her motel room. Slender hands caress taut belly and sleek waist. Her eyes close, and her head tilts back in ecstasy, as they slide in erotic self-exploration up her sides, until they cradle firm breasts. A small moan of desire escapes her lips as she fondles the soft, willing flesh. Soon, if she has her way, another's hands will replace her own.

Time to prepare.

Her clothing is laid out in readiness. The choice of attire is, for once, gloriously simple. Only certain items are right—are fitting for tonight.

The first item to attract her attention is a pair of black silk panties. They are delicious and decadent, and gloriously inviting, both to the wearer and to any observer lucky enough to be granted a glimpse of their forbidden beauty. She takes them into her hands and rubs the glossy fabric against her cheek. They have a subtle, ephemeral musk—not an *odor* (for that would be coarse and crude), but rather a deeply arousing *memory* of passion past—and a promise of pleasure to come. Seating herself on the end of her bed, she bends from the waist, the pressure of her thighs against her breasts a momentary distraction as she slips first one foot, then the other, into the silken garment. Soon, she feels its close embrace against hip, cheek—and the very heart of her desire. She cannot resist, and the fingers of her right hand trace her womanhood, now pressing the silken fabric within herself as the fingers of her left hand caress her face—stroke her warm, moist lips. She lingers for a moment, but there is more to do; and finally, with a soft sigh, her hands return to their work of selecting the next item of clothing.

The bra is a poor substitute for the caress that she desires, but the satiny touch against her eager breasts will have to do—for the moment. She slides first one strap, then the other, over her shoulders, pausing each time to flick her golden tresses over the opposite side. Then, with a simple flick of her hands, the snaps are fastened behind her back, and her bosom nestles within the shimmering fabric. She smiles at herself in the mirror. A small victory is attained; a small rite of passage is completed.

Bra and panties—but these are the final treat, the penultimate morsel for her lover's delight—to be concealed and withheld, until the moment is right. Now she needs to attend to that which she will display for the entire world to desire—that which she will first use to tempt and tease, incite and inflame.

The garter belt with its straps and fasteners is just snug enough around her waist that the whole provokes a delightfully wicked mental image of bondage and restraint. Usually, this is not something that she desires. But tonight, who can say what her lover's pleasure will be? Will silken cords encircle her ankles? Her wrists? Wrists that she will lift in tearful supplication to her dominating lover? And if her beseeching face and helpless tears sway him, then who shall be the conqueror, and who the conquered?

The stockings have always been her special favorite. What can be more feminine than the silky, shimmering gauze that caresses her and that lend her the illusion of flawless tanned flesh; that slip like a dream between her thighs, as they move against each other; that allow her skirt to flow over her legs with such a liquid grace?

But they are delicate, these stockings. One does not simply stick a foot into them, and tug them into place. That would be tantamount to violation! No. They must be handled gently. Lovingly. Her legs must *insinuate* themselves into the stockings' silken embrace, just as her lover must tenderly cajole and caress, if he wishes entry into her most intimate realm.

The shoes are a passionate, evocative red. Just shiny enough to make one wonder if they will betray by reflection the closely-guarded secret of their wearer's under-dress.

The dress is the crowning glory. It too is red, the color of passion and flame. It hugs her hips, and dips low over the cleft of her bosom. It reveals by concealing. It accentuates each achingly feminine curve. It hints at wild abandon, yet admits nothing but virginal modesty. It conceals all of her carefully prepared secrets—shielding her silk and lace from all but that one man fortunate enough to be admitted at her whim. And until she grants that one special man that special boon, the red dress offers her substitute comfort, by fondling her legs with an invisible lover's touch; the dress caresses with each movement.

Her makeup is carefully considered. The rose shade of lipstick that might call to mind other rosy, moist flesh. Blusher to counterfeit a maiden's innocence, even when her thoughts are wicked and wild. Subtly dark eye shadow and liner, to magnify the deep azure of her eyes, creating a depth that can encompass and entrap any man.

Finished, she once again stands before the mirror in critical contemplation. Then smiling in anticipation of the conquest of which she is now certain, she spins with a dancer's grace. Her hands aid the billow of her skirt as it grants one last fleeting glimpse of the silk, lace, and concealed treasures that she will henceforth deny to all but he whom she eagerly awaits.

****

His knock on her door is promptly answered.

He can't help but smile at her choice of wardrobe, just as she grins in recognition of his own familiar blue blazer, shirt, and tie. She steps aside, granting him entry. He closes the door behind himself; and then moves to take her in a strong, masculine embrace. She surrenders for a moment, but then presses her hands against his shoulders.

"Gene! Please!"

Does he read shock and flustered desire in her wide-eyed smile? Or is she only pretending outraged modesty in an attempt to lure him on? The increased pressure of her hips against his, as her hands continue to press him away, leads him to think it is the latter.

She frees herself from his embrace. "I'll be ready in just a moment. I have to fix my face."

"How do you fix perfection?"

That earns him a musical giggle, as she disappears into the bathroom with a swirl of fabric and the click of heels on tile. "Flattery just might get you everywhere!"

Smiling, he seats himself in his accustomed place on the end of the unused bed. His experienced eye has already informed him that her makeup is complete. She is just teasing him, forcing him to wait upon her whim. So that is how the game will be played tonight? Fine. Let her have her moment. He has a stratagem of his own that should pay back all her clever deceits and wiles.

After what seems an unduly long wait (but is in fact only a few minutes), she emerges from the bathroom and stands with hands folded modestly against her skirt. "Well? Do I look good enough that you won't be completely embarrassed to take me out in public?"

"You're a vision." And so she is. (A petty little stab of jealousy clamors for attention, but it is easily ignored.) He stands and holds her faux fur coat open for her.

She allows herself to bundled within its embrace; then turns to favor him with a seductively soft smile, as she gathers the fur collar against her throat.

The evening is a delicious reprise of the night before. She flirts and teases. She hints at wanton desire, and then professes demure shyness if he tries to act on the hint. She insists on all female prerogatives. He must open each door, and allow her to precede him. He must hold each chair, must help her to remove, and later to don, her coat at each new locale. She seems to delight in selecting the most expensive items from each menu, and then perversely takes only a few bites.

She won't dance to any but the slowest, most romantic tunes. Their first "close dance" is a bit awkward. By the third tune, he has begun to understand the fundamentals of "leading." She simply presses herself against him, forcing him to make all the decisions. On the floor, she flaunts her soft curves against his taut physique, as she occasionally smirks mischievously into his eyes.

On the stroke of midnight, he offers to her, her coat. "Come on. I've got a special treat planned."

When she realizes that he is returning her to the lodge, there is a genuine note of disappointment and resistance in her voice. "Gene! It's too early! If you think you can have your way with me for this little effort, you've got another 'think' coming!"

He parks the car near the front entrance, then takes her hand in his and presses it to his lips. "Who says that I don't have something very special planned?"

She turns away, facing forward once more. The coquettish vamp is back, as she folds her hands in her lap. "Humpf. Well—we'll see."

He alights, then opens her door.

She offers him a languid hand, and allows herself to be assisted out of the car. Her nose is held high in mock disdain, as her hips swing in a sultry strut to the front door of the lodge.

He pauses as they pass the front desk. "Just a second. I've got to get my key."

The desk clerk comes out of the back office at the ring of the desktop bell. "Yes? Ah, Mr. Cavanaugh! Everything's ready. Here's your key."

With a wicked gleam in her eyes, the scarlet-dressed temptress shamelessly takes his left arm, and rubs herself against his side. "Darling, please hurry." Then she grins wickedly at the desk clerk, as he tries to maintain a neutral expression.

Gene simply takes the key from the clerk's hand, and gives him a knowing wink.

Pamela moves off with that same sultry strut, but he stops her with a hand on her shoulder as she moves off down the hallway. "No, hon. This way." He indicates the elevators; and is secretly pleased to see a flicker of genuine surprise and uncertainty on her face.

She points off toward their rooms, their *former* rooms. "But—?"

He shakes his head, and again indicates the elevators. "Uh-uh. This way."

The elevator opens on the top (third) floor of the lodge, and he takes her arm in his, leading her toward the suite that he previously "scouted out" this afternoon. The key turns in the lock, and this time he insists that she "enjoy" her prerogative as he stands aside, bowing her into the darkness. She takes a few tentative steps inside, then he switches on the lights, and closes the door behind them.

"Oh, Gene, is this—?"

"Yep. It's the Bridal Suite."

With a wonderfully mischievous grin, she slips her hands beneath his blazer, and strokes his chest. (He feels a secret, electric tingle that no other man would feel if a woman's hands pressed against that part of his body.)

Her lips come close to his and he can feel the warmth of her breath. She comes just close enough to make him think a kiss is imminent; but at the last instant, she pulls away again, still grinning mischievously. "Does this make me 'Mrs. Cavanaugh'?"

He offers her a salacious leer, and lays possessive hands on her hips. "No. This makes you 'Mrs. Smith.'"

She murmurs a pretended whimper of consternation, and bites her lower lip in sham dismay. "But what about my reputation? You'd let all the world think I'm just a cheap little slut?"

Before he can answer, her hands are guiding his hands down from her hips, and then up beneath her skirt. "I guess there's nothing I can do now but to make the best of it."

They spend the next minutes undressing each other. She prolongs the operation as much as possible with repeated demands for caresses and kisses, often removing his hands from their manipulation of her clothing, and directing them to fondle and stroke recently bared flesh.

Finally every item of clothing lies discarded upon the floor. She wraps one leg around his, and presses his face between her hands. She presses her lips against his. She forces her tongue between his barely-parted lips.

She disengages only when he sweeps her off her feet, and into his arms. She shrieks with laughter as she is carried out onto the enclosed private balcony. The laughter dies when she sees what awaits them there.

A bubbling hot tub that is just large enough to accommodate two in intimate closeness.

He holds her for a moment, her arms around his neck, as she regards the steaming water. Then she offers him another kiss.

This time she can sense that there is no sham or pretense in his ardor. He allows himself to be lowered into the warm water, then helps her to climb in.

In just a moment, the heat and the water begin their metamorphoses.

Each explores the other's disguise. Seeking entry; seeking reality; seeking the eager, genuine flesh beneath the façade.

Chapter 4-7
Love Amid The Ashes

In the night

I don't know if I started to awaken when Jean slipped out from beneath the covers; or whether I never noticed her departure at all, and it was something else that awoke me. I only know that I drifted to wakefulness, and realized that I was alone beneath the silken sheets. I looked around in the darkness, at first confused by my surroundings. Then in a diffuse glow coming through the unfrosted glass above the hot tub, I saw Jean sitting cross-legged on the balcony, gazing upwards.

Softly, I too climbed out from the warm comfort of the bed and joined her.

She didn't acknowledge my presence. She just kept looking upwards. I followed her gaze. Landscape-lighting bathed the lodge building in a soft-white glow. In that ethereal light, I could see that clouds had gathered again after we'd retired. Snowflakes drifted downwards out of the black infinity of sky, appearing as if by magic out of the gloom. Each crystalline flake materializing as a delicate point of light. It would swirl and dance in each errant breeze it encountered on its descent, then finally come to rest on the pane of glass over our heads.

There, the heat still lingering from our tryst in the hot tub rapidly transformed the delicate crystal into a shimmering drop of water that ran, tear-like, down the pane before it ultimately vanished from sight.

I gently rested my hands on her shoulders as I knelt behind her; like her, I was mesmerized by the spectacle. She placed one hand atop mine, and with the other hand, she reached up and tried to brush tears out of her eyes.

"Why are you crying?" I asked, confused.

She gave up trying to conceal the tears that I could hear in her tremulous voice. "I'm afraid."

"Afraid?" I slid my hands down her back, then encircled her waist. She hugged my arms within her own and leaned backwards against me, seemingly trying to lose herself in my embrace. "What is there to be afraid of?"

Still she watched the dance of the snowflakes. "The future."

I nuzzled her neck, drinking in the perfume of her hair. "Are you afraid that this is just a one-night stand? It isn't."

"No. That's what frightens me. Oh, god, PJ, I think I've fallen in love."

We just remained like that for a moment, my arms around her waist, her arms drawing mine tight, drawing herself against me. Then I brushed my lips against the top of her shoulder. The quiet but fervent words seem to come, of their own volition, from somewhere deep within me—

"Fallen in love? Jean, I know I have."

I felt the warmth of her tears as they fell upon my arms, tight within my embrace.

"What will we do?"

"We'll hold each other. And love each other. And we'll make it last forever."

She disengaged herself from my caress, and turned to face me. In the reflected light I could see the crystalline shimmer on her cheeks, so alike to the glistening brilliance on the window above. "Make *what* last forever? A *lie?* We met because of a lie. Every day at work—another lie. Can we live like that? I don't think I can."

"What I feel for you isn't a lie. What we have—I've never felt this way before. This is *real*. Jean, I love you. We can find a way to make it work."

"For how long? A month? A year? The rest of our lives? I've only just met you, and already I know that's what I want—a lifetime with you. I love you. And you love me. Peter loves me. And I want that, like nothing I've ever wanted before."

"Great. So there's no—"

"But every day, we'll have to hide the thing we want most. We'll go to work, and we'll pretend to be something we're not. Maybe for a while we can play at 'Gene loves Pamela.' But that's a game. It's not real. And because of that, it will come between us, this masquerade. After a time, it won't be a game anymore. It'll be . . . a barrier. A hindrance. Because it's *lying*."

I couldn't bear to see the pain on her face, and I gathered her against me again. "Somewhere there's an answer. We'll find it, we'll make this work."

"Will you stop being Pamela? Can you? Can I stop being Gene?"

I just held her and stroked her hair, trying not to acknowledge the sudden uncertainty—

Trying not to feel the fear.

****

The next day, we left for home and a return to the normal routine.

We tried, Jean and I. Or rather, "Gene" and "Pamela."

For a while, it worked. We became fodder for the office gossip mill. Gene brought Pamela flowers. Pamela left silly, sappy cartoons on the net for Gene. For a while, we managed to play at 'Gene loves Pamela' just as Jean had predicted.

And as the weeks turned into months, it became a hindrance. Again, just as Jean had predicted.

I could see "Gene" anytime I wanted. I could touch "him," hold "him." But I was "Pamela," so I had to do it in a soft, feminine way. I had to play my role. I had to live the lie. I couldn't sweep Jean into my arms and just hold her. Feel her soft against me.

After a time, seeing "Gene" only made me frustrated. Angry. Seeing "Gene" only reminded me of what I could not have, till after work and on the weekends. The woman I loved was right beside me, yet completely inaccessible for five-sevenths of my life. And that on a good week!

My work started to suffer. My inspiration had evaporated like those snowflakes on the window over the hot tub. Near the end, the firm probably would have had as much luck giving one of the secretaries an "Etch-a-Sketch" as by depending on me for commercial artwork.

The company's intranet—which had been running so smoothly that I *had* begun to wonder how we'd gotten along without it—started to suffer more and more serious breakdowns.

It was all falling apart.

****

It happened on a Friday.

I came into my studio, dreading another day of work. Dreading another eight hours of playing my role. There was an image on my computer monitor that hadn't been there before. Eagerly, I sat at the screen and studied the picture. Sometimes I got messages or notes from "Gene." Messages that hinted of Jean's authorship as far as was possible.

There on the screen was that little stick-figure, holding the bunch of cartoon daisies.

The caption read; "I love you. I'm sorry. I can't do it anymore."

I sat staring at the screen for the longest time.

Then it all just became a disjointed series of memories—

The computer room where "Gene" kept his office. Still to be found there were the hum of air conditioners, the diffuse white lighting, the flickering monitors—but no Gene.

In the corridors—

My repeated question, "Has Gene been by this morning? Have you seen him today?"

Always the same answer: "No."

On the bus—

I rode the bus toward Jean's apartment in the middle of the morning. I wondered if they'd miss me at work. I wondered if it mattered to me if they had.

Her apartment—My key in the door—

The note on the counter: "Please try to understand. I need to be alone now. I need to think. But always know how much I love you."

It was neither addressed to me, nor signed by her. It didn't need to be.

She was gone.

Chapter 4-8
What We Do For Love

Monday morning

I arrived in my studio at WN&A, as Pamela, for what I'd determined was the last time.

Josh's secretary took the phone message for him. With steel in her voice, she told me in no uncertain terms that he was in a meeting and *wasn't to be disturbed*. (And this time, she by-God meant it!) He'd be down to see me as soon as he was available. I thanked her and hung up.

I pulled out my letter of resignation and reread it one more time.

Jean had asked me, "Could you stop being Pamela?" I'd thought about that all weekend. Finally, sometime Sunday afternoon, I'd realized that if it was a choice between Pamela and Jean, then there really was no choice at all.

If that meant I couldn't be an artist anymore, then so be it. To have Jean, I'd happily stock shelves at the local discount store. Or pump gas. Or wait tables in the restaurant down the street.

Just before nine o'clock, Josh strolled through my office door and seated himself in his familiar spot on the edge of my desk.

"You wanted to see me, Ms. Wright?"

I handed him my resignation in silence.

He took it, glanced once at his wristwatch, then quickly skimmed the page. I didn't really know what reaction I'd get from him. I confess I was shocked when he simply nodded once, and handed the letter back to me.

"I wondered how long it would take for you to finally get around to this."

"That's it? You don't care that I'm quitting?"

"Of course I care. You're a damn good commercial artist, and the firm will hate to lose you. But far more than that, you're my brother and I hate to see you throw away a good job. But as your brother, I'm also glad you're finally willing to stop this charade."

I shook my head and just stared at him. "It was your idea in the first place, yet you've never really approved of it."

He wouldn't meet my gaze. "No. I never have. In the beginning I saw it how you once described it: 'A desperate response to a desperate situation.' But when the desperation was gone, and still you kept up the act? No, I never approved of that."

"What do you mean, 'kept up the act'? What choice *was* there? What choice *is* there?"

At last he looked up and met my eyes. "PJ, I'm the managing partner now. I run this firm. I can hire whomever I want. If I want to hire my brother, who's to say I can't?"

I think I actually smiled, though I'm sure it was a rueful smile. "And nobody will think it odd that 'PJ' for 'Pamela Jane' walks out the door, and 'PJ' for 'Peter James' walks in? You don't think that one or two people might think that's one hell of a coincidence?"

Josh just shrugged and looked at his watch again.

Then he said, "So? It's a coincidence. An incredible one. People might even wonder if Peter is Pamela or Pamela was Peter all along. But considering how well you've pulled off the deception, I doubt that supposition will seem any less unlikely than the coincidence. And if they do wonder? Let them. I won't tell them the truth if you don't. And after a year or two, folks may still wonder occasionally. But what difference will it make?"

We just stared at each other for what seemed like an hour or two.

Josh was right.

I didn't need to be Pamela anymore. It would be strange for a while. I'd get odd looks. Conversations would die when I walked up to the water cooler. For a while, it would be uncomfortable.

For a while.

But no more uncomfortable than I was now.

Josh broke the spell by looking at his watch *again.*

(Needless to say, I felt angry that he had something he considered more important than this conversation.)

Josh stood to leave. "Well, think about it. You've got time to decide."

He started to go, but I stopped him in the door.

"You're right, Josh. There's really nothing to think about. My resignation as Pamela stands. You'll be getting Peter's résumé this afternoon."

He just nodded, and smiled over his shoulder at me. "I think we can find a place for him in the firm."

I returned my brother's smile. "People are still going to think it one hell of a coincidence, though. You've got to admit."

His smile softened.

If ever I've wondered if my brother loves me, that smile put the doubt to rest.

He said, "So what? There are lots of strange coincidences in the world."

Another glance at his stupid watch!

Then he stepped aside, and I understood what it was he had been timing so carefully. With a smile, Josh said, "Hell, I just got out of a meeting with the new Computer Manager. Would you believe, I've just replaced one 'Gene' with another one down in Computer Maintenance?"

Jean was standing there, *had been* standing there, hidden behind Josh. Now she was holding a tool kit in one hand, and a bunch of cartoonish daisies—real ones this time—in her other hand.

****

And that's my story.

I suppose this sounds a little final. It shouldn't. I'm not at an ending. Quite the opposite. These last few months have been very much about new beginnings.

Jean and I, some things are just meant to be.

It's been three days now since Jean abandoned her former guise and assumed another. I think this one will last. Like "Gene" before her, Jean Cavanaugh is no more.

For three days now, she's been Mrs. Jean Wright.

We're on our honeymoon, sharing a certain Bridal Suite in a certain Idaho resort community. We came by our occupancy honestly this time.

She's funny, and smart, and beautiful. A woman I've always dreamed of—recognized for the first time just down the hall, on a magical night not even one year ago.

We share secrets. And fantasies. And dreams. She's my soul mate, my partner, and my best friend.

I think I love her more with each passing day.

And we have something that very few couples have—understanding.

****

And what of Pamela, you ask?

As I say, Jean and I have a unique understanding of each other.

So, if you gentlemen are ever in a bar some night, and you spot a gorgeous blonde with china-blue eyes, make sure you find out her name before you get too serious with her.

If she tells you her name is "PJ," it's probably best to move on. For though she's hot and sexy; though she'll flirt with you shamelessly; though she'll tease you, and tempt you, and make you think that it's all there for you—don't believe her. It's just a game. You'll never get her home.

You see, she's not really interested in you. She's just killing a few minutes, waiting for her *real* lover to arrive.

She's just waiting for Mr. Wright.

PART 5
Femme Fatale

Chapter 5-1
Storm Warning

In the L.A. apartment of Peter and Jean Wright

I was on my way back to the sofa, and the Sci-Fi Network's Japanese Anime festival, after a quick trip to the fridge for a refill on my glass of diet Coke.

That meant I was passing right by the extension phone when it started ringing. Jean was up to her elbows in the sink, prewashing the baking dish that I'd used to make tonight's casserole. (We traded off each night; one of us cooked, the other one did the dishes.) So I knew that she'd have to dry her hands to answer the phone.

"I'll get it, hon," I said as I lifted the receiver. "Wright residence."

There was a short pause, then a male voice sounded in my ear: "Good evening, may I please speak to PJ?"

It had been so long that I'd been living 24/7 as Peter James (almost six months now), I didn't even think to answer any other way than "This is he."

There was another pause. "No, I'm looking for Pamela. Pamela Wright. Do I have a wrong number?"

I gave the excuse that my brother Josh, with his usually inventive sneakiness, had devised to ease my transition from Pamela to Peter at WN&A: "No, this is the right number. I'm Pamela's twin brother Peter. And I'm sorry, but Pamela's out right now. May I take a message for her?"

The male's voice was more assured now; apparently he was buying my story. "Yes, please ask her to call Alan Armour. My number is—" The phone number that he gave had a prefix I recognized to be in swank Century City.

I jotted the phone number down. "Got it. May I tell her what this is in reference to?"

"Tell her I have a business matter to discuss with her. One she'll find interesting. Do you know when she'll return my call?"

I tapped the pencil I'd used to take down the number on the pad of paper. "No, I'm sorry. I really don't."

"This is rather important. If she could return my call as soon as possible—?"

"I'll see that she gets the message the moment I see her."

"Thank you."

And he hung up.

Jean was standing in the archway that separated the kitchen from the dining nook, drying her hands on a towel. "What was that all about?"

Holding the now-silent phone in my hand, I turned to her. "I have no idea."

****

Josh was pacing.

Add to that, the fact that he'd just returned from wherever that extended business trip had taken him, and we all knew: Something was up.

And it wasn't good.

The rest of us senior staff just sat at the conference table and waited for "El Presidente" to get to the matter at hand. Finally he sighed, and rested his fists on the head of the long, polished table.

"We've got trouble, folks."

Department head Joe Norway was the first to respond: "What's the problem, boss?"

Josh glanced up from his study of the grain of the table. "We lost the Adagio Motors Contract. They won't be renewing this fall."

That bombshell produced a worried frown on the rest of our faces, to mirror Josh's own frown. Though the loss of that account hardly spelled the doom of our firm, Adagio had been a major client. We'd feel their loss.

I piped up with, "Who'd we lose out to?"

Josh's face now showed a touch of anger to go with his concern. "AdCon. Again."

Now there were worried mutters to go with the worried expressions. This was the second major client we'd lost to that upstart agency that had opened only two months ago.

Josh brought the meeting to a close with, "I want to hear from all of you about possible cutbacks in each of the departments."

He quickly waved a hand, to cut off the protests that, from the sudden intake of breath from all the assembled throats, clearly was about to burst out. "I'm not saying we're there yet. Nor am I saying that we'll ever get there. I just think we need to start considering options, if worse comes to worse."

And on that cheerful note, Josh dismissed us.

Chapter 5-2
Storm Watch

I think, of all the things that might have given me away—I mean, might have tipped off anyone at WN&A that I, Peter, was the same person who used to go by the moniker *Pamela*—it would be my constant inability to make appointments to speak with my (still-unacknowledged) half-brother Josh.

I just strode past Josh's blonde receptionist, heading for his inner office door.

"Mr. Wright, you can't—Wait a—*Hey!*"

But the closing of Josh's office door cut off the remainder of her objection.

I perched on the corner of my brother's desk, and watched him stare out the window with a troubled frown on his face. After a while, he sighed. I guessed that this was all the recognition I was going to get, so I spoke first.

"How bad is it, really?"

"It's not good." He finally swung around in his high-backed chair and faced me. "Oh, it's not like losing those accounts is gonna sink us. But—"

I nodded. "*But*, how many more clients are we gonna lose?"

A glum nod was my reply.

It just wasn't like my brother to behave this way. He had always been such a never-say-die go-getter. But perhaps carrying around the weight of responsibility, for all the people who were depending on WN&A for their livelihood, was starting to wear him down.

I tried to perk him up. "Come on, bro. We've been in worse scrapes than this. So, what's the plan? How do we turn this around?"

But halfway through my little pep talk, he'd slowly spun his chair back to the window. His reply was a distracted, "I don't know, PJ. I really don't know."

****

I thought things couldn't have gotten any worse as I walked out of Josh's office. (As his receptionist's glare burned a hole between my shoulder blades.) Not get worse? Little did I know—

It's times like this that a man needs someone to turn to. Someone to listen to his problems with a sympathetic ear, and to reassure him that everything's going to be all right.

Someone like a wife.

Fortunately for me, I'd picked up one of those oh-so-useful items (a wife, that is) six months ago, so I knew just who to call once I got back to my office. I didn't even need to dial an outside line. I thought that all I needed to do to speak to my darling Jean was to punch in 7128 on my intercom line, and my call would float down two floors to the Computer Center where my mate kept her offices.

The phone on her desk rang. And rang. And rang.

On the seventh ring, a rather out-of-breath male voice answered, "Computer Center, Barry here."

My wife's junior assistant; Barry Snyder. "Hey, Barry. It's PJ. Is my lovely wife around, or is she out on a trouble call?"

"Oh, um, Mr. Wright. Uh, Mrs. Wright isn't here right now."

"I kinda gathered that, Barry. Where is she? I need to talk to her."

"Uh, she's—she's not here right now, Mr. Wright."

"I understand that. I'm asking—"

Suddenly, a little imp of fear went skating down my back. "Barry, what's going on? Where's Jean?"

"She, um—"

"Where's my wife?"

"I—I'm not supposed to tell you. She left a couple of hours ago."

"Where'd she go?"

"She—"

"Barry!"

"The doctor's office. I wasn't supposed to—"

I didn't hear the rest. I'd already punched down on the "hang up" buttons, and was dialing my family doctor's number.

****

Though there'd been benefits to being Pamela, I have to admit that getting around had always been a pain. I mean, a modern Los Angelino without a car (because "she" couldn't ever figure out a way to get a driver's license) was a real square peg in L.A. society's round hole.

Now that Pamela had become Peter, it was a problem I no longer had to deal with. Today I was very thankful for the speed and maneuverability of my red Italian sports car as I weaved my way through traffic, heading back home from the office.

Our family physician had refused to say anything to me, and had deflected all my increasingly-anxious requests for information with the repeated assertion that it was a matter I'd simply have to take up with Jean.

I admit, by the end of the call (before he hung up on me), I was getting—dammit, I had good reason! Jean was my wife, I had a right to know!

But he hadn't seen it that way. He'd just said that Jean had left the office an hour ago, mentioning that she was heading home.

So without so much as a note to Carl, my secretary, I'd jumped into my car to challenge the mid-morning rush of L.A.'s freeway system. All the way home, part of my mind had been conjuring up more and more horrifying possibilities; as the other part, the rational part, kept arguing that I was surely overreacting.

Until I remembered the day before yesterday, when Jean had been so pale when she got up. And had been so listless and lifeless, for the rest of the day. How she'd just dismissed it as a bad night with too little sleep. And I'd believed her, because Jean and I never kept secrets from each other.

Until now?

But thinking about it, I realized that she'd been quiet and withdrawn since then. And yesterday morning, had her eyes been puffy and red? Had she been crying in the night? Was I just imagining things? Was I reading too much into common, meaningless stuff?

You can bet that by the time that I got to the front door of our apartment, it took a second of trying before my shaking hands managed to get the key into the lock.

She wasn't downstairs. A quick tour convinced me of that.

I found her sitting on the edge of our bed, staring out the window of our upstairs bedroom with an expression that was like Josh's distant, distracted frown of this morning. Hearing me arrive at the door, she turned to me, a little smile finally tugging at the corners of her mouth.

I moved quickly to her. "Jean?"

"Hey, babe."

"What's going on? I just called the doctor, but he wouldn't—"

By now, I was sitting on the bed beside her, her hand that had been resting on her lap, now clasped in mine. I said, "Jean, please, tell me. Are you all right?"

Deep-brown eyes searched mine. With her free hand, she stroked my cheek. It was like those old movies where they shoot the actress's close-up through cheesecloth, to give her features a soft, glowing appearance.

"I'm all right, PJ. Actually, I'm *very* all right—"

Then her smile bloomed, and I knew even before she said—

"—I'm also very pregnant."

****

I did all the husband-things that first-time expectant fathers are supposed to do.

Of course we kissed, and I held her, and she held me. She asked me if I was happy; and then immediately abandoned the question, because my grin was so big and goofy that I don't think I could have spoken to save my life. I got another kiss for that.

I finally found enough of my voice to ask if she needed me to bring her anything. If she needed to lie down, or—

That got me my first gentle lecture about how she really and truly was just fine. That she didn't need to be pampered or treated like spun glass. *Yet.* (But the time was coming when she expected to be cranky, and helpless, and waited-on hand-and-foot, so don't waste it now. All this was spoken with her devilish grin.)

But for now, knowing that I was as happy as she was, what she really wanted to do was to celebrate. The time was coming when a night on the town would probably be more trouble than it was worth, so we might as well make the most of the present opportunity.

We went out dining and dancing. Most of the night is kind of a blur; I just couldn't concentrate on any one thing for very long.

I remember Jean's face, that glow still making it so feminine and radiant, smiling at me over the rim of her glass of nonalcoholic champagne. (It's not a cliché, pregnant women really do have a "glow" about them. Well, maybe one that only their husbands can see.)

I remember a slow dance. (I absolutely refused to let her "boogie." That got me another mini-lecture, but this time I held firm.) I recall Jean's soft curves pressed against me as I held her, and realized: *I'm holding the two most important people in the world in my arms.* Corny, but what are you gonna do?

I put her to bed at about ten. I doubt it had anything to do with the pregnancy. It had just been a very busy day for my very lovely wife, and she was asleep almost as soon as her head hit the pillow. I curled up beside her, "spooned" against her, with my chest to her back. She gave me a contented little murmur, snuggled a bit closer against me— and was soon softly, gently snoring.

I lay there in the darkness for a long time, just feeling her beside me and listening to her sleep.

I couldn't sleep. My mind still wouldn't focus on anything; too many thoughts, circulating too fast.

After a while, I very carefully slid back out of bed. Jean gave a sleepy little snort, a little moan—and then hugged tighter into the curled-up huddle that she usually slept in. In a moment, she was again peacefully dreaming.

I went downstairs and got myself a cup of tea. Then I padded back upstairs to my studio. Every man has someplace in his home that's uniquely his. His sanctum sanctorum. My studio is mine.

I gazed out the window for a while. I sipped my tea. I tried to marshal my thoughts, because now I was not only a husband, I was going to be a father; and that was more responsibility than I've ever had in my life.

After a while, I started to sketch with charcoal on a big tablet that I had set out on my easel. I wasn't really even concentrating on what I was doing.

It was kind of the artist's equivalent of doodling on a scratch pad. I lost track of time. I don't know, maybe it was a "waking dream," the kind of thing where the body's awake, but the mind has gone . . . somewhere else.

Anyway, the next thing I knew, the first pastel glow of morning was brightening the edge of the sky; and there, gazing back at me from my easel was Jean. Turned in three-quarter profile. Her dark eyes shining at me over her shoulder. Her smile just starting to bloom, and the words just starting to form on her lips.

On the day I'd married Jean, I'd been truly, completely happy. And now it was again Jean who gave me a day of perfect happiness.

****

Word about Jean's pregnancy spread like wildfire down at WN&A.

I couldn't stick my nose out of my office without being swarmed by well-wishers. Jean was getting the same thing.

That's all right. Maybe our troubled world would be a better place if we could all be so filled with the wonder of life all the time.

Even Josh's funk dissipated. For a while. I guess finding out that you're an "expectant uncle" is something of a thrill too. (But I knew that one of these days, I'd have to find a mate for my brother. This feeling of—hell, "immortality" and fulfillment—was something that Josh just had to have for himself.)

Things settled down after a couple of days, and the office returned to its usual bustle.

Then the dark clouds of our troubles with our new competitor started to roll in again.

****

Josh had left for another week of meetings somewhere. He was starting to spend more time out on the road than he was in the office.

Once he returned, he called another staff meeting, and informed us that AdCon was wooing several more of our biggest accounts. Most worrisome of all: a rumor that AdCon had approached our flagship client, The Sprague Group. Fortunately, all our clients decided to stay with WN&A.

For now.

We were tasked with redoubling our efforts to make sure that our customers stayed happy with our work. We'd begun a brainstorming session about the best way to mount a counterattack against AdCon when somebody asked, "What do we know about these guys? Starting with, who are they, anyway?"

Josh leaned back in his swivel throne at the head of the table and steepled his index fingers. "From what I've been able to learn: AdCon's core people are a bunch of mavericks from several East Coast agencies. I guess there was some kind of pogrom back there, and the most dangerous young Turks got handed their golden parachutes."

Beth DiAngelo asked, "What makes someone in this business be 'dangerous'?"

Josh said, "The guys who are the most aggressive, hardest chargers. The kind that make 'The Establishment' nervous. Apparently a bunch of them got together, pooled their severance pay, and used it to start up AdCon."

Beth sighed, "Just our luck they choose to start up in our fine city."

Josh shrugged. "Well, they're here, and it doesn't look like they're leaving. So, the question becomes: What do we do about it?"

I stuck my oar in: "What kind of talent do they have? Artistic, I mean. Let's not be unduly modest here, we've got some impressive artists, both writers and graphics. Can we outperform them there? Beat them by the relative quality of product?"

Again, Josh shrugged and glanced away. "I don't know. Not much on the grapevine about that. But that's one to look into. I know that, at the moment, it's business-savvy that's their strong suit. There's no question that they have some genuine talent there."

Joe Norway asked, "Who's their head man? Who's driving the business end?"

Josh replied, "Some guy named Armour—Alan Armour if I've got the intel correct."

Chapter 5-3
Storm Surge

That afternoon, at home

The pleasant female voice on the phone said, "One moment, Ms. Wright, and I'll connect you."

I stood there, loosening my tie and listening to on-hold Muzak. I probably should have taken the tie off while I was waiting for the voice-spray to kick in. The last time I'd been Pamela was a little over a year ago; so I'd forgotten that the chemical didn't immediately change my voice from baritone to contralto—

I heard, "This is Alan Armour."

"Mr. Armour, good afternoon. Pamela Wright returning your call."

"Ah, Ms. Wright, thank you for that. Did your brother tell you what I was calling about?"

"He mentioned that you had some kind of business offer. I should say, I'm really not looking for any investment opportunities or—"

A warm, masculine chuckle, then: "Oh, nothing like that. I represent an advertising agency that's just recently moved into the area. Your impressive reputation as a graphic artist is known to us, and we'd be interested in offering you a position."

I let that thought hang for a moment, pretending to recover from such a "surprising, out-of-the-blue" offer. "Uh, goodness, I—good heavens—"

More masculine charm. "I realize that this is quite unexpected. I'm sure you'd have a hundred questions that we'd need to answer, before you could even begin to reply.

Would it be possible for us to sit down some time, for lunch perhaps, and discuss this?"

"I—of course we can. Surely. Yes."

"Excellent! How about day after tomorrow, two o'clock at The Cedars?"

"That's fine. I'll be there."

"Wonderful! I look forward to meeting you then."

Again I stared at the now-silent phone in my hand. In a little bit of déjà vu from the last time I'd been in this pose, at that moment the key turned in the lock, and Jean strolled in. I hung up the phone as she set her purse on the counter. We met in the middle of the room, and she wrapped her arms around my neck.

"Hello, my darling husband."

I gave her a little peck on the cheek. "Hello, my beautiful wife."

I don't know which of us was the more surprised at how incongruous that greeting sounded when spoken in a light contralto.

Jean pushed me away at arm's length, and regarded me with a puzzled, intrigued grin. "Hm, I remember that voice from somewhere, but I can't seem to place the face." Then she chuckled, "What the hell are you up to?"

"Well, you see—"

There was a playful little threat in her tone. "PJ?"

"It's, um—here, let's sit down for a second."

I led her over to the couch and she sat down next to me, her legs curled under her with that lithe, feline grace that I find so arousing.

I tried to figure out a way to broach the subject of what it was that Josh and I had determined to do. But I was so embarrassed, and that made me tongue-tied.

I guess Jean misread my frown for embarrassment of a different kind, because before I could begin to explain, she was running a long, slender finger down my arm. "It *has* been a while since we played, hasn't it? Yeah. And in a while, we won't have the chance for a while so—"

Then she was cuddling up closer, and nuzzling my neck; and in a sultry purr, whispering, "But how about if we talk dirty a little before we slip into some*one* more exciting? You know it gets my motor running when Pamela—"

"Whoa, girl!" I gently pressed myself away from her, with hands on her shoulders, as she looked at me with renewed puzzlement. "This isn't play. Believe it or not, this is serious."

"Serious, how?"

"Do you remember, last week? When I got that phone call? The one for Pamela that we couldn't figure out?"

Jean nodded.

I continued, "It turns out it was from Alan Armour!"

Jean didn't look horrified, so I had to explain: "He's the head of AdCon! That new agency that—"

But Jean's now-thoughtful expression indicated she had realized the significance of the phone call. "What the heck does he want with Pamela?"

Before I could reply, *thoughtful* turned to *oh-ho*. "AdCon wants to hire Pamela! So that's why—"

I nodded. "Yeah. See, once I figured it out, I took what I knew to Josh. He thinks—"

"He wants you to take the job. He wants somebody inside AdCon."

I braced myself for the flood of protest. "Exactly."

But the flood didn't come. Instead, Jean just nodded. "Fine. When do you start? I mean, when do you have your first meet with this Armour guy?"

Needless to say; I was stunned. I decided Jean couldn't have understood this correctly, because she was taking it all so casually. "I—Lunch, Friday afternoon."

Again, Jean only nodded. "So, for how long is this going to go on? Any ideas?"

"No. I'm not even sure what it is that I'm going to— Hon, you *do* understand what we're talking about here? I pretending to be Pamela so I can get into AdCon, and"—I shrugged, peering closely into my mate's eyes.

"I get the picture. What can I do to help?"

" 'Help'? Jean, I'm going to be *spying* on somebody! Using Pamela to *steal* secrets and—oh hell, I don't know what all."

Jean lifted her chin. "I see. And you were expecting some kind of outrage from me. I'm supposed to tell you this is all terrible and amoral, after which I try to talk you out of it, correct?"

Again I could only shrug in my confusion.

She took my hands in hers, and her voice became very quiet and serious. "Okay. Let's talk about this. I got the 'Black Monday Memo' day before yesterday."

(The 'Black Monday Memo' was what we were calling the printed result of our study of just where and how WN&A could cut back, if worse came to worse in our financial situation.)

Jean continued, "Data Systems has a 50 percent rollback goal. You know what that means? There's only Barry and me down there. He saw the memo too, PJ. He took it like a real trooper. Didn't whine or complain or anything. Oh hon, he just smiled and shrugged, and went back to work. I saw him a few hours later in the lunchroom. He'd fished the Help Wanted section of that day's paper out of the garbage can, and he was looking through it. He tried to hide it when he saw me. I'm *not* going to fire him, PJ. Not if I can help it. Understand?"

"But hon, I mean—"

Jean's tone got a little more heated. "Okay. If Barry's situation isn't enough for your conscience, how about this one? WN&A got along for quite a while without an intranet. I'm sure that if the first job cuts aren't enough to feed the bulldog, Data Systems is going to get a *one hundred percent* axe. Remember what it took for me to get that job in the first place? Think it's going to be easier or harder for me to land the next one? And let's not forget, the next time 'Gene' is out pounding the pavement, he might be a lot more 'portly' than he was the first time he started answering Help Wanted ads."

The baby! I haven't even thought of that! I haven't even thought of what an additional burden the baby will be on both our paychecks—if there are even two paychecks when the baby arrives. And what about all the hospital bills?

Oh sure, Jean's health plan would cover the bulk of the costs—so long as she still worked for WN&A.

She could read me well enough to tell that I was considering all the implications that her fears had raised, so she didn't push me further.

I thought hard. Then I realized I had only one real choice—though I was still very uncomfortable with my own nagging fears and doubts.

I gave her hands a squeeze, and gazed into her eyes. "Returning to your original question: I don't know. How can you help?"

Strangely, in the entire conversation, neither Jean nor I wondered why Armour had never tried to recruit Peter, only Pamela. But we *should* have wondered—and worried.

Chapter 5-4
Into The Wind

Tuesday afternoon, The Cedars restaurant

It had been a while since I'd worn high heels. Only six months, actually, but still—

Oh, I remembered how to walk in them—how to balance in them so I didn't turn an ankle with every other step. I remembered how to walk like a woman:

Shoulders erect. Take smaller steps. Put each foot on an imaginary line that ran straight out in front of you. Swing your hips a bit. *But* not exaggerated, not slinky, just a little more rolling than came naturally for the male who I really was. Just different enough that I had to remember to do it, rather than not thinking about it at all.

The shifting weight of an unrestrained pair of breasts, beneath silk blouse, beneath linen jacket, was sufficient reminder to keep me within my role. Jean had picked this outfit for me. She thought that Pamela should be a bit more confident, a bit more assertive if she was going to play power games with "the boys." So—no bra today, only a lacy little camisole. Beneath which, Pam's luscious bosoms bounced with each step.

But Jean had kept everything classy. The stylish blazer that I wore, concealed most of the jiggle, leaving only an enticing hint of brazen femininity with each subtle shift of my jacket.

I'd walked through the door a little after two o'clock, enough time to let Armour arrive before me, so I could make a grand entrance. The maitre d', once he'd discovered my name, informed me that "my party was waiting," and he led me through the afternoon chatter of a popular restaurant to an intimate little table near one of the windows.

An expensively and tastefully dressed, vaguely Latino-looking fellow rose when he realized that the maitre d' was bringing me to him. So this was the boogeyman who had Josh (and all the rest of us, for that matter) running scared?

He was neither handsome nor unattractive. *Ordinary* would be a good word. He had curly, jet-black hair worn stylishly short. His dark (almost black) eyes were just slightly magnified by steel-rimmed glasses. Other than that, a well-tanned, unremarkably-featured face and trim figure completed the individual.

"Ms. Wright?"

I nodded, and offered a polite smile and a softly feminine handshake. "Mr. Armour?"

I got a polite smile, a gentle clasp of my hand, and a nod in return. "Thank you for coming. Please join me."

I almost blew it. I almost reached for my chair, before Armour could step behind me and pull it out. *Manners, Pamela, manners. Allow a gentleman to seat you.* I perched, very lightly, on the front edge of the chair, bearing as much of my weight on my feet as possible. More squatting than sitting. That was the rule: you had to let the man show how much of a gentleman he was, by seating you. You, in turn, had to make the chair weightless—very easy for him to then slide forward a bit.

With an unconsciously resurfacing habit, I tucked a lock of hair behind my ear; and smiled at Armour, once he had reclaimed his own seat. I said, "I wouldn't have missed this meeting for the world. If for no other reason than to satisfy my curiosity."

****

Lunch was polite and pointless, and full of inconsequential chat about nothing in particular.

We'd finished a pretty good meal and a nice cup of coffee when Armour glanced at his watch, then said what I'd wondered if I was going to hear.

"I have some material you might be interested in, upstairs in my room. Do you have a few more minutes you could lend me?"

I folded my napkin on the table, and favored him with Pamela's patented sultry smile. "Why, of course."

In an almost perfect echo of the word and tone that I'd heard once before, after accepting an invitation up to a different high-powered executive's hotel room, Armour fixed me with a meaningful smile and purred, "Excellent."

****

It's odd sometimes, how life seems to move in great, curving circles. How we seem to always be returning to some place, some situation, that we've visited before. Maybe it's in how we deal with these constant "returns" that gives us clues to how much we've grown. Perhaps we arrive at some predicament, then we say to ourselves, *I remember this. Maybe this time, I can do a little better than when I was in this scrape last time.*

Or maybe we just keep plodding in circles, for no particular purpose.

Armour had a suite (sitting room, kitchenette, bedroom) up on the hotel's ninth floor. Yes, I knew Armour had some ulterior motive for this invitation—come on, he lived here in L.A., so why get a hotel room unless he wanted some place private to take Pamela once he had her in his clutches? But it wasn't until he opened the door for me, and then stood aside, that the memories of another very similar situation hit me in a tidal wave.

Kevin Sprague and my first real initiation into The Game.

But this time I was older and wiser in the contest, and knew how to give as good as I got.

Armour followed me in, and motioned me to a large couch that was set against one wall. "Please make yourself comfortable. Can I get you something? I know it's a little early in the day, but—"

I faced him with a smile, as I lowered myself to the waiting cushions of the couch. I made no attempt to modestly tuck my skirt beneath me. I'd be willing to bet that from where he was standing, Armour was getting a wonderfully provocative flash of the lacy hem of my slip, which was just visible beneath the "accidentally" immodest disarray of my dress.

For good measure, I crossed my legs without bothering to hike the hem down. Now Armour probably could see all the way up Pamela's sleek thigh, to what I call "the warning track": that narrow, slightly more opaque band of material that circles a woman's leg just below where the thicker, darker hem of her stocking begins. (Again, it was Jean's idea for me to be wearing garter belt and stockings today, instead of pantyhose. As with the braless camisole, these were items that would have made Jean feel more powerfully feminine, sensual, and bold if she'd been wearing them; so she'd included them in my ensemble. Luckily for me, the teasing allure of those stockings now gave me another weapon for my seductress's arsenal.)

I said in contralto voice, "Oh, I think the sun is probably below the yardarm, somewhere in the world. Some sherry would be lovely if you have it."

It was not much more than the flick of his eyes, but I caught it.

There is something about the opportunity to peek up a woman's skirt that men just can't resist. (Lord knows, I sure can't, anyway.) With just the hint of a smile, that could very easily be read as blithe ignorance of Armour's sudden interest—or as a sly acknowledgement that we both knew just exactly what I was doing—I primly slid the hem of my skirt down over my knees, tucking the material tightly beneath my thighs in the process.

That was the "freebie," Armour. If you want another peek, you're gonna have to work for it.

Let the seduction begin. May the best man win.

With no loss of urbane poise, Armour gazed into my eyes and nodded. "I have a pretty good dry white wine I can offer. A Riesling. Will that do?"

Again I tucked a stray lock of Pamela's blonde mane behind my left ear, and continued to smile. "That would do nicely. Yes."

In a moment, he was offering me a wineglass, which I accepted. Then, to my surprise, he took his own glass of— well, maybe it was rum and Coke—Coke for certain, dark and fizzy and lots of ice—and sat down across from me in one of the room's chairs.

Was it possible that I'd misread the situation? Were we only going to discuss business?

Boy, was this the story of my life or what? The last time that I'd been in this situation, I'd have given anything if Kevin Sprague had just sat in a chair across from me and talked shop. Of course, that hadn't happened. This time, when it would have been so helpful if Armour made a grab for me so I could start spinning my own little webs, he just plopped down in his seat and started sipping his drink.

When it became apparent that Armour was perfectly content to silently sit there, I decided that I'd better get the *real* discussion started. I said, "Perhaps we should get down to business?"

He nodded, setting his glass aside. "Indeed. I suppose I could bore you with the details of all the work benefits we're prepared to offer you, but let's simplify this and just assume for the moment that AdCon is willing to make your decision an easy one. I promise, without hesitation, that you'll do better with us than you're doing now with WN&A."

Obviously he was confused about "Pamela's" employment history. But I needed to be tactful, so I said meekly, "Mr. Armour? There seems to be some confusion. I left WN&A just a little over six months ago. I don't—"

He waved a hand and smiled. "Please, enough formality. All of the senior staff at AdCon is on a first-name basis. So, call me Alan. And I'll call you PJ—"

"—unless you prefer Peter."

Chapter 5-5
Rip Tide

I was dressed like Pamela, I looked like Pamela, but Armour had just called me *Peter*.

I don't think my jaw dropped. I think—I hope—my expression remained neutral. "Peter?" I repeated.

I tried an airy little chuckle; it came off as a nervous giggle. "Peter is my brother."

Armour stared into my eyes for a moment longer, that urbane smile still playing around his lips. "Going to whip that dead horse all the way to the finish line? As you wish."

Before I could reply, Armour had turned to a slender briefcase that was sitting on the floor beside his chair. From it, he withdrew a file folder, which he opened in his lap.

He read aloud, "Peter James Wright. Born April 3, 1975. Mother: Julia. Father: Michael. Parents separated in August of 1981. Julia remarried to Aaron Arjer in June of 1983. Peter apparently decided to retain his father's surname, because that's the name that appears on his diploma from Juilliard."

He glanced at me over the top of his glasses. "There is no mention anywhere of a twin sister named Pamela. No birth records. No academic records. Nothing. It seems that she just sprang into existence a little over two years ago, when she showed up on WN&A's doorstep and immediately landed a very prestigious position in her stepbrother's firm—"

"Mister Armour—"

"I am informed WN&A handles the account of a company named NuGen—"

Oh, god!

"—which manufactures a very intriguing little item called a"—he flipped through the folder—"transgender appliance. Informally, it's called a 'bodysuit.' "

How ironic: I'd become so adept at being Pamela—it had become so much second nature to me—that long ago, I'd stopped worrying about being "read," or having to pass any kind of suspicious scrutiny. I used to have so many contingency plans for how I'd handle the situation, if it ever arose.

But Pamela had been such a foolproof disguise, and I'd become so comfortable playing her, I'd become complacent. I'd forgotten all of my planned schemes and defenses.

Not that any of them would have worked in this situation.

Armour had me. Cold. I could only sit there, feeling like a dozen different kinds of fool.

A guy in a plastic suit, and lady's underwear.

Surprisingly, Armour's voice held neither condemnation nor triumph. He just continued in that same urbane tone: "Did you think that once we'd become interested in hiring a former member of the WN&A staff, we wouldn't check, very deeply, into her background?"

I couldn't look him in the eye anymore. "I. . ."

No words suggested themselves. Now, there was no artifice at all in the way I hugged my skirt against my knees, trying desperately to conceal as much of what was beneath that material as possible.

Quietly I asked, "How did you get those records?"

Armour ignored my question. "I'm curious: Why the deception? If it's too personal, you don't need to—"

"No! It's nothing like that! It—Josh wasn't the managing partner then. He wasn't a partner at all. That happened several days after I was hired. I—"

Armour was nodding his comprehension. "So it *was* an attempt to take advantage of some hiring quota, wasn't it?"

I could only nod, my eyes once again fixed on those beautiful, feminine and horribly *fake* fingernails that were nervously plucking at the hem of my skirt.

Armour shrugged, and gave me more of that knowing little smile. "It's not important, really. I like to think I'm cosmopolitan enough that it wouldn't have bothered me if it was a matter of *personal preference,* and not just some kind of necessity."

I was so embarrassed at this point that it came out as a snarl. "Okay, fine, you've had your little laugh. Have I made enough of a fool of myself that we can call it 'good,' and I can leave?"

He cocked his head. "Do you think that was my only purpose? That my sole intent was to call you up here just for the chance to embarrass you? Peter, I assure you: My offer of employment is genuine. We are very eager to have you working for us. Of course, it would be Peter we want to hire, not Pamela."

I started to stand. "Look, let's just—I'm not leaving WN&A. It's my brother's company, and—"

Armour waved me back to my seat. "Don't be too hasty, Peter. *Is* it Peter? I admit, under the circumstances, I'd be more comfortable calling you PJ. It's just too incongruous to address such a beautiful woman by a male name."

"If you know my real name, call me Peter," I said sullenly.

Armour shrugged. "The technology of your bodysuit, it's really quite remarkable. I confess, the illusion has been a constant distraction since you walked into the restaurant. I have to keep reminding myself that I'm dealing with another man. Especially since you play the woman's role so well. Wow, that trick you just did with your skirt—"

He chuckled, and playfully wagged his finger at me—

And I wanted to just curl up into a ball and die.

Returning to that quiet, businesslike tone, he continued. "In any event, I urge you to take some time and carefully consider my offer, before you make any decision. Your loyalty to your brother is both understandable and admirable. But loyalty can be carried to misguided extremes. Be sure that you don't throw any chance at a career away, solely for blind filial devotion."

I managed to muster enough audacity to make my reply sound—well, better than a whimper. "How can loyalty to one's brother be misplaced? Is business really that much more important than family to you?"

Armour leaned back and crossed his legs. "Perhaps I should rephrase. I don't urge you to abandon Josh. But the time is soon coming when your brother won't have a company for you to be loyal to. At that point, it would be sad indeed if you'd burned all your bridges with AdCon. Besides, if I have my way, your brother will eventually see the handwriting on the wall, and he'll become a valuable addition to AdCon's executive staff as well. And then your refusing me would truly—"

This bragging was getting on my nerves. A feminine voice is superior to a male's for some things, particularly scorn. "Don't you think you're counting chickens a bit early? I grant, you're giving us a run for our money, but you're a long, *long* way from burying us. Or hadn't you heard that five of our largest accounts decided to stay with us, rather than falling for you?"

Armour cocked his head and stared at me in such a challenging manner that I couldn't maintain eye contact. "Yes. They've decided to stay with you. *For now.* I wonder though, what will happen when word of some of WN&A's business practices comes to light?"

That jerked my head up. "What do you mean? What business practices?"

Armour shrugged. "How about an agency that stoops to disguising males as females, just so they can boast about the 'uniquely feminine perspective' they bring to their ad campaigns? And what, I wonder, would the Department of Labor and Industry say about a company that flagrantly violated an equal-hiring quota by—"

I was on my feet before I realized I was standing. "That's—that's *blackmail!*"

His eyes went as cold and hard as onyx. " 'Blackmail' is a very ugly word that you should be careful using. You don't want to increase your difficulties by adding a lawsuit for slander to your troubles. It may be 'sharp business practice,' that I grant you. But bringing to light the dishonorable, to say nothing of illegal, activities of one of our competitors could also be seen as nothing more than admirable service to the marketplace. Besides, to be blackmail, doesn't there have to be some kind of extortion involved? Where's the extortion here?"

"You—You're threatening to expose—Unless I come to work for you—"

"PJ, *really*. Are you really going to try to claim that the offer of a significantly better-paying job is some kind of *duress*? Besides, I never said that the exposure of your past misconduct had anything at all to do with your coming to work for us."

"But then what—?"

He waved me to silence. "Of course, we would reconsider our decision if it would be against our best interest to make our discoveries about WN&A public. I mean, we don't have a *duty* to make these facts known, now do we?"

"And what might make it in your best interest not to rat us out?"

Armour chuckled. " 'Rat us out', that's an unusual business term. To answer your question: It wouldn't be in our best interest to make our findings public if we'd hired several of the principal players from the firm that we were considering exposing. And it certainly wouldn't be in our best interest if we eventually acquired that particular firm as a wholly-owned subsidiary—as we intend to do."

I just stood there, stunned by the magnitude of what was going on. I'd always thought Josh was a wheeler-dealer of the first order. But my poor brother only knew how to play for money and prestige. He had no experience in the vicious game of "conquer and devour." Josh simply wasn't a predator like this jackal, Armour.

With a sickening feeling in the pit of my stomach, I realized that AdCon was going to eat WN&A for breakfast. It looked like the only question remaining was how many bones would they be spitting out?

Armour could apparently read that realization on my face, because he leaned back in his chair and smiled—and suddenly all I could see was a jackal, grinning as it circled its exhausted prey. "I've stated my case. I'll have a prospectus sent to you, so you can review the concrete benefits of working for AdCon. I'm sure you'll see I'm not exaggerating the advantages. Why don't you take some time, look through the materials, and think about it? I'll give you a call later this week."

With that he stood, and showed me to the door.

At the door, he looked me up and down, from head to toe, like I were a naked store mannequin.

The bastard *chuckled*. "Astonishing. Part of me hates to bring this meeting to a close. I admit, my curiosity—well, some other time."

Chapter 5-6
Broaching Seas

Jean was once again curled up beside me on the couch, but this time I was just too distracted to appreciate her lithe grace. Femininity was not particularly attractive right now. I'd shrugged out of my blazer, kicked off my high heels, grabbed a beer, and then plopped down on the sofa to tell her all about the horrifying afternoon I'd just spent.

She reached over, brushed Pamela's hair off my forehead, and then gave me a gently-encouraging caress on the cheek. "So what do we do now?"

A feminine voice might be better than a masculine voice for some things, but it has the oddest habit of turning snarls into whimpers. "I have no fucking idea! Talk about a deer in the headlights!"

"We've got to call Josh."

I struggled not to take my anger out on Jean. "I tried. Don't you think that would be the first thing I'd think of? Turns out, he's off on another of those damn extended business trips. Can't be reached until next Tuesday."

"PJ, what are we going to do? Do you think Armour would really—?"

"In a heartbeat! He has nothing to lose, and everything to gain. He's got us, and he knows it. Frankly, I don't know why he's even bothering to be so polite."

Jean's smooth brow furrowed into an angry scowl. "Maybe the slimy little asshole just likes watching his prey squirm before he bites off its head."

The jarring reminder that this radiant, pregnant angel who was curled up beside me was also a former (and still occasionally salty) combat sailor cooled my incipient anger a bit. "I wonder how Armour got all that info on me?"

Jean folded her hands in her lap. "It's all open record, isn't it? Your diploma from Julliard, your folks' divorce—it's just a matter of looking, isn't it?"

I gazed into Jean's eyes and asked, "But how would you know to look for *Peter* Wright's records if you started out investigating *Pamela*? Where's the connection? How would you get from her to Peter?"

Jean shrugged. "I suppose any examination into the Wright family—"

Suddenly, a nagging little doubt was tickling the back of my mind—still ill-formed, but growing more noticeable. "Wright's a very common name. There are a couple of hundred Wrights in metro L.A. alone. Must be close to a thousand in L.A. County. And there's no connection in Pamela's files to Peter; that would have given the joke away. Josh and I just made up a life history for her when we filled out the employment application. Enough of a past that it looks okay on the surface. You wouldn't notice anything fishy, unless you really started to dig; unless you started comparing Pamela's life story with Peter's."

You could see Jean was trying to burst the bubble gently. "Well, hon—don't forget you've been telling that 'twins' story for some time now. Surely, once Armour dead-ended in Pamela's files, he'd start looking at the rest of her—" Then her voice trailed off as she clearly spotted the flaw as well.

I nodded at Jean's sudden insight. "How would Armour have heard 'the twins story,' *unless he had an ear inside WN&A?* I mean, it's not like Armour was just wandering the halls down at the office, picking up useful little tidbits of gossip. No, he *knew* when he called here the first time. Otherwise, why call *Peter* to talk to *Pamela?*"

But Jean was shaking her head. "No. That doesn't work."

"What?"

"Okay, let's assume that Armour does have an insider feeding him useful bits of info. Who at WN&A could have spilled the secret? Who besides Josh and me knows the truth about Pamela?"

I wracked my brain for a second. "Emma Huddleston knew. But she retired last year, right after Mr. North. And she was about as loyal to old Wilson North and his firm as a person could get. I doubt she's the leak."

Again Jean shrugged. "Well hon, I'm sure Josh isn't torpedoing his own company. And, cross my heart, I promise the snitch isn't me."

I raised Jean's hands that were clasped in mine to my lips, and gave her a sly little grin. "Well, I suppose I'll just have to trust you."

She returned my evil expression, while kissing the air between us.

I sighed and lowered her hands, which were still held in mine, to the cushion between us. That suspicion had fallen back down to a nagging doubt—

How had Armour done it? How had he learned my secret in what must have been just a few short days, when nobody else had cracked the secret in two-plus years?

****

There was a FedEx overnight letter waiting on my desk when I got into work the next morning (Wednesday). Sure enough, it was the prospectus from AdCon.

I glanced through it. I had to admit the perks for working for our rivals were impressive indeed. They had all the standard benefits. A very generous 401(k) retirement plan. Stock options. Profit sharing. The Works. There was even a Comprehensive Medical Plan, including coverage of spouse and family members. At least I'd be able to provide first-rate medical care for Jean and the baby when the time finally came.

All I had to do was to abandon Josh and WN&A to get it.

It wasn't until I was glancing over the prospectus for the second time that I noticed that most of the really big-ticket items were "projected." That is to say, though the pay and benefits were quite nice right now, if you read between the lines, you could see: AdCon was betting heavily on a rosy future to fund a lot of the more expensive promises.

Of course, that wasn't all that remarkable. They were a very young firm, after all. It wasn't surprising that they were engaging in a little *I'll gladly pay you Tuesday, for the work you do today.*

Besides, given the remarkable inroads they'd already made on our business, it seemed at least an even bet that they'd be able to make good on the promises they were making. This was especially so, when you considered the weapon they had to use against WN&A, if we didn't play along and fold our tents in the very near future.

I was still browsing through the literature when Carl buzzed me. In a tight voice, Carl said, "Call for you on line six, Mr. Wright. A Mr. Armour from AdCon."

I frowned, and set my reading aside. "Thanks, Carl. Hold my other calls, okay?"

I punched the button on my phone, lifted the handset, and paused for just a second before growling, "PJ Wright."

"Peter, good morning! I hope I haven't caught you in the middle of something important."

The bastard. He sounds so smug. Of course, why not? He's holding all the aces, and he knows it. Why bother hiding your satisfaction over your latest conquest?

Aloud I said, "Nothing important. I was just glancing through your prospectus."

"That arrived, did it? Good, good. So what do you think? You can see I wasn't exaggerating when I said that the benefits of working for AdCon—"

"Look, Armour, let's save ourselves the tap-dancing, all right? We both know what my decision is really going to depend upon, and it isn't my weekly paycheck."

"Peter, please. I hope there is some way that whole business can just be set aside. It's so much better for all concerned if our relationship is based on mutual benefit and respect, rather than on some kind of implied coercion."

It was becoming a real struggle to keep my anger in check. I snarled, "I'm so sorry, it's hard for me to accept your offer of a friendly handshake after you've kicked me in the groin."

Armour gave a rather theatrical sigh. "I admit our first meeting was, of necessity, unpleasant. That's why I'm calling today. Several members of our staff are taking the weekend off, and going up to our condo on the Oregon coast. It would be wonderful if you'd come along. I think you'll—"

That does it! Angrily I said, "You're out of you mind if you think I'm going to spend a whole weekend cooped up with you! Wasn't our little luncheon date enough fun? You want a whole weekend to snicker at me? You may think you have me by the short hairs, but I'll be damned if—"

The kid gloves had come off and Armour's voice was now cold steel. "Peter, you need to reconsider that decision. I've already said that my intention is not, and never was, to embarrass or belittle you. I sincerely hope that you'll find this weekend most interesting and informative. Are you *sure* you won't reconsider?"

God, this was so frustrating! There was just no room to maneuver with this guy, as long as he had Pamela to hold over my head.

I gritted my teeth, and took a deep breath. With a voice still angry, but at least now controlled, I replied, "Fine, I'll be there."

Armour was again all smiles and urbane politeness: "Excellent! I truly do think you'll be interested in some of the other folks who'll be attending our little getaway."

I just shook my head, and massaged the beginnings of a tension headache. "What kind of clothing should I tell Jean to pack?"

"Jean? Oh, your wife. I'm sorry, but we were expecting you to come alone. Not that your wife wouldn't normally be most welcome. After all, she too is going to be a member of our corporate family one of these days. But this weekend—"

I didn't feel like resisting anymore. It was pointless anyway. "Fine, whatever. Just me."

You could hear that his smile was more smug than ever, now that it was clear to him how deep my surrender was becoming. "Excellent. I'll send over directions, and a set of airline tickets for you. I assure you, I really am looking forward to this weekend. I really do want to try and finally get off on the right foot—"

It was petty and rude, and I probably shouldn't have done it: Hanging up on him in mid-sentence, I mean.

****

At first, Jean took it all with stoic calm. I don't think either of us liked being separated, all of a sudden. But she didn't start out with any kind of fuss. She knew who was calling the tune that we were all going to dance to—at least for as long into the future as any of us could see.

So she just helped me pack with as much quiet support as she could muster.

But her calm failed her when she saw me opening Pamela's underwear drawer and removing items from there. She stood silently for a moment, and I could feel her eyes on me.

"PJ, honey? Why—?"

I stared into the depths of my suitcase, looking for a place to stow a trio of bras. "It was in the set of directions that Armour sent. 'Bring some play clothes, and something that would work for a casual client dinner. For both of you.' The *both* was underlined."

Jean hugged her arms to herself, stared at the floor, and thought about that. Then she said, "What do you think it means?"

I willed my suddenly-clenched fingers to loosen. "It means that Armour has some use for Pamela this weekend, and that's the real reason I've been 'invited' to come."

"What reason?"

I could only shake my head.

Jean's stoic calm finally crumbled. "PJ, I don't like this. Maybe you'd better reconsider—"

I glared at her over my shoulder, a pair of pantyhose wadded up in my hands. " 'Reconsider'? Reconsider what?"

Jean shrugged her shoulders, her arms hugging even tighter. "This whole thing. I mean, Armour's up to something. The fact that he's insisting that Pamela—"

I turned back to my packing. "Of course he's 'up to something'! He's been working some plot since this started. The fact that he wants Pamela there, confirms that."

Maybe it was the rising note of panic in Jean's voice when she said, "But what if he wants you to do something wrong? Something illegal? You could get into trouble—"

It's the first time I'd ever raised my voice to my wife. "I 'could get into trouble'? I seem to recall that it was just fine for me to do something wrong, when you thought *we* were calling the shots. When you thought that Pamela was going to go spy on AdCon. But now when it's not something you want to do, *now* it's worrying you?"

Jean started to reply, but I cut her off. "You know, I'm getting awfully tired of this. Everybody is so quick to have me jump into my Pamela-suit when it suits *their* purposes. But when it doesn't, all I ever seem to get is a lot of sanctimonious head-shaking and I-told-you-so moralizing."

I slammed my suitcase shut, as I growled, "I sure wish you people could make up your minds!"

What a wonderful way to leave my distraught, pregnant wife.

Chapter 5-7
Shipwreck

I'd been booked on United from LAX to Portland International. (First class, of course. Armour's way of rubbing it in some more, I supposed.) From there I made a connection on a little puddle-jumper commuter airline that was going to take me back down the coast to Coos Bay. Armour himself was going to meet me at the airport, and drive me out to the AdCon company condo on Cape Arago.

That is, such was the plan.

In a portent of things to come, the whole trip was a disaster from the get-go.

The flight's arrival at Portland was delayed by thunderstorms, so we wound up circling for an hour. They were seriously considering diverting to SeaTac when the weather finally lifted sufficiently for us to sneak in between cloudbursts.

Of course, no sooner had I reclaimed my luggage and had made arrangements for a seat on a later flight of "Puddle-Jumper Air," the weather closed in again. I got to cool my heels in the airport lounge for another two hours, waiting for the clouds to lift so I could finally be on my way.

To meet with Armour.

I don't know if I was rooting more for the storms to lift, so I could get the trip over with; or if I wanted the clouds to descend with such finality that I could justify spending the rest of my life eating Beer Nuts, watching ESPN on the over-bar TV set, and listening to the female voice on the PA system announcing flight delays.

When I finally arrived in Coos Bay, I was almost four hours behind schedule. Needless to say, Armour was nowhere in sight. As I understood it (from the taxi driver who was supposed to carry me on the final leg of my journey), Mr. Armour apparently had another guest (a person of greater importance than me, evidently), whom he had met earlier. Instead of waiting around for me, Armour had departed in his hired limo with his other guest, and I got to ride in one of the local taxis to my final destination.

Just as well.

It turned out to be a little over an hour from the airport to the oceanside condo. If I'd been forced to take that ride while cooped up in a car with Armour—well, I would have acted much ruder than hanging up on him in mid-sentence. Of this, I'm quite sure.

Finally, just as the sun was setting into a cloud-obscured west, in a particularly gray and unattractive ending to an especially gray and unattractive day, I arrived on AdCon's condo's doorstep.

Armour met me at the door, all urbane smile and good-host-bonhomie. "Peter, welcome! Goodness, what a dreadful flight you must have had! Here, don't worry about your bags; the boy will get those. Come in, come in."

I found I was just too tired at that point to joust with this smiling bastard, and I trudged past him without comment. Armour was content to let my feeble snub slide unremarked. Why not? He had so many barbs waiting for me that he could "graciously" allow me the little, ineffectual jabs.

He called after my retreating back, "You just go up and get some sleep."

The tone of his voice made me stop dead, and look at him over my shoulder.

Armour's jackal's-grin was back: "Pamela's got a *very* busy day tomorrow. There are some people here who are just *dying* to meet her."

****

I don't think I ever put Pamela on with the same feeling of shame as when I "became" her the following morning. I've done things that made me uncomfortable as Pamela—that made me *desperately* uncomfortable, in fact—but I'd never had such a sense of dread and embarrassment so as to tie my stomach in knots. I felt misery as I slid "the flesh" of her legs up over my own, slid my hands into her arms, and felt the sudden pressure against my groin that signified Peter had vanished inside the *lie*.

I guess that was the fundamental difference—"The Lie." Before, I'd always had a mask to hide behind. It wasn't *Peter* doing all those sinful, shameful things. It wasn't *Peter* who seduced boys, who bedded men to further his dirty little schemes, and who took horrible advantage of his gender to get his way. No, always it was beautiful, wicked Pamela. Peter was out of sight, unsuspected and undetectable beneath the disguise.

But this time, the people I was going to face knew just exactly who they were dealing with. The "disguise" only served to heighten my shame this time, not to conceal it. Worse yet, this time it was all out of my control. It wasn't for my agenda that I was doing this.

Armour continued to call the shots.

I could have railed and fought, I suppose. For all the good it would have done me.

But why waste energy fighting the inevitable? So when I got up that morning, I just bit my lip and filled the tub with water, and tried not to think about it too much.

It finally became unbearable when I started dressing. I couldn't bring myself to put on any underwear. It was just too humiliating, all of a sudden to go to the effort of strapping those fake tits into satin and lace, or to pretend modesty for that make-believe pussy by concealing it beneath feminine little bits of silk.

I pulled on a baggy, shapeless sweatshirt and a faded pair of jeans.

Squaring my shoulders, I turned and strode for the door—

—and felt those huge, plastic lumps jiggle beneath my shirt.

I was braless. When she was choosing my outfit for my first meeting with Armour, Jean had said that going braless was supposed to make you feel assertive and self-confident.

I clawed the sweatshirt off, and donned the plainest bra I'd brought. Then I surrendered, slid off the jeans, and tugged on a pair of unadorned cotton briefs as well.

Once again dressed, I headed off down the hall to Armour's suite. My arms were tightly hugged to my chest. My head was bowed. My eyes were staring fixedly at my toes. Unintentionally I was presenting the epitome of cowed femininity to anyone who saw me.

I unfolded my right arm long enough to knock, once, on Armour's door. I'd just managed to hug that arm back inside the other arm when the door opened.

There was Armour. He was smiling—*leering*—at me.

"Pamela! My, my, don't you look chic? Come in, come in."

He stood aside, and with my eyes once more firmly fixed on the carpet, I crept through the door.

An oddly familiar female voice greeted me with, "My God! Alan, you've got to be kidding!"

I glanced up—turned my head to peer into the aristocratic face of the redheaded siren who was reclining with casual, regal ease on Armour's sofa.

She looked me up and down, with a smug little smile playing around her lips. "I'm supposed to believe that this is PJ? *This* is a *man*? Alan, come now. Who's kidding whom?"

It was a nightmare. That was the only explanation. All of this was simply a nightmare, and soon I'd wake up. I'd be lying beside Jean, in my bed at home, and none of this would be happening; because suddenly it had just become all too surreal—

Armour chuckled. "The joke's on you, my dear, if you choose to believe your eyes. Go ahead, *Peter*—tell Karen."

Before I could work up the will to speak, Armour continued: "Where are my manners? Peter James Wright, please allow me to introduce Karen Sprague. No doubt you know that name?"

I dumbly nodded. I knew the name. Karen Sprague was the wife of Kevin Sprague. Kevin Sprague was CEO of The Sprague Group—and the man who had viciously raped me one night, so long ago.

Armour prodded me with a "Well? Come now, Peter, where are your manners? Do say 'hello' to the wife of one of your largest clients."

I nodded, then murmured, "Mrs. Sprague." With a voice that surprised both her and Armour for that voice's lack of emotion—and which was clearly masculine, because I hadn't bothered with the voice-altering spray.

Her hand flew to her mouth to cover her bark of surprised laughter. "God, it *is* a man! Oh, Alan! When you said the technology was—I had *no* idea!"

She uncoiled from the couch, and with casual grace, circled me once—all the while muttering "I can't believe it."

Standing once again in front of me, and in a tone that suggested she was used to having her commands obeyed, she ordered, "Take that baggy top off and let's see—"

It didn't matter anymore. It was all just too dream-like (nightmarish!) by this point. With small, precise movements, I slid the sweatshirt over my head then held it loosely at my side.

Again Karen's hand covered her laughter. "My goodness! No wonder Kevin was so interested in you. He does have a weakness for big-boobed women."

She turned to Armour. "Does he know how to play the role?"

I didn't need to look at Armour to know his expression matched that of the woman standing in front of me, staring with unashamed amusement at my counterfeit breasts. Armour laughed, then said, " Yes. You can be sure of that."

Karen cocked her head on her shoulder, and gave me a wicked little grin. "Show me. Show me how you seduced Kevin."

I just closed my eyes.

The smile was gone from Armour's voice. "Peter—"

Karen interceded on my behalf, in a voice that dripped with patently sham concern. "Now, Alan. Perhaps the poor thing's embarrassed. Why don't you be a dear, and run along for a few minutes and leave 'Pamela' alone with me for some girl-talk? Maybe that would make her feel a bit more at ease, while I explain the little job we have for her."

Armour's urbane chuckle floated over my shoulder. "Very well. I'll be down in the game room, when you two hens are through cackling. Don't say anything bad about me just because I'm leaving."

I heard the door close behind me. I stood there, arms at my sides, staring at the floor.

At that moment I wanted, more than anything, to fall through that floor.

Chapter 5-8
Castaways

Karen turned away, moved to the window, and stood with arms folded. She watched the waves roll up onto the beach below.

After a moment, and for no particular reason, I shrugged back into the sweatshirt, then again just stood there. I honestly couldn't think of anything to say.

The figure at the window sighed. Then, still gazing out at the surf, she quietly said, "You don't know how scared I was when you walked through the door just now. I was afraid you were going to blow it when you recognized me. I had planned to catch you at the airport last night in order to set this up, before Armour showed. But when your flight was delayed, and *he* showed up instead—my god. You handled it very well, though."

I stared at the carpet. "So, Josh, *this* is where you've been going when you take your trips?"

The "woman" I'd once known as Jessica finally turned and faced me. "PJ, there's so much to say—so much I *need* to say—but if we take more than a little while, Armour might get suspicious, and that's something we can't afford right now. So, you and I will just have to find some time to sit down and talk, *later*. But for now, you need to know what the plan is, and—"

I snorted and shook my head. I could feel the sardonic little smile on my lips. " 'Plan'—I should have known you'd have a plan. You always do, don't you?"

Then a light clicked on in my head, and my still-baritone voice went flat, emotionless: "You, it was *you* who clued Armour into my secret. *You—*"

"PJ—"

"*You gave me up*, Josh—put me through all this *shit* just for—for—one of your goddamned schemes!"

"No." Then, for just an instant, Josh slipped back into his Karen persona to simper, "It was Karen Sprague who tattled your dirty little secret to dear Alan. That was part of my entrée into his good graces: the wonderful little tidbit I figured out, all on my own, while I was looking into my darling, cheating husband's 'affairs.' "

Then my brother folded "her" arms, and gazed back out at the sea. In quiet tones, he continued. "An entrée that I needed, if my plan could hope to succeed. Now I'll tell you the plan, and it's fairly complicated. Pay attention, because you play a crucial role in it."

****

It was almost two hours later when we finally met with Armour down in the game room. "Karen" still wore the casual (but oh-so-expensive) blouse and slacks that I'd first met her in.

But I was now wearing one of my Giancarlo originals (thoughtfully provided by Josh, though I'd lie that I'd brought it, if anyone asked.) It was a slinky little dress: wine-red and skin-tight with spaghetti straps, a fairly daring neckline, and a miniskirt that ended barely mid-thigh, but which still forced me to take mincing steps. Top it off with four-inch heels, and the outfit was just barely on the "sunny" side of appropriate for casual afternoon wear.

My arms were still hugged beneath my imitation (and now openly displayed) breasts, and my eyes were still downcast.

A little of my apparent shame was acting now, but most of it was still very real. "Karen's" presence no longer daunted me; she was as much a lie as I was. But there the similarity ended. Josh's mask was still intact. Armour didn't know that Karen was as phony as Pamela, and so

Josh had the luxury of being as brazen as he wanted, with no genuine shame attaching.

At least, not for his alter-ego's wickedness.

As to whether or not Josh was feeling any shame for other reasons—who knows?

In that dangerous, sultry purr, "Karen" folded her arms and smiled at her co-conspirator. "So, Alan, what do you think? Isn't this just the *perfect* little bit of bedroom bait?"

When Karen and I entered, Armour had glanced up from the *US News and World Report* that had apparently been occupying his time since our separation. Now he stood and circled me once, just as Karen had done upon first meeting me upstairs.

When he spoke, his tone was coldly analytical. The calculation, the evil *impersonality* of that tone sent a shiver skating down my spine:

"Karen, are you quite sure? I think this is way—"

" 'Too obvious'?" My brother used his borrowed voice to counterfeit a wicked feminine chuckle. "Poor, dear Alan. You boys like to think you're always so much in control. And usually, you are. But we women have our resources as well. Trust a wife to know what will enflame her husband. Rest assured, my darling Kevin will be blissfully unsuspicious of, and predictably lustful after, our little decoy's charms. 'She' will be a flawless lure."

Of course I would. Josh's plan simply could not fail; that was one of the beauties of it.

What a luxury—to be so assured of victory. Of course, if Josh is wrong, he won't be the only one paying the price.

Armour stood before me, arms akimbo. His expression was still nothing more than analytical.

I felt like some kind of—machine. Tool. A *thing*, not a person.

Finally, he shrugged and smiled. "I suppose I'd be foolish not to trust your judgment in this matter."

Then he glanced at his watch. "Look at the time: almost noon! Your husband will be arriving any minute now. Do you have any last-minute instructions, as to how dear Pamela should behave this afternoon? You and she won't get many other chances to talk, once things get rolling."

Karen laid a pair of possessive hands on my shoulders. *God! How can Josh do this so well? So effortlessly? Where did the ability to so flawlessly portray this cold, evil bitch come from?* I thought I knew my brother. But this—

Karen gave another wicked chuckle. "I don't think any instructions are necessary. After all, she's accomplished what we want her to accomplish once already, simply by being herself. So let's 'let nature take its course.'"

Then Karen purred in my ear, "Don't you think so too, *dear?*"

In one syllable, it was all there. The condescension. The loathing. The unavoidable but inadmissible hatred by a woman betrayed, for the hussy whom she perceived to be one of her betrayers. All there, in that one little word.

And all so perfectly, believably portrayed.

No, I didn't know Josh. I didn't know him at all.

Chapter 5-9
The Drowning Man

Kevin Sprague arrived in Armour's limo a little after noon. (No taxi rides for *him*, Armour's star guest!)

I'd forgotten how poised Kevin Sprague was. How regal.

You'd never know, to look at him, what kind of ugliness lurked just beneath the surface.

Armour, Karen, and I met the latest arrival out on the condo's little patch of lawn. Armour, all smiles and calm elegance of his own, grasped Kevin's hand and spouted some kind of welcome.

I didn't hear it; I was having a panic attack. What would happen when Kevin met "Karen"? Would the whole thing fall apart? Would Armour suddenly realize he'd been duped when Kevin stared at the sham woman standing before him, a look of confusion on his face as he said, " 'Wife'? That's not my wife! Who is this imposter?"

Of course, that didn't happen; Josh wasn't that careless.

When Armour released Kevin's hand, Kevin side-stepped and then wrapped his hands around Karen's waist. Kevin purred, "Hello, darling. Did you miss me?"

It was just so perfectly played. Karen snuggled into her husband's embrace, an adoring smile on her lips but just the right degree of coldness in her eyes.

I wonder: Where was that coldness coming from? It certainly played perfectly—it was just what you'd expect from the genuine Karen. But when it appeared in Josh's eyes, was it the product of distaste at being groped by another male? (Kevin's hands had slid down from Karen's waist and were now fondling "her" ass.) Or was it disdain for the person who had so abused his brother?

I would have liked to believe it was the latter.

Karen cooed, "Hello, sweetheart." Then at just the right moment, she turned her head sideways, so that the big, wet kiss that Kevin had been aiming at her lips landed on her cheek instead.

Again, Josh was playing the role perfectly. There was no love in Kevin's and Karen's marriage; anybody who knew anything about them probably knew that. Of course, since Kevin knew this woman wasn't his wife, her teasing wasn't disconcerting him a bit.

Quite the contrary.

When it came to be my turn for his genteel handshake, the cold, predatory light in Kevin's eyes made his growing excitement obvious. There were two females available for his attentions this weekend. Two females over whom he had no legitimate claim, no legitimate right—but who were very definitely "in his power."

For Kevin, nothing was more arousing.

Before Armour had time to speak my name, Kevin purred, "No need to introduce Pamela; we already know each other. Don't we, my dear?"

I didn't want to look at Kevin's smug face, but looking around was no improvement. *Everyone* was wearing smug, disdainful grins of their own. Especially Karen.

****

Josh's scheme was really obvious when you stopped and thought about it.

Armour had announced a midnight cruise on the hired yacht. Soon before the boat had left the pier, Kevin spoke of a "sudden headache" as his excuse for not boarding the yacht. Meanwhile, I—or rather, Pamela—confessed to being prone to seasickness, and admitted my supposed worries about being out on that "big, frightening" ocean at night, as my own reasons for remaining at the condo.

All these things were according to Josh's plan.

Yet Josh's scheme was not so obvious at all. Not when you looked at it from Armour's point of view. Which was the only viewpoint that really mattered, right? Armour was the only one who had to be fooled by any of this.

Given Kevin's lustful nature, his desire to wind up alone with Pamela for a few hours shouldn't be too hard for Armour to believe. Especially when Kevin's very own wife was assuring Armour that, if given the chance, this was indeed how her husband would behave.

Karen acting unsuspicious might have seemed strange. That is, unless someone knew (as Armour *thought* he knew) that she was in on Armour's entire scheme, and was secretly hoping for things to proceed just as they were.

What did Armour think Pamela was up to? Simple: He was pulling her strings. So of course she would give Kevin a window of opportunity. She'd been coached on her excuse for not going sailing, in order to set up that very thing.

No, from Armour's point of view, everything was going exactly as planned.

Indeed it was. Just not according to *his* plan.

****

Kevin stopped me outside his bedroom door by grabbing my arm.

All the images that came with the memory of his fingers clenching my wrist came flooding back. I felt my pulse pounding beneath my skin, beneath his hand.

He said, "You're clear what to do, right? You fuck this up, you little—I'll make you regret it. You've already caused me far more trouble than you're worth. Understand?"

I bit my lip to hide the trembling, and nodded.

He peered into my face with a dark, animal frown. "Christ! You look—well—maybe it'll look like passion to the camera. You remember what you're supposed to say?"

"I remember." I finally managed to gaze into his eyes.

I couldn't believe it when I saw it.

Fear.

Kevin was *afraid.* Oh, not of me, of course. In his mind, I was just the little toy he'd once used, perhaps ill-advisedly. The tangible reminder of what had now become the real worry—the real threat. I was nothing. He'd conquered me once already. Completely. Indisputably. Now I was just the means through which he'd clean up the mess that his carelessness had caused.

Kevin repeated, "Don't fuck this up. I mean it."

That's when I found the strength. Strength from the sudden realization of how small and ignorant and—

Worthless

—this *little* man really was.

He didn't see the tension go out of my neck. He didn't notice that my lip finally stopped quivering.

Once, he'd had all the power, all the control.

Now, though I didn't have power of my own, at least I was the instrument of power. So be it.

Time to be free of Kevin Sprague and the memory of him raping me—by my own hand.

It was I who opened the door and led him into his bedroom.

****

Funny. When I look at that DVD now, even though it's been months, you'd think there'd be—

—something.

Some kind of emotion that I feel.

She practically drags him into the room. No sooner are they inside, and the door shoved closed, but she's all over him. His face is between her hands. Her lips are crushed to his. Her body is pressed against his with urgent need. One leg is wrapped behind both of his as she wriggles against him.

Her voice is a deep, hungry growl. "I was beginning to think we'd never be alone!"

"Pamela, I—"

"Shh, don't talk."

More hungry kiss. Her right hand is under his pullover shirt, teasing, fondling. Her leg that is wrapped around his, continues to draw him tight, to press his manhood against her; as her left hand curls behind his neck, forcing his face to hers.

She says, "Oh, Kevin, you don't know—Ever since that night so long ago, I've wanted you. <u>Needed</u> you. It's never been that good again."

It would be almost comical, his sudden confusion, his sudden reluctance. These were the right words for Armour's script, but her aggression wasn't in Josh's script. Her apparent eagerness—what was going on? "Pamela, wait, I—"

Poor Kevin. He'd never been raped before.

But his shirt is off, and now both her hands are out of sight of the camera. Hands furiously working at something between them—at waist level.

For a moment, her back is still mostly to the camera. Pamela hikes up her skirt, then pushes her panties down—

Then she spins Kevin around, and forces him to lean against her and to press her to the wall. Now it's his back and her face we see.

"Let nature take its course," fake-Karen had said. And so it does, with Kevin. The sex-rhythm is irresistible, born of blood and instinct, not rational thought—

—at least for him.

It <u>sounds</u> real for her as well, when first she whimpers—then pants—then finally snarls, "Harder, Kevin, HARDER! . . . Oh! OHH!—"

Perhaps he doesn't hear even her loudest cries, because clearly his attention is elsewhere. The video never shows him looking at her face. So he doesn't see those cold, empty eyes that never leave the mirror, behind which she knows that the video camera is unblinkingly watching.

Chapter 5-10
Again On Distant Shores

Josh's plan was simple. Now it was just a question of again letting nature take its course—in this case, the "nature" of one venal, conniving man: Alan Armour.

According to our little vacation's schedule, we were all going to depart together for the airport after a leisurely breakfast.

It was over that leisurely breakfast that Armour was going to bushwhack Kevin Sprague. At least, that was Armour's plan, as Karen/Josh had explained it to me.

****

Breakfast was excellent. Omelets made to order, perfectly prepared by the caterers. Nothing but the best for prospective clients of Advanced Concepts, Inc.

Everyone was casually (if expensively) dressed. Karen had a straw tote bag hanging off the back of her chair. I'd have to ask her sometime, where she'd bought it.

It was while we were lingering over coffee—Well, the others were lingering, I was just staring out the window at the sea, no longer interested in any of this—that Armour sprang his trap.

He took a casual sip of his coffee and then smiled at Kevin. "I hope this little get away has helped you relax a bit, Mr. Sprague." A charming smile: "Forgive me—Kevin."

I'd forgotten how urbane and handsome Sprague could be. When he wasn't pawing at you—forcing your legs apart so he could—

But that was gone now—banished. Exorcised.

Suave Kevin replied, "Delightful, Alan. You have a wonderful place here. I must see about acquiring some condo space here myself. My stay was very nice."

Armour waved an airy hand. "Oh, please. Allow us to take care of that. We have very good relations with the agents of this property. It's the least we can do for a client."

Sprague chuckled. "I give you high marks for enthusiasm, Alan. But I'm sorry"—he gave a sad little smile, and a shake of his head—"we won't be changing over from WN&A anytime in the foreseeable future."

Armour pursed his lips and pretended disappointment. "Are you sure you won't reconsider? That's going to make things so *inconvenient*, you know."

Sprague continued to smile though now he managed to look a bit perplexed as well. " 'Inconvenient'? For whom?"

With a little "tsk" and a snap of his fingers, Armour signaled to the flunky waiting in the wings with the combo TV/DVR on the wheeled cart. The flunky rolled the cart in, pushed "Play," then quickly retired, closing the dining-room door behind him.

I watched my video-recorded performance for the first time.

In a wonderfully subtle bit of business, just as the image of my hands began to slide down toward Kevin's and my waists, "Karen" took a casual sip of her coffee.

The recording ended. After a moment, Armour, with a very theatrical sigh, rose and turned off the television.

He reclaimed his seat and folded his hands on the table. He sounded so *concerned* when he murmured, "It brings me such *sadness* to think of the horrible pain, and how terribly wrenching it all will be. Particularly when the jury in your divorce has to view something like this. Should you contest your heart-broken wife's suit, that is."

Karen's wry smile confirmed her understanding of her role in the proposed scam. No doubt Armour believed she'd make a very convincing "woman betrayed."

Armour delivered the coup de grace. "Not to mention, and I know this can only be a very secondary concern, but how terribly disruptive it will be to your business interests when control of The Sprague Group moves to your wife as part of her property settlement."

Sprague made a little moue of his mouth, and studied the tablecloth for a moment. "Why, Alan. If I didn't know better, I'd think you were trying to blackmail me."

Then he raised those dark, dangerous eyes to Armour's.

Give Armour credit, he didn't flinch a whit. He only returned Kevin's cold smile. "*Blackmail*, what an ugly word. And forgive me, I'm no lawyer, but don't you need proof before you may make accusations of that nature?"

Here he turned a smug little smile to Karen. A smile she returned in kind.

Armour turned back to Kevin, and spread his hands. "I wager you won't find too many friends among the people assembled here." He nodded to me. "Dearest . . . 'Pamela' has very good reason to be . . . shall we say, 'reticent' in any matters that impinge on AdCon's interests."

Then Armour smiled again at Karen, and cooed, "And as for your lovely wife—well, as the party who stands the most to gain by maintaining that the DVD was anonymously delivered—"

Considering the magnitude of the bomb he was dropping, Kevin delivered the next line with enviable aplomb. "My wife? My wife is currently vacationing in Aruba. She's been there for the past month. And as far as this little DVD goes—"

Armour's façade cracked for the very first time. "What do—"

Armour quickly glanced at Karen.

Who again, and for answer, calmly sipped her coffee.

With an increasingly vicious smile, Kevin completed his thought. "As far as my wife goes, mutual knowledge of *mutual* indiscretions has led to a very 'amiable' marriage. I'm afraid that your video will only add to her collection. Though, unless I've lost count, my collection is still larger."

By now Armour's brows had furrowed, and he was glaring at Karen. "But then who—"

She set her coffee cup down, pulled the straw tote bag off the back of her chair, and reached into the tote bag. From it she withdrew a cell phone—

—which she made a grand show of hanging up, then she returned that cel phone to the tote bag on her lap. She calmly reached for the coffee cup, then went back to sipping her coffee, her expression Sphinx-inscrutable.

Armour stared at her for a moment longer. Then to my surprise, he *smiled*, as he struck his forehead with the heel of his fist. "Note to self: If it looks too good to be true, it probably is."

He turned to me, that same, innocent, horrible smile on his lips. "I was clever enough to carefully investigate the *subject* of the message. But in my eagerness"—another glance at Karen—"I quite forgot to examine the *messenger*."

He shook his head, then turned his attention back to me. "Would you do me a favor? The next time you see Josh, please tell him I said, 'Well played.' It's really quite a pity that you won't be joining us. Either of you. At least, not for a while."

All this was proceeding above Kevin's head, but he really didn't care at this point. He had his victory. Never again would the managing partner of his advertising agency be able to hold the threat of exposing the rape of one of

WN&A's employees over Kevin's head. Kevin's copy of the DVD would render any such accusation rather absurd.

Next time contract-renewal rolled around, Josh would just have to find some other lever to use against AdCon.

Armour glanced at his watch. In a perfectly conversational tone, he said, "But we really must be on our way if we're going to catch our flight."

That line was pure Armour: Urbane, sophisticated, and not quite human.

Chapter 5-11
The Survivor

It was illegal, what I was about to do.

But given all that had just gone before: the lies and schemes, all the blackmail, and all *the other things*—

A violation of the county's no-open-fires ban seemed trivial.

Besides, of all the ways I could do it, this way felt the most—

—*right*.

****

The trip back from Coos Bay had been—

Josh and I were exhausted, I guess. There were no strong emotions left. Once we'd taken our leave of Armour and Kevin, Josh had gone to the airline counter and had exchanged a first-class ticket to Chicago (which was "Karen's" return trip home) for a first-class ticket to L.A.

First Class wasn't that crowded, but Josh and I still sat together. Two well-heeled businesswomen on some high-powered errand from Portland to L.A.; you saw it all the time. Nobody paid us much attention, except for the stewardesses, and their ministrations were predictable.

Nobody paying attention to us was just as well. I didn't realize at the time how much concentration Josh was expending to maintain his "Karen persona." He didn't have the years of experience at counterfeiting a woman that made it all second nature, so for him it must have been a constant struggle not to make any obvious mistakes.

But once we were on the plane, and "Karen" finally relaxed—

Fortunately, nobody noticed when I reached over and surreptitiously patted her on the thigh. The touch was a reminder that, while crossing her ankles was a perfectly acceptable posture for a decorous woman to adopt while seated, she still had to remember to keep her knees together.

We didn't talk.

Which was funny, because there was so much to say. *Who was the man who cheated on Jessica, who broke Jessica's heart? How did Jessica find out? Did Jessica cry?* And yet I said nothing.

I had my car waiting at LAX. Instead of "Karen" grabbing a taxi, by wordless mutual assent, Josh just followed me out to the parking garage and threw his suitcases in the trunk along with mine.

I drove straight home.

I don't know whether subconsciously I wanted Josh with me when I faced Jean; or if I was just so drained and oblivious to things that I drove home by rote. Instead of I taking Josh home first, I mean.

Jean must have been waiting at the window, because she opened the door for Josh and me before I could even get my key in the lock.

Jean peered curiously, neutrally at the strange woman I'd brought home with me. (Jean had never met "Jessica.") I brushed past Jean with a muttered, "It's Josh."

Jean's expression went through surprised puzzlement to—

Jean has a very intense, very quiet kind of anger. You can tell she's mad when her brows knit together, her lips thin, and she gets these two little—well, you can't call them *laugh lines*, but that's what they look like—at the corners of her mouth.

My wife is no fool. She'd put enough of the clues together to deduce that whatever had happened during my "weekend on the coast," Josh had played some kind of role in the affair. Given his reputation as a wheeler-dealer, plus his current role as Jessica/Karen—it didn't take a rocket scientist to figure out that his involvement in the whole tawdry business didn't amount to anything good.

I have to also say, though my wife and my brother get along well enough—particularly in the professional setting of the office—still there's no love lost between them. In fairness to Jean, her first meeting with Josh—when he'd flatly refused to consider her for a position with the firm, solely on the basis of her gender—probably entitled her to a measure of coolness.

But now the atmosphere was positively glacial.

Things didn't warm up when Josh and I took turns relating the weekend's events, in as brief and clinical a fashion as we could manage.

Trouble is, how do you make seduction, rape, and blackmail come across as clinical?

Jean listened to our tale, her eyes fixed on her toes, those "laugh lines" becoming more and more pronounced. After Josh and I ran out of narrative, Jean sat quietly for a moment.

Then, without meeting either of our eyes, she asked Josh, "That cell-phone call. At breakfast. Where did that call go? To the police?"

Josh shook his head. "What would that have accomplished? If I'd narced Armour out, he'd have just used his own ammo against us, and taken us down with him. No, I'd set up an answering machine with a tape recorder back home."

Jean nodded and sneered, "Sure. That way you now have a gun you can hold to Armour's head. Now everybody's got a gun pressed to everybody's head. Mexican standoff. Except for Sprague, that is. He gets to rape PJ *again*, and this time it gets him off the hook! Brilliant plan, Josh."

Seeing how tired Josh was, and that there was going to be a real fight between my brother and my wife, I tried to intercede. "What else was there to do? And it's not like Sprague raped me this time. This time, *I—*"

Jean whirled on me and snarled, "This time you think you were so clever. This time you got to have your revenge by fucking Sprague for a change. Right? That's how you think it went down?"

My jaw dropped open as Jean charged ahead: "He *fucked* you again, PJ. Just like Josh *fucked* you! And Armour *fucked* you! Everybody's fucking you over, PJ, and you're just too—too—*GOD!* Can't you see anymore? Don't you understand?"

Now I was getting mad. " 'Understand' what? What are you insinuating?"

I said Jean had a "quiet" kind of anger, but there was nothing quiet about it now. Now she was shouting and stabbing a finger into my fake bosom. "I'm not 'insinuating' anything, I'm telling you straight: *It's got to stop!* How many more times? Hmm? Is this how it's going to be from now on? Life throws PJ a curve, so he just jumps into his girl-suit and lets Pamela deal with it?"

Josh piped up with, "What other choice was there? You have to admit, there was a symmetry to this."

Jean turned on Josh. "And *that's* the justification? *'Symmetry'?* Is that how you're going to rationalize this? It's not wrong if it all fits together nicely?"

With a regal curl to Jessica's full lips, Josh growled, "Being a bit high and mighty, aren't you? Playing roles is okay if it gets *you* what you want—like a computer job. But it's all tawdry and dishonest when it works to someone else's advantage?"

I snapped, "Now wait just a minute! Whose fault—?"

But the battle had passed me by, and Josh just charged ahead. Now he was stabbing a well-manicured finger at Jean. "You might want to remember all this was in *your* best interest too. Or have you forgotten who it is who signs your paychecks? Who it is who's paying for your medical plan? PJ was trying to save the business. But he was also thinking about *you* when he did this. About his wife *and his baby!* You should be less quick—"

Jean bounded to her feet, and brought the debate to an end with a shouted, " 'Everybody else is doing it, so that makes it okay.' That's a three-year-old's excuse! It was *wrong* when I did it. It was *wrong* when PJ did it the first time. And this—this whole—*it was WRONG!* Pile as many wrongs up as you want. It still won't make one 'right.' "

Then she stormed up the stairs, and slammed the bedroom door.

Josh said nothing more in my living room, except to pull out the cell phone and call for a taxi.

****

"How many wrongs make a right?" With Pamela, it always seemed to come back to that.

That question circled in my head for the following days.

Meanwhile, Jean was quiet. Closed off. I don't know, maybe Josh's jab at Jean's masquerade had touched a nerve. Maybe that was part of it.

But that wasn't the largest thorn in her side. Across the dinner table the next night, I tried to work it out with her. The discussion didn't get very far. Only far enough for her to give me another little morsel to chew.

"PJ, don't you see? Don't you understand how—You say you're doing it for the baby. Okay. I believe you think you're doing the right thing, but—What are you going to tell him?

Or her? 'Daddy's having a little trouble at work, or with the neighbors, or—or whatever. So he's going to put on this magical suit, and he's going to be a girl for a while. And you get to play along. Won't that be fun?' Is that what you really want to do? Is it?"

That was the clincher. Oh, I agonized over it for a few more days. But I just couldn't get past that mental image—trying to explain to my son or daughter about Pamela.

So in the end, that's why I was standing out here behind our apartment complex's garage, watching the smoke rise from the old, rusted 55-gallon drum that the tenants sometimes used to break the county's clean-air ordinance when they didn't feel like taking the trouble or expense of toting something out to the dump.

Funny, for all the impact she'd had on my life, you'd expect Pamela to go out with more fanfare. A big rush of flame like a Viking funeral pyre or something. Not just one anticlimactic puff of black, burning-rubber-smelling smoke.

With a shrug and a feeling of ill-defined loss, I turned and trudged back to my wife and the child that was to be.

Jean had seen the truth of it. No amount of "wrongs" ever added together to produce one "right." Life didn't work that way.

But in our lives together, two Wrights had combined to produce another.

And it was to make room for that other—that little Wright-To-Be—that Pamela had passed out of my life.

The smoke rose into the air behind me. Maybe—sometimes—one wrong can make it right.

THE END